The Secret Keeper

Shirley Eskapa was educated at the University of Witwatersrand, Johannesburg, where she took a degree in sociology and psychology as well as a post-graduate degree in international relations. Her first short story was published in 1961. Since then her work has appeared in various magazines, including *Cornhill*, the *Telegraph Magazine*, *Fair Lady* and *Woman*. She lived in Geneva for eleven years and now lives in London. She is currently working on a major non-fiction project called *Woman Versus Woman*, a study based on case histories of the tactics used between wives and their husbands' mistresses.

Shirley Eskapa

The Secret Keeper

Academy
Chicago
Publishers

Published in 1985 by

Academy Chicago Publishers
425 N. Michigan Ave.
Chicago, IL 60611

Printed and bound in the USA

Library of Congress Cataloging in Publication Data

Eskapa, Shirley.
    The secret keeper.

    I.   Title.
PR6055.S4S4   1985   823'.914   85-1364
ISBN 0-89733-126-5

For Raymond

'No one ever keeps a secret as well as a child'
Victor Hugo, *Les Misérables*

1

On Thursdays children in Geneva do not go to school. Some, but only very few Swiss go to one of those despised, foreign and exorbitantly expensive international schools that do not close on Thursdays. And on Thursdays even the clear air of the Mont Blanc golf club of Geneva is invaded by something closely resembling excitement; an only just permitted happiness, rare enough in Switzerland to approach hedonism, disturbs the profound humourlessness of the club's elegance. For the golfers start sweeping up the immaculate driveway at about eleven in the morning.

It is said of Geneva that everything that is not forbidden is prohibited which means that the bankers, the industrialists, the lawyers, the doctors and even the ambassadors who desert their desks experience, on Thursdays, a delightful sense of near sinfulness.

In the golfers' dining-room – where spiked shoes are permitted – the waiters hover over their blindingly white tablecloths, and Philipe, the chief barman, who has the talent of appearing to be every member's personal butler, checks the precision with which his surgically bright glasses are stacked. Philipe, who has an encyclopaedic knowledge of the private lives of all his members, knows that on Thursdays they feel something not entirely unconnected with friendship for one another, as if they are meeting at a party, and not at a reception.

Nigel Pritchett-Ward, the managing director of Nekker & Cie, a subsidiary of one of the oldest merchant banks of Britain, climbed the sweeping staircase with more than his usual Thursday speed – he was known as one of the fastest walkers on the course and most golfers had almost to run to keep up with him. He was one of the better golfers with a handicap of three, but in the ten years he had been in Geneva he had not yet won the club championship. He paused briefly to greet the Austrian who, in real terms, was one of his lesser clients, and his dimple augmented his smile the way his accent augmented his French – both his smile and his French were perfect. Of course in the banking world his golf was a great asset, and he was much sought after. People liked playing with him because he was always ready to play with those who would always be beginners, and because he was a true sportsman (rare in golf) who knew how to lose and who never griped about the greens. People felt at ease with him because he had an almost magical quality of restraint mixed with warmth. His movements were natural and easy, and his clothes were worn with just the right kind of carelessness. He usually changed as soon as he got to the club, but had been too impatient this Thursday, and still wore his checked cash-mere suit, Ilsa's favourite.

Ilsa was where she had said she would be, and he saw her immediately. Not once, in the eight months he had known her, had she been late. She appeared to be studying the menu, though he knew she was not; he halted momentarily, simply to observe her, and because she did not know he was looking at her it was as if he was seeing her during a moment as private as sleep, and he knew he could never get enough of seeing those heartwrenchingly sad and helpless cheeks of hers. Suddenly she looked up and waved casually, and it took all his self-control not to race toward her. Instead, he slowed his pace.

He slid beside her on the black leather bench.

'You could say it was a rough morning,' he said. 'A complicated morning. I didn't have time to change.'

'A currency crisis?'

Nigel's aim, in the metal markets, was no less accurate than it was on the putting green; he almost never failed to sink a putt. It was his long game that let him down. 'No. No currency crisis. I came straight from home. I did *not* go to the bank this morning.'

She said nothing, but her eyes widened.

'I'll tell you later.'

Because Philipe joined them, last Sunday's golf and the weather were discussed. Ilsa selected a *croque monsieur* and Nigel ordered one too. Philipe suggested a white wine, and they agreed, and when he left Nigel let out his breath.

He said quietly, 'Caroline is leaving.'

'What did you say?'

'Yes. She is. Leaving.'

'My God . . . Oh my God. You'd better give me a cigarette – '

Ilsa now smoked his brand, which pleased him. He longed to place his already lighted cigarette between her lips, but that would have been unseemly. He took out his pack and said, 'We had another of our serious talks.'

'But you've been talking for fifteen days.'

'Yes. Fifteen days. She was very good, and very brave.'

'The poor woman.' They spoke in English because her accent thrilled him. 'The poor, poor woman,' she said again, and bit her lip. These days she wore no lipstick, only lip salve, because their kissing demanded it.

'True,' he said miserably. 'Poor kid.' And he added, 'She seemed to muster all her dignity. She was so damn dignified!'

'I would never be. Not after twenty *days*, never mind twenty *years*.'

'*You* will never have to be.' He pressed his knee to hers and she responded. 'She's going to leave Geneva.'

'You can't really blame her for that.'

'That's exactly what she said. She also said that she wanted things to be civilized, amicable, dignified, not only for Peter's sake, but for the sake of our twenty years . . .'

'You English – I have to admire her . . . It's only fair . . .' She floundered and looked away. They had been going through this kind of anguish (on Caroline's behalf) for months, ever since things had begun to run out of control.

He looked out toward the golf course, and beyond to the lake, and beyond that to Mont Blanc. 'She said she was doing her best to make it – to make things easier for me – she understood that neither of us wanted to hurt her . . . But it was – painful – just the same –' He raised his arm. 'I think I need a whisky.' He rarely drank spirits during the day.

Philipe was beside them almost at once. 'In the middle of the day monsieur? Certainly monsieur. And Madame du Four?'

'Philipe, you think of everything. But I'll stay with the wine.'

'Philipe doesn't miss a trick,' she said. She was imperious with the staff, and Nigel liked that; he and Caroline were too democratic, almost subservient in their dealings with domestics.

One daring afternoon he and Ilsa had driven into France. Hungry, they'd stopped at a *boulangerie*, and he noticed how Ilsa had not waited in the queue, but had merely called her order from the back of the little shop. She'd been served at once. It was this public air of authority, of expecting nothing but deference, that he found so – well, compelling. He wanted to say this to her now, but he said, 'Caroline says she wants to – well, I'll tell you exactly how she put it – she said she wants to diminish Peter's suffering as much as possible. Thirteen is a particularly vulnerable age, of course – '

Ilsa was used to men thinking out loud, and muddling. She said soothingly, 'I know. I know.'

'Yes,' he said, 'you *do* know.' He tried a smile, his dimple flashed, and he went on, 'Caroline's been very generous, actually. She told me that she will always love Peter's father, and of course I assured her that I will always love Peter's mother. Which is true, you know, in a strange sort of way it's very true – '

'I suppose so. In a way.'

'But of course she understands that I'm *in* love with you. Though she still insists it's the mid-life crisis kind of love – '

'Nothing mid-life about you!' Ilsa flicked her tongue rapidly across her lips.

She must know that drives me mad, he thought. 'She

doesn't know that about me. It's not like that with her. It's never been – ' And now he thought of the way Ilsa stripped, how she managed to leave her clothes precisely folded, and yet was naked while he still fumbled with his socks.

'It's never been like that – as you put it – with anyone else, either,' Ilsa said with as much wonder and seriousness as if she were telling him for the first time. And because this had become a recurring theme of theirs – they could never hear enough repetition of it – they both laughed.

'You are so beautiful, Ilsa,' he said. 'Caroline understands that neither you nor I wanted things to develop – to snowball – to come to this. She's a good-looking woman. She'll find someone else, I'm sure.' He added, teasing, 'She's got an excellent figure – '

'Don't talk to me about her figure. I don't want to hear about it. This is not a game we're playing – '

But it had become a game, as they both knew. They had discussed Caroline's figure so often, managing to shape their conversations into something that closely resembled a shared property. This flattered them both, though for different reasons: after all Caroline's excellent body provided Nigel with near-perfection – to give up – for Ilsa. His not inconsiderable sacrifice therefore reflected on Ilsa, too, and most favourably – for if he was ready to give up a more than ordinary wife for her it followed that at the very least she must be, as they say, one hell of a woman . . .

'Caroline's an odd girl,' he said. 'D'you know she refuses to discuss finance. She's ready to leave all that to me. She trusts me.'

'She's clever,' Ilsa said. 'She's a very clever woman. In Switzerland women do not fare at all well in divorce settlements.' She flicked her tongue again and then smiled, 'In any case you are a gentleman, Nigel, and I expect you to treat Caroline the way a real gentleman should.'

'London will be better for her. The theatre and all that. She never really fitted in here – '

Ilsa shook her head sadly. 'I know.'

'She confessed that all this is especially hard on her,

11

because she had honestly believed that we'd had a happy marriage. She feels her existence has been negated. And it is true, I had thought we were happy, too, but of course I didn't know what real happiness meant – '

'I wish we didn't have to play golf now. I wish we could go to our little hide-out.' She passed her fingers through her hair. 'Pretend, at least, to eat,' she whispered. 'I want to touch you. Everywhere. . . . I want to touch you everywhere. You look so – so exhausted and miserable. So drained. It kills me to see you looking like this.'

He shut his eyes. He was thinking – irrelevantly – of how efficiently, how neatly and how speedily she always made their bed . . .

They were in the quarter-finals of the mixed fourball championship. It was part of a knock-out series and unthinkable to cancel.Besides, they'd been drawn against Guy and Michelle Bouvier, a serious challenge because the Bouviers were both better than their admittedly low handicaps. Ilsa was the reigning women's club champion; she'd won the championship twice, and Nigel thought she had the sexiest golf swing he'd ever seen. She was short and slender and her cleverly cut trousers discreetly emphasized her taut buttocks. Her hair was a brilliant black and she tied it back in an elastic band whenever she played golf, and when she did not she wore it loose with a bandeau to keep it in place: both styles reminded Nigel of a cute nine-year-old, he liked to think of her as a little girl though she was thirty-eight, and only twelve years younger than he. It was those knee socks of hers that had finally undone him, and which undid him still. And even now, as through his cashmere trousers her much-known knee pressed against him, he felt the double thickness of the cuff of her sock, he could not resist looking down at her feet shod in the flat black patent moccasins of an American teenager, could not resist marvelling that he alone knew those feet in all their nakedness, those sensual toes in all their dexterity, just as she had shown him what, unclothed, the tempo of that sexy golf swing really looked like. She was rather keen on feet and had once demanded, 'Let me see your toe-nails – I want to see if they're really clean!' Which was how his preoccupation with his toe-nails had begun and which had in turn, he remembered, led to Caroline's suspicions . . .

He said now, 'I *am* whacked. Caroline and I talked through the night. In fact we went on talking until about two hours ago – '

'Poor Nigel. All this is so hard on you, I know – '

'It's harder than I had thought, I can tell you that,' he said almost bitterly. 'The thing is that she wants to leave Peter with me. She does not believe mothers should bring up sons – not after a certain age, and certainly not after ten – '

'Wait a minute – are you telling me that she's ready to give him up?'

'Yes. That is exactly what I am saying.'

'Give up her only son? Her only child? You've got to be joking,' she said.

'I asked her that very question in that very way. She maintains that she's not prepared to be selfish. She said – '

'But that's unnatural,' Ilsa interrupted. 'Caroline must be an unnatural mother. Look at my Jean-Pierre – when his father died he had to be brought up by his mother, and even if Luc had not died . . . This is too much for me. Why didn't you mention this at once? What an unfeeling, what a cold, what an unnatural female. Why, she's a disgrace to womankind!' In her agitation Ilsa withdrew her knee.

'You could never do that, I know. Not you, you're all woman, you see. Put your knee back, and I'll try to explain my wife to you – '

'Please don't.'

'Wait!'

'Please call Caroline by her name. You know how unhappy the other makes me.' Ilsa returned the knee she had momentarily confiscated.

'Of course. Sorry. I forgot. Rejected wives, Caroline believes, are peculiarly dangerous to their sons. They often turn them into queers. She is very very upset, you know. She can't sleep. She looks drawn. She says her hands

13

shake. She insists that she does not want Peter to be harmed or damaged by seeing her in this state. She adores the boy. She's always been almost afraid of the mother-son relationship and believes she would have been wary of this even if we – that is if she – had had more than one child . . .' A note of simple satisfaction entered his voice, he couldn't help it. 'She's always been my best propagandist, always told him what a great father he has . . . She honestly believes that Peter could more easily take being separated from her than from me . . .'

'I see. To be honest, I don't really see at all – but for the moment, spare me, will you, from Caroline's amateur psychology!'

'You don't mind? I mean you've always said you loved Peter.'

'Of course I love him. Everyone does. He is an adorable child.'

'I knew you'd say that.' He forgot himself, forgot that they were at the club and took her hand and squeezed it. Ilsa, however, did not forget; she withdrew her hand. 'Caroline told me that in Switzerland the courts tend to award boys who are over the age of eleven to their fathers, anyway.'

'She's not Swiss!' Ilsa burst out. 'I can't understand this. I've never heard of anything like it. All I know is that I'd kill anyone who tried to take my little Jean-Pierre from me . . . Caroline's crazy – she *must* be! Peter's such a nice little boy. He could only be an asset to her!' Her eyes narrowed. 'Do you think she could have someone else?'

'No. She doesn't even want to – not ever – ' Ilsa snatched another cigarette. Nigel stopped to light it for her. 'You couldn't, I know that. You could never give up Jean-Pierre.'

'I couldn't live without him.'

'I know that.'

'Poor Peter, I pity him, having such an unnatural mother.'

'I can't understand her myself,' Nigel admitted. 'This is not in the least like her. But it's clear to me that she's at breaking point. She is simply not able to cope with Peter – '

Ilsa adjusted her knee, and he felt its increasing pressure. He stared at her, and staring, saw her again as he'd seen her once before, shortly before the beginning of their affair. He'd been watching her having a drink out on the terrace and when Jean-Pierre came up to her she put down her glass hurriedly, and picked him up and held him and hugged him, and distributed kisses; and she'd been so graceful and so loving, and so feminine and so sexy. She'd caught Nigel's eye, and smiled her awareness of him. She'd seemed both passionate and maternal, a combination that appeared somewhat at odds with that controlled sporting air of hers. He had found her behaviour with her child remarkable, so remarkable that he had that evening discussed Ilsa and the strength of her maternal instinct with Caroline, even though Caroline had never met her.

Ilsa looked at her watch with that movement he dreaded because he had come to associate it with her leaving him to fetch her son. He had neglected his bank, told all sorts of fragile, convoluted lies only to have her look at her watch – she could not be late for her son. Jean-Pierre, who was eight. She fetched him daily from school. Once, after a particularly energetic four hours, she had been too late to find a parking place on the school-gate side of the road, and one of the other children she collected had dashed across the road, been knocked down and had her arm broken. Ilsa had had to take the child to hospital. After that she'd left Nigel at three thirty instead of four.

'What time are we teeing off? I've forgotten,' she said.

'In about five minutes. We'll be late. I'll have to go and change.'

Philipe had left the bill and Nigel signed it quickly.

She turned her fullest, her most meaningful gaze on him. Then she giggled and said, 'I must change my shoes.' She stood up. 'We're going to win this match. I feel it in my skin.'

And so they did.

2

My Mom bought me this diary before she left. She bought a whole stack of things before she went away. She said it was a shopping spree, and we went shopping for clothes for four consecutive days. We went on the little *mouette* across the lake and into town and she got the driver to let me steer the boat. But my Dad and I don't live in that flat on the lake any more, so I don't know when I'll get to go on that little boat again. Mom used to tell me not to say 'get to' because that is American from the International School and she wanted me to speak real English. Now I say 'get to' as much as I like, and Dad doesn't mind.

The first things my Mom bought after the diary were a medical kit and two dictionaries. She didn't actually buy the box with the medical kit, she took quite a large white shoe box, and painted a red cross with nail polish on it, and bought things like bandages in lots of sizes, and sun tan oil, and aspirins and vitamins, and a thermometer, and also a special kind of gauze for really bad burns. I suppose she got the burns stuff because she used that once when I'd been badly scalded, and so I didn't have to go to the hospital. My Mom always included a medical kit when she and our housekeeper Frederica packed my things before I went away to camp. I tried to pretend I was only going away to camp, because even though I don't like camps, I wished it was a camp I was going to. In any case this kit is much bigger than any of the others and I can tell that it is meant to last for a long time.

The dictionary takes two large volumes. It is called *The Shorter Oxford Dictionary*. Inside the dictionary my Mom wrote:

> *To my darling son, for his crossword puzzles,*
> *with love from his Mother.*
> *1st March, 1981.*

My Mom said she had to buy a whole new wardrobe, and

got me two new pairs of golf shoes even though my old ones still fit. At least she bought bigger sizes. And stacks and stacks of underpants. She was so uptight about my laundry, because our housekeeper also went away. Frederica went back to Portugal. Mom says she's a bit neurotic. She was so upset when she heard Mom was leaving that she started to wear black, everything black, even a black scarf over her head when she was in the kitchen. And thick black stockings, too. Even her face looked black. It was horrible. And then she got hold of a rag doll, and started sticking it with pins, and Mom found it sitting in the fridge, started screaming and crying and laughing and we had to send for Dr Kohler who came and gave both of them an injection. And then Mom said that the doll would have to be a secret – *even from Dad*. She said she was sorrier about that than I could ever know.

And then she bought me this diary. She said it was for my secrets. She told me that most boys of thirteen have secrets, even when the family is not divided. And then she took me to meet a doctor who specializes in secrets, a psychologist.

Mom thought that I should meet this Dr Gaud so that I could discuss any secrets that made me very very unhappy. The doctor wasn't too bad. He explained that changes in routine make everyone – even the bravest of men – feel strange, and said I could phone him if I felt like it. He thought the diary was an excellent idea. He liked the lock and key, and said that I should write in the diary whenever I felt like it, and not only when I had a very special secret. It was possible that I would feel lonely sometimes and he told me that it would be normal and natural for me to miss my Mom sometimes and he said something very strange indeed. These are his exact words, and when he spoke he sounded just as strict as my golf pro. 'You must not feel ashamed when you miss your mother. I command you not to feel ashamed about missing her, and furthermore I command you not to feel ashamed about anything to do with this tragedy. None of this is your fault, never forget what I am saying to you now. None of this is your fault.' My Mom was blowing her nose a lot – I heard her – I was too

17

embarrassed to really look at her while he was talking to me – and then Dr Gaud asked her to leave the room.

I began to be afraid that I would cry. I didn't want to do that. He said that he knew I would be going to live with my Dad who would be living with Madame du Four in her house next to the eleventh hole at the golf course, and with little Jean-Pierre du Four and with Raffles, my dog. I must try to understand that my Dad was also sad that we would not all be living together. Even Madame du Four was sad, but adults do not always know how lucky they are, they don't always value the really important things like having health and enough to eat . . . He was sighing a lot while he was saying these things.

Then he said he was going to do something he did not usually do, and he said he was doing it because I was being so brave, and because my mother was one of the most unselfish women he had ever met. A long long time ago he had done the same thing as my father was doing, and he had regretted it ever since . . . Young people see their parents as super-beings, he said, but they are only ordinary human beings, and even the Bible is filled with stories of adults like Adam who made terrible mistakes. Of course we were speaking French, and he said that there was a name for what had happened to my father, it was called *le démon de la lune,* and it happened to men, and sometimes to women. It was like a disease over which they had no control, though most of them regretted having been careless enough to expose themselves to this sort of infection, this vicious germ. Doctors had not yet invented a vaccine against it, he said.

He had to emphasize that he was talking to me almost as if I were an adult because I was such an intelligent young man. He seemed to know so much about me, about my chess, about my being on the merit list at school, even about my golf and that this is only my second season. But I wasn't really surprised that he knew so much, I could tell that he was a very wise man like my friend's grandfather. My grandparents died long ago, when I was very very young.

He said that my mother was going to live in London for a while because she wanted to give me the chance to settle down, and because she did not want me to be too upset by her sadness, and above all because she believed that a boy of thirteen needed his father more than he needed his mother, though of course she knew that I loved and needed her, too, but that she felt too fragile at this stage to be able to actually see my father and Madame du Four together because Geneva was such a small place that she would not be able to avoid seeing them together, but that she would probably come back and live there just as soon as she felt a little stronger, which, in time, he was sure she would . . .

I started to cry then. I really cried. I cried and cried, and the doctor told me that those tears were the medicine of the heart, the best cure and had I not seen that press photograph of Gary Player crying when he thought he had lost the British Open? When I shook my head he took the clipping from his drawer and told me that even Gary had not been ashamed of his tears, and what is more he had gone on to win other British and American Opens. He wasn't a golfer himself, he kept that picture to show it to people sometimes. He said that real men knew how to cry, some men, and even some women, are too babyish to cry.

It sounds crazy to me, but he's a psychologist, so he must be right.

I've been writing for ages, and my hand is tired. The diary was a good idea, after all. Because something so terrible happened that I cried in front of *her*, it feels as if I've been crying for years, and to tell the truth I've been crying all the time that I've been writing this. I was going to write about what happened, but it is too terrible, and I can't.

3

Ilsa was only spending the day in bed because Nigel had begged her to; she was not the sort who would allow a mere head cold any importance. But under the weight of Nigel's need to demonstrate his concern she had capitulated – that morning he had brought orange juice, croissants, lemon tea and honey up to their bedroom, it was now ten o'clock in the morning and he had already telephoned twice to sympathize, and to tell her that he would be bringing her some high dosage Vitamin-C tablets, and of course he would collect little Jean-Pierre from school, give him lunch and take him back again. Peter lunched at the International School, but Jean-Pierre, like most Swiss children, lunched at home, which meant that Nigel would fetch Jean-Pierre at the usual time of eleven thirty.

Which hour Ilsa blessed.

For she could not have contemplated the thought of not seeing Jean-Pierre for seven or eight unbroken hours each day. Except for Thursdays, when he did not go to school at all, and Saturdays when the school day was only a morning, Jean-Pierre spent seven hours of every day at school. But those hours, thank God, were in two shifts. She supposed, sometimes, that it was because Jean-Pierre was asthmatic she needed to see him, needed to satisfy herself that an attack was not imminent or worse; but whatever the reason that break from eleven thirty to one thirty ensured the shape of each day, and guaranteed its validity. She could shop *and* play nine holes; the pressure of time acted as a stimulus, or challenge; and the effect was an all-round increase in efficiency, even to each golf shot. Sometimes during those hours with Jean-Pierre she would shampoo his hair, or give him a manicure, a pedicure; she would read to him, or as was happening more and more, he would read to her.

But each day, unfailingly, she tested his spelling, both in French and German.

It was a well-balanced relationship, Jean-Pierre's and hers, Ilsa believed, because the dependence was mutual. And it was this sense of mutuality, so fairly weighted, that bound them in weightless bands of permanent, unqualified security. Simply having Jean-Pierre within her line of vision did something to her, and for her. It was partly physical, she knew, for she felt herself change – become softer, become brighter, become calmer . . .

When she was with him she could laugh; she did not need to giggle.

Perhaps in her son she found not only her *raison d'être*, but herself. In his presence, all restlessness left her.

Things had moved so fast, Ilsa told herself, that a day of silent and serene contemplation was not only needed, but in a way, deserved. It was fifteen days since Peter and his father had moved in with her and although Ilsa had an accurate sense of time – she would remember the exact month in the exact year of all sorts of events, meaningful as well as meaningless – a certain sense of timelessness went with these past fifteen days. Of course Peter's presence was something she had neither planned nor bargained for, thus the fact that he was with them added a distinct measure of respectability to their liaison; which factor, Ilsa deduced, must have been left out of Caroline's calculations – whatever they might be.

Nor was this the first time that Caroline had unknowingly protected her rival's reputation. From the outset Nigel had known that Ilsa was not the sort who would meet married men in a flat casually borrowed from a friend or in an hotel, and certainly not in Jean-Pierre's and her own home. Her house, after all, abutted the golf course, and besides, her neighbours were members. So Ilsa's surrender – it never was a seduction – had finally taken place in Caroline's guest room, under Caroline's bridal photograph which stood on top of the bookcase across the way from the bed. Because Caroline insisted on having books everywhere and yet her flat was irritatingly beautiful, even elegant, having somehow surmounted all its endemic disorder . . .

At the same time Ilsa had thought the photograph fitting,

though she had told Nigel that it had been strange to make love to him – for the very first time – under Caroline's watchful eye. Nigel was filled with remorse, he ought not to have been so thoughtless, but they made love many times that first time . . . And now that they were actually living together with both their children Ilsa had made certain to intensify this activity so essential to the sustenance of all her real desires . . .

That bridal photograph had acted as some sort of presence – almost supernatural – rather evil, rather sad . . . As well as frightening, almost terrifying. Deeply afraid, Ilsa had expected anything but fright, the ensuing shock brought genuine tears to her eyes, and to this day Nigel was still unbearably moved by that moment, those tears – he had felt as if he had been about to take a (willing) virgin, and had said, 'But you're frightened – ' Ilsa could only nod and tremble. 'And shy – ' At that Ilsa had struggled with an almost overwhelming urge to giggle. She nodded again; the effort not to give way to the kind of laughter that threatened all the complicated planning that had gone into that very moment muffled and thickened her voice.

'Please,' she said, 'you'll have to show me, Nigel. Please . . .'

'Oh – you poor darling.' Masterfully, then, as Nigel liked to think, he had shown her everything.

Now she lay back against her sheets fingering them. They had shopped for them – she and Nigel – because Ilsa had insisted on new and pure sheets. Their newness and their purity and their perfection (they were of the very best Irish linen) would be the symbol and the emblem of all that lay ahead of them. Besides, they planned on needing dozens and dozens of sheets, didn't they?

It was when Ilsa had first seen Nigel playing golf with Peter that she had made up her mind that she would – as she put it to herself – try to get him. Nigel was the sort of father she had in mind for Jean-Pierre. He was everything her son needed.

But she was to tell Nigel later, 'I made up my mind to get

you the first time we played golf together.'

'You made up your mind.'

'Yes. And it wasn't easy. You didn't make it easy for me.'

'That was because I hadn't dreamed that you found me attractive – '

'Not even when you asked me what we should play for, and I said a weekend in Paris, maybe?'

'Well, I did wonder about that, but then you made it clear it was only a joke. But I do admit that the mere mention of a weekend brought a special tension into the game. You almost beat me, too.'

'Yes. I had an 82 and you had a 79 – '

'Of course it was those cartoons you gave me that did it. You remember how you climbed over the fence between your house and the golf course, and met me at the eleventh green, and told me that you had something to give me, but you were a bit shy about giving it to me?'

'I made you beg – '

'My God you did. And of course you were wearing those sexy knee socks of yours! Then you gave me that envelope, and I didn't dare open it until I had left the club. And there were all those cartoons you'd drawn so painstakingly, and the little raindrops you'd made out of our initials. You spelt it all out, literally – '

'I couldn't help it. Mr Pritchett-Ward didn't notice me hanging about my garden in my bikini.'

'The hell I didn't! Thought I admit I didn't know you were doing all that for me – '

Like all lovers, Nigel and Ilsa loved going back over the phases of their courtship, because lovers need to remember and to marvel at the fact that there was a time, once, when neither even knew of the other's existence. Because the joys, the agonies, the uncertainties of their relationship made the present more solid, more comforting than had the prior high excitement.

Only last night Ilsa had added another detail to the history of their courtship. She confessed to having watched him, spied on him, actually, from her balcony, with the aid of her binoculars. It was many many days before she'd had the courage to climb over that fence, to give him that envelope with those cartoons . . .

The little drawings were kept in Nigel's private safe at the bank. Even now he would take them out and marvel at them; it was as if they were her very essence, like her they were minute, child-like. But their lines were firm and strong, as powerful as her swing. She was muscular, but very feminine, and especially with those knee socks she was like a delicate miniature revolver, hand-finished in ivory . . . Because he knew from the outset that she would be dangerous, that she would never be, so to speak, a mistress on the sidelines.

Indeed, four months were to pass before they met under Caroline's bridal photograph, and the very day after that eventful Wednesday he had presented her with a Russian wedding ring, made by Cartier, in three shades of gold.

Ilsa played with these rings now. She loved handling them, caressing them, she would arrange and rearrange their colours, the white, the yellow and the gold – they might have been Greek worry beads, or a rosary.

Because, however naive Nigel might have been, only Ilsa and God knew the precise combination of planning and prayer that had gone into bringing her to the point at which she was now.

For three long years Ilsa du Four had protected and cherished her reputation as an honourable and dignified widow and mother. It had become her cause, and the fierceness of her determination was matched only by the relentless zeal with which it was applied; in the end people (well, those who counted, anyway) came to look on her as not only honourable but noble. The single relatively simple factor in the whole long exercise of her widowhood was that in Geneva the people who counted were all members of the Mont Blanc golf club. Still, all things considered, the acquisition of a reputation of respectability had been no mean feat. For even if she had not begun life in Switzerland as an *au pair* who had genuinely come to the country to perfect her French (and she had, she had, to the point where her German now bore the inflection of a French accent), and even if she had been the daughter of a count she still would not have been a Genevois. That she had been married to a Swiss had helped of course, but she had observed that Swiss women, and for that matter, Swiss men, who had come from a different canton, say, Zurich or even the adjacent one, Vaud, had not in the home of Calvin won complete acceptance.

At least Ilsa had had the advantage of knowing exactly what she wanted; acceptability followed by respectability, and, finally, nobility. She had the first two, and as for the third – well, she would settle for the Genevois notion of that. Nigel was, after all, a Swiss banker. Nigel's genius lay in his having not only persuaded his own British bank, Coombes, to put in a bid for Nekker & Cie, Geneva, but in having persuaded that illustrious bank to accept Coombes's admittedly excessively generous offer. Nekker & Cie was one of the Big Seven of the private banks.

That bankers, in Geneva, are at the pinnacle of the hierarchy, is not to be disputed. In Calvin's time lace and jam were forbidden, the place for the franc was in the bank. That has not changed. The Rolls-Royce (or its near equivalent) is rarely seen at the Mont Blanc golf club. The secret Swiss like to think of all the secret Soviet money in their many secret Swiss vaults – which means that Swiss bankers undertake the noblest of all duties; they are the defenders of neutrality, because they are the protectors even of the gold of their enemies. The private bankers of Switzerland are revered. And soon a former *au pair* would be admitted to their ranks.

Ilsa's late husband, Luc du Four, had not been anything like a banker, though he had been stolid enough and unimaginative enough to have managed a branch of one of five large public banks. His photograph, its classically simple Jensen frame (one of the two frames acquired after his death) so carefully tended by Ilsa, still stood on her bedside table, and another, also in a silver frame, was on display in the salon.

Ilsa kept a squash ball beside every telephone – that way

she was able to strengthen her wrists and palms and fingers while she spoke on the telephone. That way no time was wasted. When the phone rang she automatically grasped her squash ball.

'Nigel, I've spent the whole morning thinking of you.'

'I'm bringing home some smoked salmon, and on my way I'm collecting some broth that I've ordered from the Richemond.'

'You're so good to me you make me want to cry.'

'And I'm also bringing home a surprise for little Jean-Pierre. And then after I've taken him back to school I'm taking the day off to look after you know who.'

'I must get a cold more often. It's worth it!'

'You sound all bunged up. Have you got a temperature?'

'Should I have?' she teased.

'I can't wait to see you.'

Ilsa allowed herself to feel very deeply pleased, because even if she had come to believe that Nigel was no more than her due, no harm could come from taking pleasure from the achievement of an ambition, especially when one knew – as only she knew – of all the years of effortful planning, to say nothing of the privations, the frustrations, the patience and the discipline that had gone into it.

Luc would never have telephoned; he believed in frugality and lived by it; he was ready, on Saturday mornings when he used his car, to wait until someone – usually a foreigner – drove out of a parking space before the meter expired. This kind of dedication to parsimony meant that he saved twenty centimes; and centimes, carefully hoarded, have a way of accumulating, which is partly why Ilsa had been left so well off. Like his son, Luc's father had been an insurance agent; staff discounts meant lower premiums which meant that hefty life insurances had been taken out when young Luc was only a toddler. And of course there had been accident insurances; Luc's death on the autoroute to Lausanne had been instantaneous which meant that the policy on his life had doubled instantaneously, too. Hence the house in Cologny, adjacent to the eleventh hole, in which she and Nigel and Peter and Jean-Pierre now lived . . .

Ilsa laid aside the squash ball, and, on impulse, looked, really looked at Luc's photograph. She had – she realized – come to think of Luc as the frame, the frame had become more important than the photograph, but then it was more valuable, and besides, she excused herself, four years is a long time. Looking at the photograph now she saw that she had not looked at it for years, the man who stared out at her with that uncharacteristic smile was thin-lipped, sharp-nosed, and his narrow and unsmiling eyes conveyed his life-long dedication to duty and to order. She felt a pang of something like loyalty; Luc had certainly been a good husband. Indeed, as husbands go, he had been excellent. The Swiss Civil Code gave him absolute rights over her, of course, but he had allowed her the occasional game. Eleven years passed before Jean-Pierre had been conceived, and when Ilsa found out that the infertility was Luc's fault and not hers, she had been too canny to tell him so and persuaded their doctor to do likewise. The doctor understood the fragility of male virility . . . Luc was disappointed, naturally, but he bore his disappointment with stoicism and even with optimism – this sort of adversity, he believed, made faith stronger. Well at least Luc knew he had a son, she thought now, feverishly polishing the frame on the sheet. Luc du Four died on that highway when Jean-Pierre was only four years old.

Nigel knew this, and to set her mind at rest had for the past months taken a different route to Lausanne. She valued Nigel's thoughtfulness but would not have settled for anything less. And why should she have, she asked herself, when she had enough of everything to be able to choose? Because she had worked for it *all*, even the golf. Nothing had come to her easily, and luck was for other people, she knew. There were those who would think she was lucky to have got hold of Nigel – well, she'd let them think so, more, she would go as far as she had to, to help them think she'd been merely lucky.

The real truth was that the acquisition of Nigel represented the culmination of the kind of planning that was not too dissimilar from the accumulation of all those twenty centimes of Luc's.

Ilsa put the photograph aside and reached for her tweezers and mirror. She would not be totally idle today. Oh yes, if she didn't know better she could easily fool herself into believing that everything had just happened by luck, or by accident, or by chance. Her life had been made to be something like her eyebrows, whose perfect shape came from constant attention, whose style came from hard thinking and much study, and whose body came from dedicated and not painless plucking and pulling.

True, she owed a lot to golf, she knew, although – unlike Caroline – she had not had the luck to have had a golfing father or anything remotely like one. But she also knew that no matter how well she played, or how good she could have become, she would not have got anywhere if she had not joined the Mont Blanc golf club.

She had first heard of the golf club when she had come to Geneva as an *au pair*. Then she had been sixteen and frightened, but, like a true and good German ready to work hard for Maître and Madame Pachoud and their two sons. Oh, she had worked hard . . . Which was why (much to Nigel's delight) she had refused living-in help ever since. She helped the boys. Marc and Alain, with their German grammar, and at the end of term their marks had improved so appreciably that the family decided to take her out for a German meal which marked a great step forward and was a promotion of a sort.

Spring came soon after their momentous dinner and several weeks after watching the Pachouds and their sons practising golf in the garden she felt daring enough to ask them if she might try. She had been good at games at school where it had been generally conceded that she had an excellent eye for a ball. She had never picked up a club but had watched Gary Player and Lee Trevino and others on the little screen. True, she had natural sporting abilities, and true, it seemed mere chance when she hit the ball so well; only Ilsa knew of the books taken and studied from the library on her days off. The Pachouds were average but dedicated golfers. Ilsa's first golf swing was almost as good as Maître Pachoud's, but it soon became apparent that it was more than beginner's luck. In time they allowed her to accompany them when they went to the golf club. And it was at that golf club, in France, in Divonne, that Ilsa first heard of the Mont Blanc.

That was the first time that Ilsa du Four, or rather Ilsa Grundheim as she was then, began to make up her mind about things, and she made up her mind to be a member.

It took about twelve years, and although she knew that as long as she was Madame Luc du Four, membership was out of the question, she had never given up hope.

But for her golf Maître Pachoud would not have noticed her, but though Ilsa had not as much as tried to forget about all that, she preferred not to think about it now.

One thing was sure, though. When Nigel came home she would have a surprise for him, too. His photograph would be in both those silver frames. Luc would be consigned to the bottom drawer in which he had always belonged.

Which, as Ilsa was to think later, was a stroke of pure luck.

When Nigel came upstairs with Jean-Pierre he noticed that absent photograph at once. 'Oh, Ilsa, darling,' he said inclining his head in the direction of where Luc's photograph had been because Jean-Pierre was with them. 'You've put it away. That's a very sensitive thing to have done – '

'Well – '

'I know, it wasn't easy – ' And then, as if to divert a little child, he put a large orange envelope in her hands. The envelope was made of fairly thick paper, banks were given to using these envelopes whenever they wished to be declarative instead of secretive. 'Now you have a look at what is inside this, and I'll go down with Jean-Pierre and we'll fix a tray for the three of us. O.K.'

'But what *is* this?'

'You'll see. Banking documents. Nekker & Cie need your signature, it seems.'

In her excitement Ilsa had picked up her squash ball. Now she laid it down. An honest tremble seized her, and she felt unaccountably afraid. She longed for a cigarette but, because of Jean-Pierre's asthma, cigarettes were not allowed in her home. She discovered a rather thick cheque book which was encased in a leather cheque book holder on which *Banque Nekker & Cie* was stamped in gilt lettering. Opening the cheque book, and inspecting the blue cheque forms she read:

ILSA DU FOUR et NIGEL PRITCHETT-WARD.

Ilsa had been very very careful not to discuss money; clearly, she had not been wrong. There was a form to be filled in – all that was required was her signature. She considered making a little ceremony of it, of waiting for Nigel, but rejected the idea. She would not make too much of this, nor would she ask what sort of capital sum had been put into this new joint account. No, that would appear too mercenary, too practical. Of course, it would be nice to know the really relevant details. But wait, there was another smaller envelope. This one contained credit cards – American Express, two departmental stores, and Banque Nekker & Cie's card. Ilsa had never owned a credit card in her life, nor even dreamed of such things. This is the small stuff of which power is made, she thought, small things mean large numbers.

She was reminded of the afternoon at Madame Pachoud's when she'd bent to retrieve the bits and pieces that had spilled from Madame Pachoud's friend's handbag. She'd picked up all those little metal-feeling cards, and the friend had taken them from her, and without as much as saying thank you, had turned to Madame Pachoud, her hostess, and said, 'My dream in life is to live with a little dog and a cheque book, and no husband – ' and with that the guest had swept away. Ilsa never saw her again. The woman had actually looked like a Pekinese herself, Ilsa remembered now.

She signed the cards, as instructed, with a ball-point pen,

and then she signed the bank form. When Nigel and Jean-Pierre came in carrying their trays they found her giggling.

'Look Maman, look,' Jean-Pierre said excitedly, 'look, Dad bought me a water pistol.' And to prove it, sprayed her with a small jet.

'Don't, Jean-Pierre. Don't. Your mother's got a cold.'

'It doesn't matter,' Ilsa said. 'It doesn't matter. I want to hug both of you.'

The phone rang. It was for Nigel. He would not be able to spend the afternoon with Ilsa after all, something was happening to the price of gold, in only two hours it had jumped forty dollars. Decisions were required.

'It's like living with a doctor,' Ilsa said. 'Only men like you are so much more important than doctors. Of course I understand that you must go back to the bank!'

A few minutes later, when Nigel was about to leave, Ilsa said, 'I filled in the form for you, hope I put my signature on the right line. I'm not so good at that sort of thing . . .'

Ilsa could stay in bed no longer; it had all been too exciting, even unsettling . . . Jean-Pierre had called Nigel 'Dad'. Ilsa could not believe it. Everything was going almost too well – and if not too well, then so well that – Ilsa cursed her superstitious nature. She would rearrange Jean-Pierre's shelves; it was the sort of therapy that was almost as good as golf.

4

21st March

A second bad thing happened.

John-Pierre has started calling *my* Dad, Dad. Not Papa, but Dad. Of course he can't speak English, he can hardly read French – my Mom told me to be very very patient with him because he's a tiny bit slow, she said, as well as

31

asthmatic. Actually, she suspected he was a little bit retarded, and she warned me never never to use that word if I could possibly help it. He's not a bad sort of chap, he blinks a lot, though, and cries a lot, too – he follows me around like a puppy. He thinks I'm the coolest, I can tell, but I can't get used to him calling my Dad, Dad. It's not fair! You should see how my Dad smiles when Jean-Pierre calls him Dad, you'd think he'd just won the club championship. It makes me sick. My Dad told me that he could never love Jean-Pierre the way he loves me, he said he would like to be like a father to him, because Jean-Pierre's own father had died when he was only four. I'm sorry for Jean-Pierre, but why should he have *my* father?

I just want things to go back to normal again. My Mom told me never to give up hope, and I won't.

My Dad says I have not actually given up Raffles, because I can go and see him. So far my Dad has only taken me once. Madame du Four – I only call her Ilsa when I have to – when my Dad is around I don't call her anything at all if I can help it, and when he's not, I call her Madame du Four, because I know she doesn't like it. Once or twice she's asked me to call her Ilsa, and wanted to know whether I remembered her name, and I mumbled something about being used to her as Madame du Four. Meanwhile Madame D is being patient with me, she thinks she'll win me over, she told that to my Dad.

Well, she won't.

Long ago, before any of this happened, Mom and I invented a nickname for her – lots of our friends have private nicknames – it was fun making them up. We called her the Tick, because she sort of stuck to my Dad, and when he had coffee or a drink with her, she would always send me down to the basement of the club to give Jean-Pierre some sort of stupid message, at that *garderie des enfants* the club provides for its members. I hate that place, and so does poor Jean-Pierre – he's the only boy there. The Tick says it doesn't matter at this stage of his life, because he's safe down there. She's always worried about that asthma of his. I feel sorry for him, because he can hardly breathe when he has an attack, but the truth is that Jean-Pierre is allergic to dogs, so, after two days, Raffles was sent away, I can't believe it!

I can't forgive him for it, either. I got Raffles when I was two years old, and now my poor best friend is at a kennels. They said he would have house privileges, but that crazy woman who looks after him has her own horrible whippets – she says they are perfect specimens, but I think they look more like perfect skeletons. It's gross. She's got ten of them living in her house, they all sleep on a special bed in her living room, and the boarded dogs sleep in cages outside. Those horrible whippets must hate Raffles. Raffles cried and whimpered and howled and jumped when my Dad took me to see him – the place is very very far away, in the country, and the Tick has offered to take me, although she can't go in and actually see Raffles, because of the dog hairs. My Dad made me change in the car before I went in, and he changed, too, and then we had to change again before we went back to the Tick. I love Raffles, but I don't want to go with *her*. I'd rather walk. But my own Dad will take me back there very soon, I'm sure he will. But I know what will happen, she'll come with us, for the drive. Perhaps she won't – she hates to leave Jean-Pierre.

My Dad keeps telling me what a wonderful mother she is, and he wants me to like her, I know he does, he's always reminding me how she has helped my golf. I'm using a squash ball, too, now, to strengthen my wrists the way she does, and my grip has improved. I admit that, so has my putting. We practise in her garden. The Tick has got a beautiful swing, no one can deny that. Mom should've played golf, she tried, but she was hopeless. I tried to help her. She did not miss the ball too often, but she had the clumsiest swing I've ever seen. She only began playing last season. She took lessons every single day.

My Mom used not to go to the club very often. She used to laugh about it being my Dad's territory – she thought she wasn't masculine enough for the game. Besides, she didn't very much like it there – the members somehow reminded her of the darns on the club tablecloths, because they seemed to be held together by millions of tiny stitches, like those darns, that's why they were so stiff and humourless – they had to be, to protect all those careful stitches. Where else in the world, my Mom used to say, would anyone take all that time to darn tablecloths?

I wish I had not told her that I had overheard the Tick saying to Madame Koechlin that my Mom was making a fool of herself trying to play. My Mom was so upset when I told her, because she did not know that I knew who the Tick was. My Mom didn't even know what she looked like, so I had to show her who she was. The day I told Mom what the Tick had said about her golf lessons was the day we made up that nickname.

I remember the day I showed her to my Mom. We were sitting under the pure white umbrellas on the patio having a *jus de citron*, and watching the putting on the eighteenth, when I said to Mom, 'That's her. The Tick.'

I could see my Mom didn't even remember anything about the Tick, not even our nickname, so I reminded her. My Mom thought the Tick had obviously made a great impression on me. I explained that it was because I didn't like the way she sent me off on messages, even if she was the Ladies' Champion. Mom started wanting to know all sorts of details and then said she decided it would probably be a good idea if she started coming to the club more often than she had been – she'd sort of left golf to my Dad and me until then.

None of us have been to the club since Mom left. I sometimes look at the players from the balcony, I can see the thirteenth and the eleventh holes very clearly. She bought a special sign that said PETER'S ROOM, in English and Dad thought that was so wonderful of her – you'd have thought she was Father Christmas all of a sudden, my Dad made such a fuss, but it's *not* my room, and never never will be – '

My Dad asked me to stop talking about 'the room I'm using', *please*, and I said I would, and if he hadn't given away my dog, I would stop. I'll never forgive him for that – I'll never trust him again. He knows that, or at least I hope he does. I don't think he really cares, anyway.

My Dad and I used to have so much fun at the club. He's very popular, and all the waiters love him, and so they are very nice to me.

My Dad arranged for me to sign our number whenever I wanted a drink, and said I could order a hamburger, or a *paillarde de veau*, in fact everything except wine or whisky. Dad hardly ever drinks those sorts of things – at least he used not to. Now – living in *her* house – he drinks wine with every meal. I suppose he thinks he's a European, now. But I liked signing our number – W53 – I had the key to Dad's locker – I still have it.

That was how the trouble started. I know Dr Gaud told me not to feel guilty about anything that's happened, but I do because I can't help believing that it's all my fault for having told Mom about the nude photograph of the Tick that I found in my Dad's locker by mistake. But he asked me to fetch him some new balls, and when I took them out of the box I saw that disgusting photograph . . . I had *not* gone snooping!

Mom said she was sure I must be mistaken, and then she suddenly said she'd take me back to the golf club to fetch it, and that was when I began to feel very very scared, because Mom looked so pale, and so kind of wild, but we went there, and I showed it to Mom, and she said I must not say anything to Dad about it, only she was going to keep it for a while. So she took me home and went out and took the picture with her, and then fetched me again, and took me back to the cloub, and said she was sorry about this, but would I mind putting the photograph back exactly where I found it? She had to think about all this, she said, and then she said I must not worry about it, and that she was sorry for turning me into a go-between – or something like that. And then she said something about the wife always being the last to know, but – there you are (and she kept on and on about this, as if she couldn't believe it herself) out of the mouths of babes, out of the mouths of babes . . . She said she loved my Dad, she kept calling him Nigel to me which was strange, and she kept apologizing and apologizing to me for upsetting me . . . She wished and wished that she had not known anything about it.

And if I had not told her, she would not have known.

My Dad doesn't know that I saw the photograph. That is a secret between my Mom and me. And I know that if I had not told my Mom none of this would happened. *Because, if you keep a secret properly, then it has not happened.* I wish I had known that when I found that photograph.

The funny thing is that writing all this down is almost like talking out loud. I feel a bit better, now. But I miss my Mom, and I hate the Tick, I wish she was dead, and so does my Mom, I heard her say something like that to Frederica. My Mom said she didn't really mean that, and she cried horribly about it.

What a stinking mess everything is.

My room though, like every room in this house, is *never* in a mess. My Mom warned me to keep it in perfect order. The Tick used to be German, she's Swiss now, and according to the Swiss cleanliness is before godliness . . . I suppose that's why she's forever nagging Jean-Pierre to wash his hands and face and *neck*, to clean his teeth, to brush his hair, that sort of thing. Or else she does it for him. It's like he has to gleam like her silver golf trophies. She speaks to him in German when she's angry, but she sticks to French, mostly. Of course she talks to my Dad and me in English. My Dad loves her accent – he's always saying so. I simply can't bear the sound of her voice. It's got something to do with the tone – it's hard to describe; it always sounds strict, somehow unkind, like a bossy schoolteacher. Or else it's like a tinned voice, the kind you get on an answer-phone, when you dial your own phone number and then dial in four digits the time you want your alarm call. When your alarm call comes you get that tinned voice again. It sounds crazy, even to me, to say this, but that is what her voice reminds me of . . . *Because her voice drives me crazy!* I hate it.

Thursday

Two things happened today, one good, and one bad.

First the good thing.

Dr Stephen Brown, our director of studies, bumped into me in the corridor today at break. He said he was pleased because he had wanted to see me anyway, he wanted me to show the project I had done on Coal Mining in the World to some eighth graders. That project was pinned up on the wall of his office, and he wanted me to collect it. Once we were in his office he told me that he really wanted to talk to me about something else as well. He hoped I would not be embarrassed by the things he was going to talk about, but he knew what had happened to the family. As a matter of fact, he said, my Mom was the one who told him. She had phoned him that morning to tell him, and of course he was always very sad when that sort of thing happened, but he had some news that would probably cheer me up. My Mom said that if I wanted to phone her I could call her collect. He was sure I would think that a good idea. He said I could call her from his secretary's office. She just happened to be out to tea at that moment. I was already jumping up to go to his secretary's office when he told me that I could come and see him at any time if I had problems, he had experience in this sort of thing. He said I was probably feeling a bit mixed up, you know, a mixture of anger and sadness, and confusion. I thanked him, I just wanted to get out of his office as quickly as I could without being rude. I wish I could learn how to stop going red and hot in my face!

That was how I spoke to my Mom. She said that she missed me lots, that she was feeling a little bit better. She could hardly believe what had happened to Raffles – as soon as she came back to Geneva she would take him to our flat. She couldn't have him in London because of the quarantine laws. She said she was shocked, and that she felt for me very deeply. We decided to keep this phone call a secret, and then she said she'd just had a wonderful idea, and what did I think of it? I could ring her any morning from the school pay phones and what was more I could call collect. This way no one would know about it. It would be our secret. She said that for some reason it was much cheaper to call London collect. She said I could write to her if I liked. She asked about the diary, and whether I was using it, and was very very pleased that I was. She was so happy about my Coal Project because she had helped me prepare it.

I don't know why, but I did not tell her about Jean-Pierre calling my Dad, Dad.

Speaking to my Mom was the good thing.

The bad thing is that my Dad told me that *all* of us are going to have lunch at the club . . .

5

The newly formed du Four–Pritchett-Ward household had waited three weeks before their first visit to the club. During this time Ilsa and Nigel had – exceptionally for both – cancelled their games. The waiting period was, they felt, only proper; at the same time the waiting had the usual edge of delicious apprehension that precedes the making of an intended public appearance while the scandal is still scandalous.

That their affair had – in the midst of the sterility of Geneva where one seldom ever saw a fly – taken on not only a life of its own – but the lives of others – Caroline, Peter and Jean-Pierre – was in itself proof (as Nigel and Ilsa admitted to one another) of its strength, of its fittingness, of its final inevitability. Had they met in any place other than Geneva, then . . . But they shuddered to think.

There are some who see Geneva as having as much charm as – but no more personality than – a prettily iced birthday cake. But even those transients who live in neutral

Geneva for no more than six months quickly come to learn what the Genevois and the settled foreigners take for granted – Geneva's personality is strong and positive and far from neutral, far from pretty. Neutrality is all very well for states, for countries, but it is not to be extended to people. Neutrality is something you work and arm for; it must be cherished as well as guarded which is why all Swiss males between the ages of twenty and fifty keep not only their assault rifles but needles and thread in their military kits in their bedrooms at home. But if neutrality means freedom it is well understood that freedom means discipline. You do not walk on forbidden green grass because that sort of thing is viewed as irresponsible, and irresponsibility is viewed with the same uncompromising distaste as sloth. You respect your neighbours, accordingly you restrict your bathing, as you restrict your hoovering, to the statutory permitted hours.

The Mont Blanc golf club is, in an important sense, the headquarters of the town's manners, and there is an assumption that everyone will conform. The international organizations such as the UN and all the many organizations that constitute it are not too well respected – indeed, they are only just tolerated, as any indignant self-important diplomat or quasi-diplomat will tell you. Of course, if you have the rank of ambassador the Mont Blanc golf club will judge you acceptable, but if you are one of those highly qualified directors general to say, the World Health Organization, you will find yourself somewhat less than welcome. The members – the non-golfing members or *membres passifs* particularly see themselves as patricians and, like all patricians, are displeased by the general propensity toward indolence among even the most exalted of the international civil servants. Because even if you are not hard at work, and even – and perhaps especially when you do not have to be – you must at least appear to be industrious, conscientious, above all, efficient. You must conform to this notion of the real meaning of life. Originality is as forbidden as sloth: and while international civil servants have never displayed any great liking for originality, they have not

39

cared to conform in any meaningful way to the belief that if work is not all, then efficiency is.

To qualify as a Swiss banker, a gnome, as Nigel had done, was a spectacular but delicate victory. Nigel was not the first foreign Swiss banker whose desire to conform was so strong that it turned him into a proselyte, and who behaved as if the heavy-handed disciplines of duty and responsibility and power were more genetic than acquired. He had not, as a young man, defied his parents – it had been neither necessary nor possible – they had been easy-going and tolerant – which is perhaps why he found his present situation so exquisitely at odds with all that he had held himself to be. It would be too simple to say that the club and Geneva represented his (undefied) dead parents – but he and Ilsa (as they both agreed) had been courageous enough and daring enough to commit this breach of taste and manners with all due rebellion – and to hell with the cost.

To brazen it out was the only way.

Still, they were not quite as brazen as they fancied themselves to be, as perhaps they both knew. Because, in leaving Peter with them, Caroline had, albeit unwittingly, allowed the lovers a measure of conformity, and, consequently, of respectability. For Nigel was taking his father-hood seriously; in this all-important aspect at least, he was nowhere in dereliction of his duty. Nigel and Ilsa would be seen together with each of their children – both sets of responsibilities, immaculately clad, immaculately cared-for, would provide the best sort of evidence: conformity had not been entirely dispensed with, after all.

Thus their first public appearance took place on a Thursday, the most prominent day of the working week. Ilsa and Nigel would play in the mid-week Stableford, Peter would caddy for them, and Jean-Pierre would spend the afternoon in the *garderie des enfants*. But before that, the four would lunch together.

In the end Ilsa and Nigel decided not to lunch in the smaller and less formal restaurant that was reserved for golfers, but in the larger and more formal restaurant that was meant for the *membres passifs* and their guests, and of course for the golfing members as well. This way they would be subjected to a greater exposure, this way they would establish the permanent seriousness that marked their new alliance.

Philipe greeted them with more than his usual show of hospitality as if he had divined their unspoken, indeed singularly private need to draw attention to their little group. He exclaimed over Jean-Pierre, over Peter, and then rather too emphatically perhaps, sang out, 'Madame du Four, Monsieur Pritchett-Ward – this way, please, your table is waiting. Please, follow me.'

And so, under Philipe's skilful conducting, the diners looked up, took note, stared, chatted, whispered. They saw Peter blush, and Jean-Pierre blink, and Ilsa glow, and Nigel beam. Table-hopping is not a characteristic of the Mont Blanc golf club but some felt it proper to waive this convention, and so strolled over to shake each of the four by the hand.

But, to merit dining in the large restaurant, something other than the more obvious criterion of a scandal had been necessary, and here Ilsa's inspiration came to the rescue. For among all the social conventions and hypocrisies of those who do not take their position – in what they fancy to be patrician society – lightly – there is nothing quite as disarming as the convention of the birthday cake. Members are forever giving birthday parties, marking the passing of the years is one of the distinctly conformist celebrations – a reminder of the future, perhaps, or likelier, of shared mortality – at any rate the iced birthday cake in the shape of a log of wood, on which stand flickering candles, never fails to produce smiles as well as congratulations.

And so Ilsa advanced Peter's birthday by about two weeks, and planned this surprise and in its execution was not disappointed. A private ceremony in a public place makes its imprint as firmly, and just as indelibly, as an official stamp on a civil document. Peter's well-wishers mistook his furious embarrassment for well-bred shyness, but it was not possible to mistake either Ilsa's glow or Nigel's beam.

There were about eighty diners in that restaurant, and one of them, a woman, rather plump, rather smug, was staring so concentratedly at Ilsa that she had the feeling she was being minutely memorized, like a dress to be described and then copied. It is especially hard, when one is unduly self-conscious, not to search out the starer whom one does not see but via some vestigial primitive instinct only feels, and Ilsa gave way, and searched and found, and was then confronted by the staring, fixedly indignant eyes of one of Madame Pachoud's long-ago guests. For Ilsa it was unsettling, it was ironic, it was bizarre, it was perfect – and for Madame Giscard Duchosal it was disconcerting, it was unfortunate, it was unforgivable – and it showed. A smile tickled Ilsa's lips and turned as usual into helpless giggles.

'Hey – What's so funny?' Nigel said. 'Let me in on the joke.'

Jean-Pierre chimed in.

Peter blushed.

Ilsa could not speak.

But signalled, and with her eyes and her head, directed Nigel's glance toward the plump and staring, openly inquisitive Madame Giscard Duchosal. And Marie Duchosal resembled nothing so much as she resembled a caricature of an indignant Swiss housewife who has spotted a crumb under a table.

Ilsa regained herself and, while wriggling her wrist dismissively, said clearly, and rather too loudly, 'I think I met that fat woman once – long ago – '

Ilsa may have appeared dismissive, but that long ago time was omnipresent, and would not be parried.

Ilsa had never met Madame Duchosal in the sense of having been formally introduced, so it would probably be more accurate to state that she and Madame Giscard Duchosal had encountered one another when Ilsa was in Madame Pachoud's service. Then Madame Pachoud had ordered, 'Take Madame Giscard Duchosal's coat, Ilsa.'

And Madame Duchosal had addressed Ilsa with the *tu*, the *tu* that was reserved for intimates, children, animals and servants. It took quite a while before Ilsa was formally introduced to Monsieur Giscard Duchosal, an esteemed client – and playmate – of Maître Pachoud.

It amazed Ilsa that she could still remember that there was a time, once, when she had not even known of Maître André Pachoud's existence – but that time – to be honest – was more like a distantly remembered nursery rhyme learned by heart, than a reality in which she had actually lived. But something of the peasant must have remained in her, for she believed, sometimes, that it was her destiny that André Pachoud would forever be as prominent in her consciousness as her own name. Indeed, when the news of Luc's fatal accident reached her, her first thought had been of André Pachoud. At first she had fought and struggled, been resentful and hostile, but finally, along with years and years of tears, resignation accumulated. There was no logic to it; she should have felt hate and rage; instead she felt adoration and hurt.

When Maître Pachoud had plucked and swallowed her with the same hedonistic enjoyment he might have accorded a luscious grape, Ilsa was sixteen and fairly innocent, just the right shape for him to have arranged as if she were one of a bowl of perfectly ripening fruit, temptation, so to speak, on display. The occasional touch, the measured caress, the distracting glance, became less and less occasional, less and less measured, more and more distracting, while consummation loomed far off, somewhere in a never-never-land.

At that time Ilsa was not, technically, a virgin; she had suffered the stumbling, fumbling advances from the peasant boys in that increasingly distant place where she had been raised. And when Madame Pachoud went off, to visit her parents in Paris, *force majeure* at his *étude* prevented the Maître from joining her. That night, as usual, even though this time they were altogether alone, he touched and caressed and teased and invited and then

43

– with an expression of something insultingly like exultation – left her and went out with his friends.

He'd had both his eyes then – the accident which Ilsa later cursed herself for half thinking he'd deserved had not yet happened – and though forty, and to Ilsa an old man, his male authority, his seigneurial bearing, his height, and his indisputably tough superiority had the sort of timeless attraction that (with neither originality nor mercy) still turns young girls into desperate young bodies whose brain and heart is attacked by the same fertile mechanisms that conceived them in the first place.

That night she'd waited for him to come home and then, clad in nothing but her long thick loosened hair and even thicker desire she stood outside his bedroom for what seemed to her to be the longest time, before she opened the door and went in.

He, of course, was unsurprised, widely experienced, expertly schooled, and unforgettably proficient. So it began, a long and wild, and for Ilsa, ruinous affair; but for Pachoud she remained the passionate serving girl who'd displayed a remarkable golfing ability. Still, it took some time before her passion lost its attraction for him, so, for all the months after Madame Pachoud's return that her attraction was to last, he met Ilsa in the little flat that he shared – for that purpose – with esteemed clients and fellow playmates such as Monsieur Duchosal, and others, of course.

And then, when he tired of her, he handed her on to Monsieur Giscard Duchosal – thus was Ilsa formally introduced to Monsieur Duchosal, as part of a non-golfing threesome. Perhaps Madame Pachoud knew, perhaps not, but after about a year Ilsa left and found that job at the English School of Leman, where she was assistant to the matron, and where she perfected the English that she now spoke with such a perfect French accent.

She continued to see André Pachoud, whenever, that is, he would consent to see her. But since his accident, nearly nine years ago, he had not agreed to see her.

Three years ago, exactly a year after Luc's premature

death, Ilsa called on Monsieur Giscard Duchosal who, though not on the Selection Committee of the Mont Blanc golf club, was none the less one of its more illustrious members. Because (during her marriage) Ilsa played so rarely she had an arbitrary handicap of eighteen, but one year (the first year of her widowhood) of lessons and practice, and discipline and drive, brought her handicap down to eight . . . So, when she presented herself to Monsieur Duchosal she had the right handicap, the right clothes, the right address and the right status – it had been a well-organized and productive year. She changed not only her neighbourhood but her bank. Thanks, mostly, to Luc's father's foresight and parsimony – his insurance policies amounted to 600,000 Swiss francs – after the sale of their little house Ilsa had a capital of 800,000 Swiss francs – enough to merit a consultation with one of the vice-presidents of one of the five big Swiss banks. As soon as she discovered that 800,000 was considered interesting, but not important, she decided to deal with one of the larger private banks where her funds would be considered interesting as well as important.

The problem though, was which private bank to choose. Her banker would be required to find her a house and arrange its financing, create and manage a portfolio and, most important of all, put her up for membership at the Mont Blanc golf club of Geneva.

But how, when one starts from scratch, does one find out who the directors or presidents of the private banks are? That Swiss banks are shrouded in secrecy is well known to everyone. It was here that one of the anomalies of the Swiss approach to law and order came to Ilsa's rescue – it is impossible in Geneva to be ex-directory. Secrecy is possible, anonymity is not. Indeed, a register of all residents is readily available – one can, if one wishes to spend one hundred francs or so, even buy a copy. Nothing is sacred, not even a lady's true age.

Ilsa, however, did not need to go to that expense; it was not even necessary to consult the yellow pages, the ordinary telephone directory, under the heading *Banquiers*, listed fourteen names – two of these were familiar to her. Both Monsieur Eric Genet and Monsieur Mara Gaillard were golfers, and both had won competitions in the senior division – fifty-five and over; she knew this because of the serious attention she devoted to golf magazines. At that time Jean-Pierre was five years old – Ilsa was sure of one thing and only one thing – her son would not have to struggle for social acceptance.

Which was where Monsieur Giscard Duchosal came in. When Ilsa called on him he agreed, at once and charmingly, to introduce her to the President of the Mont Blanc golf club of Geneva, Monsieur Eric Genet. Ilsa half feared she might have to resort to some pressure, but in the event the merest enquiry after his wife's health (and how is Marie? Ilsa had used her Christian name) had been enough. And how would he present her to Eric Genet? Very simply, as the tragic widow of an esteemed business associate, the late lamented Luc du Four . . .

The meeting with Monsieur Eric Genet took place only two days after Ilsa had called on Giscard Duchosal, and it was held, very correctly, on the terrace bordering the eighteenth green. It was Ilsa's first visit to the club, and the terrace, she discovered, not only faced the smoothest green she had ever seen (it reminded her of the green marble counters beloved by banks) but the lake, the opposite shore, and beyond that the clearly visible Mont- Blanc whose caps, even in this faltering sunlight, were still rosy. An extravagant profusion of scattered white pebbles – dazzling as hailstones and just as plentiful – made up the patio floor. The casual benches, *chaises-longues* and chairs were covered in the brightest white linen – similar in texture to the pebbles it was meant to echo – and yet, strangely, these whites were neither clinical nor sterile if for no reason other than the way in which they reflected, deflected and absorbed the miraculous greens of the spectacular fairways, and in an even more mysterious way, the pink hues off the lonely tip of the Mont Blanc. Once, in a golf magazine, Ilsa had seen a photograph of this terrace which was why she had chosen to appear in those soft sparkling pink Bermuda shorts which went so well with her brilliantly white knee socks and equally white blouse. All of this was further enhanced by her tan, by her severe but *sportif* pony-tail.

Nigel was not the first man who had gone overboard for Ilsa's impressive uniform. For Ilsa had long since divined that on a golf course, at a golf club, she could be stunning. She'd been frank enough, and sensible enough, to admit to herself that it was not just the sporting ambience that effected this magic – it would not have worked on the ski slopes, or on tennis courts, or even on horseback. There she would have been quite ordinary, very mediocre. She was an excellent golfer and as long as she was where this sort of excellence mattered she could count on its glow to make her exceptional enough to appear stunning, and perhaps almost beautiful. And, indeed, judging from the shrewd Monsieur Genet's enthusiastic responses, she was where she ought to be, where she undoubtedly belonged. The meeting lasted longer than any of the participants had imagined, and there was time enough for both men to be shown Jean-Pierre's photograph which they praised, and could not help showing how fundamentally touched they were by the young widow and her fatherless son.

Ilsa had her membership card the very next day. Candidates' names are not posted – once she had been proposed by the President (Eric Genet) and seconded by a member of Duchosal's eminence (a rare, pure *Haut Genevois*) it was a matter of informing the committee that Madame Ilsa du Four was to become a member.

Monsieur Eric Genet came up to scratch in all respects; all the appropriate arrangements were made with discreet precision; Ilsa had her house abutting the club, solid investments, and several games scheduled with good golfers as well as those lesser golfers who qualified by being socially prominent.

And now Ilsa was in her third season at the club, and now along with the correct father she had acquired for her son went the correct prestige for herself. So, all things considered, why should the sight of Madame Giscard

Duchosal's indignantly unforgiving eyes not have sent her into paroxysms of helpless giggling? Ilsa had set her sights high, but not too high. For as Madame Pachoud or Madame Duchosal would have said – she had got away with it.

But Ilsa of course could not explain the reasons behind her uncontrollable, and far too lengthy, fit of gasping giggles, the force of which made Nigel anxious for he was afraid something other than laughter must be the overwhelming power. Her eyes, he was sure, must be smarting. Could she be an asthmatic, too? But then she regained herself, she looked at, and smiled at, and touched Jean-Pierre, and then looked once more towards Madame Duchosal, and in that one sweeping glance their eyes at last locked in recognition. Suddenly, as if to make sure that Jean-Pierre was real, and to emphasize her motherhood and therefore her claim on it and on her son, Ilsa chucked him under the chin and pinched his cheeks and ruffled his blond hair. For the triumph of this moment was underscored by Jean-Pierre's presence, Jean-Pierre's being. She glanced again at Madame Duchosal. Look again, if you dare, was what her eyes conveyed. But Madame Duchosal did not dare.

Once more, and for the last time, Ilsa looked at Madame Duchosal, this time, sadly. And now, as profoundly as she giggled, she sighed. André Pachoud still hurt, unbearably sometimes, though it was a pain she had learnt to live with. Even worse. André had never seen Jean-Pierre, and that was grief.

'We'd best be moving,' she said firmly, and added, 'you're in a winning mood, Nigel. I can tell that – let's go.'

6

23rd March

Everything in my life has changed.

We used to do things together, my Dad and I. The two of

us used to go to the club – it was more or less a regular thing – either I would meet him there or he would pick me up from school. And we used to go swimming together. We'd go to the Continental Hotel for what my Dad used to call a 'quick dip' but we don't use that pool any more. She says it's unhygienic because of all those Arabs who stay there. She says that she found out that the hotel charges a huge deposit to any Arab who stays there because their suites have to be totally redecorated when they leave, because they grind chicken into the carpets because they eat on the floor. I don't believe it – we've got an Arab kid in our class and he's what my Mom calls the disgustingly tidy type. No, we go to a covered indoor pool now, and always with Jean-Pierre who has to swim because of his asthma. That's *one* thing he does well – apart from whining, I mean.

We've been in this house for twenty-three days – it seems like twenty-three months because the days seem to have more hours than they used to. The first two school days my Dad drove me to school, the way he often did, and on the third day Ilsa announced that she would show me where to take the bus, and then the tram, because that way, she said, your father who works too hard as it is, can stay in bed a little bit longer. I was thirteen, she said, sounding as if she was telling me something I did not already know. I looked at my Dad when she said that, but he didn't seem to see me. So, yesterday, I decided to ask him if he could give me a lift because I had this stack of heavy books to take back to the library. I watched him glance very quickly at *her*, somehow I *knew* he would do that, I just had to test him, I suppose, because I hoped and hoped he would not look at her as if he was asking her for her permission, but he did . . . I could not stop myself from saying, 'I'm sure Ilsa will allow you – just this once – to give me a lift to school.' She used one of those giggles of hers, and bent double, she giggled so much. I could hardly make out the words she said above all that noise.

So he drove me to school, but he wasn't pleased with me, I could tell. We didn't talk much, so the whole thing was a bit of a waste. If Doctor Gaud had not told me that my Dad caught some kind of disease I think I'd begin to think that some kind of mistake was made, that I'm not his real son, that I am really adopted, only they never wanted to tell me. Or else it's like my Dad had just found out that the wrong child was given to him at the hospital, that his son was not his real son. The whole thing is crazy.

When we finally got to school – we seemed to be driving very slowly – my Dad told me that he loved her, and that if I loved him like a real son should love a father I'd love her too. Please, he said, Peter please, do this for me . . . And you know what? You'll be happier, too. Don't disappoint me . . .

I said nothing. I'm starting to hate him, too, and that makes me hate myself, and then I feel sort of helpless, but angry. I didn't know that when you feel angry, very very angry you also feel something like the kind of pain I felt when I broke my leg a long time ago when I was nine. I feel so much pain that it seems my arms and even my ribs have turned into scraps of broken legs. It's crazy, I know.

The reason I asked my Dad to give me a lift was because I wanted to ask him – privately, when she couldn't hear, of course – to take me to see Raffles. But I couldn't ask him – it was like I couldn't trust my secret real feelings not to explode.

That day at school we were given back the project we had done last term. I got an A – Mr Holmes, our geography teacher wrote: 'An excellent project, Peter! Shows careful planning and a fine attention to detail. Well done!' The rest of my grades have not been so great, so I was very very pleased with what he had written, and I thought I'd show it to my Dad, and that that would make him not so disappointed in me, besides I felt bad because I hate to hate him – I hate hating him even more than I hate her.

This diary helps me to sort things out. I'll have to think of a code-name for it. I've started writing so fast that I don't think anyone who finds this could even real what I've written, so that's one good thing.

I always go straight up to my room as soon as I get to the house. I'm very polite – as polite as my Mom told me to be –

and I go upstairs to do my homework. She's given up offering me anything to eat because I always refuse – I have something in the school canteen before I leave. Staying upstairs until I hear my Dad's car means that Jean-Pierre gets to see him before I do – he rushes out the door and flings his arms around my Dad's legs like a five-year-old, instead of an eight-year-old. 'Daddy, Daddy,' he calls, and each time I hear that I want to throw up. Then he kisses Jean-Pierre and then *her* – he's always kissing her or hugging her or holding hands – it's so embarrassing watching your own father behave like a teenager like that – I feel stupid, even ashamed.

He must have felt bad about our drive to school because I heard him ask where I was. He said he had something for me. Well, I came down at once, and he was holding my favourite kind of chocolate – they are made in cigar-sized lengths, and wrapped in shiny purple and green wrappers, and they're the best Swiss chocolates in the world. He often used to buy then for me – it was a sort of family joke . . . Even Frederica used to buy them for me. The man in the *tabac* knew about me and my *Cailler*, even the grumpy concierge made a few funny sort of remarks about them. It was fantastic seeing them again and it seemed, for a moment, as if nothing had changed . . . You can't buy them in all the *tabacs*, so he must have visited M. Bucher, and even while I was thinking that he told me that M. Bucher sent me many greetings. I said something like 'Gee, thanks Dad, thanks a stack,' and then I couldn't help it, I hugged him. He held me tight for a few seconds until that miserable little Jean-Pierre began wailing, 'What about me Daddy, what about me?' And of course my Dad gave him exactly the same chocolates he had given me.

The Tick said something about not eating all of them at once, because I had now reached the pimply stage. I ignored that. I felt rather shy, suddenly, about telling my Dad that I had a surprise for him too, but I told him anyway and then I went off to fetch my project.

So I showed it to him at once – in front of them instead of the way I had planned. I was going to ask him to come to my room to see it. My Dad said that he thought that it really was excellent, and she said something about it being *magnifique*, but I could see her sending him all sorts of signals – rolling her eyes and eyelashes (well, almost) and my Dad obviously decoded them very successfully because he said at once. 'But Peter, have you seen the drawings of butterflies that Jean-Pierre brought home yesterday?' And while he was saying that he went to the desk and took those bright splotches, bright as the colours of my *Cailler* wrappers, and made me look at them.

I thought they were wonderful I said.

Mentally done out – that's what I keep saying to myself, telling myself that that is how I feel – mentally done out. It's the only way I can begin to describe how I feel. I just think I've got no luck any more, because that punk Michel Olivier was there when they brought in that disgusting birthday cake with thirteen orange candles made to look like golf tees. Everyone there saw, and some of them clapped, and she made me stand up, and laughed at the way I was blushing. 'Look how excited he is,' she said, dissolving into one of her giggles. 'Look at him – he's even blushing.' Some people even shouted bravo and congratulations – and then began leaving their seats and coming up to us, kissing her and then kissing my Dad on both cheeks, and then kissing me and Jean-Pierre on both cheeks and saying things like: '*Félicitations à toute la famille!*'

Michel Olivier is fourteen, and thinks he's the greatest. He's an excellent golfer, I must say, he has a handicap of fourteen – he's much better than I am, and wants to become a professional one day. He could hardly wait when we were walking down the stone steps on our way to the green afterwards, to smirk at me and leer at her, and say *in English* something about my new mother improving my game, and asking how I liked my new brother. Michel is one of those Swiss who's always talking about *sales étrangers*, and his father wanted to have a referendum about banishing all the foreigners from Geneva, so that when he said something about foreigners having no morals what with women like my mother abandoning a son and allowing him to live with his father who was living with a woman like man and wife when he was not even married to her, I tripped him, and he crashed down on his knees, and I pretended not to see, and continued walking as if nothing had happened. He'll probably report me to the committee, but they won't pay too much attention to him because his father makes a habit of complaining about foreigners. He's something of a laughing stock.

All I know is that my Dad made a terrible fool of me today, and I can't help feeling that he made a fool of himself, which is even worse. Somehow, after today, I have the feeling that I can't really respect him the way I used to.

Just before we left the club, while we were still looking at the bulletin boards in the foyer, Monsieur Lullin, the club secretary, made a big show of 'presenting' me with an envelope. He said that now I was thirteen, I could have my own locker, and in that envelope I would find the key. My Dad applied for a locker for me last season, and both of us had forgotten about it. I might use that locker for my diary – this one is almost finished. I don't know yet. My secret hiding place seems quite safe.

Still, I'm glad I made Michel fall down those rocky steps, I'm glad he hurt himself. I got my own back on him.

I'll have to pray, tonight, that no one at the club ever checks my papers and discovers that today is not my birthday – my birthday is in seventeen days' time, on May 8th. I'll never know how my father could have done that to me, but I know why, though. It was to please *her*. My Dad must think I'm stupid, as if I couldn't tell that my birthday was an excuse for everyone to congratulate her.

Sometimes I think I want to hit my Dad, really punch him, so to stop myself from thinking like that I think about *her*, and I imagine myself aiming my pellet gun at her forehead. I think of aiming, I don't think of pulling the trigger or firing. Aiming is enough for me.

The day after my Dad and I moved into her house, Jean-Pierre had an asthma attack and Raffles was taken away from me. It happened soon after I left for school, so I didn't see what it was like. We were having dinner – as we always do – in her kitchen – the way my Mom and Dad and I never did when we all lived together. She likes that kitchen, I can tell, she's always cleaning it and polishing it as if it were a silver golf trophy. It's all white and glinting, it reminds me of our dentist's surgery. It even smells like it – it's sort of disinfected like the rest of the house because of Jean-Pierre's asthma. Household dust and mites and things like that are all dangerous, she says.

She writes down everything Jean-Pierre eats. She's got a special notebook for that. She's got another notebook for her menus – her menu book, she calls it. The menu book is covered in velvet, and the Jean-Pierre book hasn't got a name but is covered in a checked plastic shelving paper. So that when Jean-Pierre had only one bite of the *Cailler* chocolate she wrote that down.

While we were having dinner Jean-Pierre began to complain about his chin having scratches on it. He looked upset but not nearly as upset as her. She told him not to worry, that a scratchy chin did not always have to mean the beginning of an attack, and she even tried to giggle. I could tell she was frightened, even though she was trying to be calm. Jean-Pierre was looking at her all the time, and then he said his lungs had become too small, and then she carried him upstairs and I saw him looking around wildly, his face was white and pale and sweaty, his lips lake-grey, but his breathing sounded ordinary to me. I suppose I thought it would sound like it does in a Western.

My Dad followed them up the stairs.

I stayed in the kitchen for a long time and then I went upstairs too and I wrote in my diary for a long time, and didn't see anyone until the next morning.

At breakfast they told me that the excitement over *my* birthday cake probably caused Jean-Pierre to have an asthma attack. I wish it had been a heart attack. No I don't. I want to forget that I even *thought* of such a wish!

I know I'm supposed to love my Dad, but I hate him more and more.

7

Nigel would have preferred to have lunch at one of his favourite lakeside restaurants, but Pamela had said it would have to be the Richemond because she was staying there, and because she would only be in Geneva for one night. She was late, as usual, but Nigel didn't mind. He quite looked forward to waiting for her; people noticed Pamela, she had a way of drawing attention and when she appeared the guests would not fail to pause momentarily, to take in – and for a moment become – that bright smile and tinkling jewelry, the stunning grace with which she had put herself together. She would walk effortlessly across the restaurant, her enthusiasm sparkling, her eyes glinting, and in some way she would make the surroundings even more elegant, the food in that five star restaurant even more memorable; women would pause to approve the obvious effort that had gone into that ensemble of perfect grooming; the shades of her stockings would be just right, at her ears the jewels that just peeped through hair that had a golden handspun look to it would be an inspiration; the men would pause to approve her provocatively shapely – though perfectly lady-like – legs. For Pamela made affluence corporeal; beside her the Madison Avenue concept seemed no more than an imitation of her idea. Everyone – even the waiters – would feel more than ordinarily privileged.

Waiting for her had intensified Nigel's self-awareness: his own pride, his own courage, his own daring, above all, his own will, made him unusually cognizant of his own appearance. Or, more accurately, the effect of that appearance. He smoothed his tie (a Dior, an early gift from Ilsa), he fingered his cuff-links (a more recent gift from Ilsa) and found their nugget shape remarkably sensual and sat waiting, with one hand in his pocket, just as he had waited when a teenager, knowing that Pamela would soon fill his pockets with all sorts of imaginative surprises. He felt something not too dissimilar from that schoolboy whose elder sister had turned up unexpectedly and charmed his housemaster into letting him out for lunch.

Pamela's arrival was all he had known it would be – it was his extra awareness (extra aliveness he would have said) that made it more difficult for him to stay in place until she reached their table. Pamela was so pleased to see him, her hugs so warm and so obviously genuine, the slight distance she forced between them while, still holding his upper arms, she examined and appraised his appearance and his health, that Nigel felt positively boyish.

And also very important.

He watched his sister approve the wine and select the fish of the lake and observed that she was a trifle less receptive than usual to the maître d's remarks on Washington. 'I have not seen my young brother for months and months,' she said pointedly to the maître. Then she just as pointedly turned toward Nigel and (in somewhat too firm a tone, Nigel thought) said, 'Well, my boy, you *are* looking well.'

'You seem surprised.'

'Hardly. I stopped in London and saw Caroline.'

'How is Washington?'

'Washington will get along without me. But it has been hectic. Election year.' She ran her eyes over him. 'Nice cuff-links,' she said. 'New?'

'Yes. A gift.'

'I thought as much. you don't have to boast, you know.' She laughed affectionately and added, 'Show-off.' She reposed for a moment her hand on his and sighed. 'Darling,' she said gently, 'why didn't you let me know about all this before? Bill and I always believed you and Caroline were so happy together. I thought Caroline was out of her mind when I spoke to her. I took the first plane out – I left everything. Bill was shocked – he would have come too, but election year – '

'Caroline called you?'

'No. I called her. I tried your Geneva number, got no reply, so decided to try London.' She went on reproachfully, 'I hadn't heard from any of you for ages.'

'You could say things were hectic here too,' he said drily.

'You should have told me!' She laid her hand on his again. 'I *was* mad with you, of course. But there's no point in going over why you didn't tell me. I suppose you didn't speak to anyone.' She played with a chunk of French bread, and even in that her movements were graceful. 'Wonderful bread,' she said fervently, and added, 'You've never been the confiding type.'

'I spoke to no one.' Nigel was obliged to stop and taste the wine. He experienced a mad urge to send it back, but thought better of it. 'Very good,' he said shortly. 'Of course I told some of my people at the bank when Peter and I moved to Ilsa's – '

His sister cut him short. 'I know about *that*,' she said abruptly. 'Tell me, Nogs,' she went on, using their very private nickname to soften things, 'Nogs, have Bill and I been wrong all these years?' She twirled her hands in bewilderment. 'It *can't* be that you and Caroline were *not* happy – I'd have put my head on a block – ' She sipped some Perrier. 'Frankly, Nogs, I'm horrified.'

'*You*?'

'I know,' she interrupted wearily, 'my third husband. O.K., so I've never been husbandless for longer than three months. OK., so I'm a romantic – at least I was a romantic. I know about divorce and marriage and his and her children. I know. So of course I'm horrified – '

'Now don't let's be melodramatic.'

'Let me finish,' she said, sipping more Perrier. 'I believed in your and Caroline's marriage. It gave me faith, and in a way that you will probably understand, it gave me stability. Your marriage was the kind that others clung to, the kind that some of us even lived by. Of course I'm horrified. I'm horrified for all sorts of reasons, not least because I now discover that it's all been a gigantic myth, a lie – you've been at one another's throats all these years – '

'Don't be stupid, Pogs, you *know* that's not true – ' Nigel interrupted restlessly.

But his sister went on as if she had not heard him: 'Of course it's all very clear to me now,' she said emotionally.

'You and Caro were mismatched from the very beginning. That's why you had only one child. I have been stupid. You've never got on with one another. It was all an act, your rushing home to Caro, her waiting for you, her face reflecting the light in yours when you met after having been separated for a whole day. And for all the twenty years that I've actually lived with both of you – sometimes for weeks on end, I've been duped – '

'Pamela! Do be sensible.'

'No, Nigel, I will not be sensible. You want me to be silent, and you choose to call that being sensible. Why, Nigel, you've been having me on all these years. Pretending to be happy the way you did. What possessed you? I always thought we had an honest-to-God sort of genuine relationship. A real brother and a real sister – Instead I now discover that you and Caro were pretending – and why were you pretending? I'll tell you why – you wanted me to be jealous of the happiness you never had.'

'Stop it, Pamela!' Nigel said, shaking his head in denial. 'Stop it. You know it's not true!'

Pamela sighed deeply. 'Well that's a relief, anyway – '

'A relief. Why?'

'Because I wasn't wrong, Nogs. You were made for each other, you and Caroline.' She bit her lip. 'Any chance of you returning to your senses?'

'If that's why you're calling me Nogs you're wasting your time.' he said bitterly. 'Did Caroline send you to Geneva? You're wasting your breath.'

'Caroline is not a fool, Nigel.' She put her knuckle against his cheek. 'Don't get like that with me, Nigel. Bill says this will have a distinctly unsavoury effect on your career. You are not Swiss, yet you've managed to become a Swiss banker – the real thing, but a non-Swiss Swiss banker. Have you thought of *that*?'

'Of course I have.'

'I don't think you have. I don't think you've thought about anything. I think your brains have descended . . . But never mind that. I want to ask you one other thing. Were you and Caroline always unhappy?'

'No. That's not true.'

'What is not true, Nigel? You were desperately unhappy for twenty years.'

'Of course I was not unhappy.'

'O.K. I accept that. You were not unhappy, but nor, for twenty years, were you happy – '

'That's not true, either. I was happy. We were happy – '

'Well, of course you were – '

'I see what you've done. You reduced this to the absurd. I suppose you think – '

'No, Nogs, not to the absurd – ' She stopped, took his hand in both of hers, and said, 'I don't think so, but of course, if the truth is absurd then that is exactly what I did do.'

'I see. . . Well, have it your own way.'

'Call it sisterly licence if you like. I can recall your having been brutally frank with me – from time to time – you know.' She sighed deeply. 'That's a relief, anyway – '

'A relief? Why? What's there to be relieved about?'

'Being truthful,' his sister said simply. 'Being able to be absolutely truthful with one another. . . You see, Nogs,' she went on, 'this comes to me as a personal blow – as if it had happened to *me*, and not to Caro. Can you understand that?'

'Can't say I do. No.'

'It's like this – well, what I mean is this: you see, my faith and not my illusions have been shattered.'

'Come on, Pogs. What's the difference?'

'For a start, I've got no illusions. None at all. Caro gave me faith, you see. She was the one wife I knew who was entirely fulfilled.'

'*Fulfilled*! Come on, Pogs please – that's not your sort of word at all.'

Pamela frowned. It was obvious to Nigel that whatever she needed to say to him, she needed, even more, to say to herself. 'Caro didn't see herself as just a wife,' Pamela said, 'because for her there was no such thing. She could have been anything, you know that – she took a first at Oxford!'

'Of course I know that!'

'Don't be impatient,' Pamela said at once, the elder sister taking over. 'I was going to say that being a wife wasn't a job – she was ambitious, but she never thought of promotion or anything like that. No, it was her vocation, or, if you like, her faith, one she embraced willingly, and she brought to it everything she had – all her considerable abilities.'

'That's true.'

'Yes, it's too true. But that doesn't count, now. You admit that you were happy, but that doesn't count either. . . You've told her you will always love her, she says.'

'Of course I will. Always.'

'And she – poor devil – loves you too much to even find that insulting!'

There was a silence.

Agitatedly, Pamela sent her silent eyes to the ceiling. She returned her gaze to her brother. He knew this movement of hers – she used it only when she was compelled to struggle for control. Nigel waited. Regained, Pamela said, 'We were talking about my faith – '

'So we were! Though quite what you meant,' he said affectionately. 'I'm not sure I understood.'

'I don't know, quite, what I mean myself,' Pamela admitted. 'Perhaps this is like a body-blow to me because Caro's vocation had nothing to do with opting out behind the brambles – she was, is, a positive, well-informed and gentle woman; stimulating and amusing, too. And very attractive – earthy and sexy and at the same time, restrained. Would you agree?'

'Of course I agree. So what?'

'You see. You see – I *knew* you would,' she said happily, and added sadly, 'But if a woman like Caro loses out, what hope can there be for any wife?' Pamela bit her lip. 'Any chance of your returning to your senses?' She did not wait for a reply but said,

'Have you been faithful to Caroline?'

'No.'

'Have you had any other affairs?'

'No.'

'I see. That's exactly what I thought. Call girls?'

'Yes.'

'I've heard about that. Not about *you* of course.'

'You sound like a lay psychologist. But then even professional psychologists can't be expected to know that this sort of thing is all par for the course.'

'Business?'

'Certainly.'

'Which means that those activities of yours were scarcely a reflection of your marriage.'

'They had nothing to do with it.'

'Ah – so you were happy with Caroline.'

'I've already said I was.'

'Until you met this Ger –' She stopped herself but not quite in time. 'Until you met Ilsa,' she amended quickly.

'Yes. Until I met Ilsa. I couldn't understand it myself. Still can't. Gave up trying – ' She brushed something from his cheek. 'Of course you're on Caroline's side,' he burst out. 'I can't say I blame you for that.'

'Come now, Nigel. Be your age. You may look thirty, but I know you're nearly fifty. I'm not on anyone's side – it's not a question of sides. But if I were you know very well whose side I'd be on!'

'I know,' he said, contrite. 'And you look thirty-two at the moment. How do you do it?'

'With diligence – and money! The infallible recipe for all things.'

They laughed again.

'Caro, all things considered, looked good when I saw her. She changed her hair style.'

'It was good of you to go to her,' he said with all the misery of one who knows he's in the wrong.

'After all she's done for me? Rubbish!'

'You don't have to rub it in! D'you think I don't know her virtues? Ilsa is an incredible mother, you know.'

'So I've been told. A touch obsessed, though.'

'I suppose Caroline told you that?'

Pamela said nothing.

'You can't expect an objective view from Caroline.'

'I suppose not,' she said conciliatingly. 'But this Ilsa of yours was left all alone in the world, she probably couldn't help developing a neurotic relationship with her child. Caro may not be objective, as you say, but even she finds that perfectly understandable. Especially since the child is asthmatic. . .You really are letting yourself in for something big, Nigel.'

'He's a sweet kid,' Nigel said defensively. 'Believe me. I'm a very lucky man.'

'Tell me about Peter. I can't help being more interested in *him*. How is *he* taking all this?'

'Giving up Peter was Caroline's one and only unpredictable act.'

'She didn't have a ready-made father-figure to give him like Ilsa.'

'This is the one thing about Caroline that Ilsa says she'll never be able to understand. D'you know Caroline hasn't written to the boy once, in three weeks?'

'Caro wanted the boy to settle – not to feel pulled. A bit too noble, I agree.' She sighed and went on. 'You and Peter golf together. She says you're Peter's hero, she's always fostered that, as you know. She said you both agreed you could give Peter much more than any housemaster could. Not sending him to your old school was a *mutual* decision. Even I remember that.'

'It was the right decision, too. It's early days yet. Peter will be O.K. His golf hasn't suffered. No problems at school, either. But he seems remote, withdrawn. He's so damn polite to Ilsa – and to me – he's helpful to the point of servility. But he'll settle down. Children do.'

'It's a lot for a little boy to get used to. I'm told you're living in Ilsa's house. Better for her child, of course.'

'We're looking for a new one. Peter knows that.'

'A new house?'

'Oh yes.'

Caroline had always wanted a house – Nigel preferred an apartment – but Pamela forbore from saying this as she had from saying so much else. Being tactful with Nigel was as tricky as it was new. She said brightly, 'Peter will be pleased. Raffles must be in bliss, having a real garden.'

'Well, we had a problem with that. Jean-Pierre, that's Ilsa's little boy, is allergic to dog hair – '

'So Raffles had to go, too.'

'Yes. But to a very good kennel. It costs an arm and a leg, I can tell you.'

'Poor Raffles.'

'Poor Peter, you mean! He's been out of sorts ever since. Quiet. Never rude or sullen. Simply quiet. Silent. But little Jean-Pierre is good company for him. He's five years older than Pierre, you see, and Pierre follows him around like a puppy.'

'You know, Nigel, silence in children is a symptom of depression. Don't you think a good child psychologist . . .?'

'No, Pamela, I don't. Psychologists are an American disease Ilsa says, and I agree.'

'I know Ilsa's type – *Alles in Ordnung!* what does Caro think?'

Nigel let that pass. He said, 'I must remind you that Caro has not, so far, made a single enquiry about Peter's welfare.'

'I see.'

'Well, I don't see. I don't understand. Nor does Ilsa. She thinks Caro's unnatural. Darling, you must meet Ilsa. You'll dine with us tonight of course?'

'No, darling, I won't. Not tonight.' She straightened a gold chain about her neck. 'Don't set your lips like that – I'm not trying to register my disapproval, you know. The truth is that I'm so upset and shattered, really, that I just want to get back to Bill as quickly as possible. I don't care which route I have to take – I – Look, be a darling, Nigel, take me to the airport?'

The urgent cable that Pamela sent from Geneva airport read:

BAD BUT NOT TERMINAL STOP INACTION STILL ESSENTIAL STOP CLEVER GIRL LOVE PAMELA.

*

After he left his sister at the airport Nigel did something very uncharacteristic – he did not go back to the bank, nor did he go home. Ilsa was taking Jean-Pierre to the orthodontist anyway (it had been Nigel's suggestion). He needed, really needed, to wield his golf clubs, and he thought he would take about a hundred balls and hit at least a hundred shots, although he never went in for more than fifty practice shots a session. In the event, however, he found himself unable to resist the golf course, and decided to play at least nine holes on his own. Because the golf course was a good place to think, or rather and more accurately, not to think. He would pit himself against the ball: this way things would sort themselves out.

Because Pamela's talk – those snide remarks and telling observations of hers – had discomfited him. She knew him so well – no one (other than Caro perhaps?) knew and understood him better. He had expected Pamela's disapproval, of course. That was reasonable enough. But he had not anticipated her distress, and he found this as unreasonable as it had been unpredictable. Still, he had never been able to fool his sister, nor, for that matter, had he ever wanted or needed to. They had always been close, which was why Pamela's reference to sisterly licence had been altogether appropriate, altogether fair.

He liked the crunch of the grass under his spikes. It was Pamela who had introduced him to golf, and now, as he took up his number one wood, and hit a perfect drive, he was transported back to his school-days, to that era of his life that had never quite become the past if only because of the obstinate way with which it intruded, for ever impressing itself upon his present, like an unpaid and unpayable debt.

Nigel's school career had not been so much distinguished as exemplary. This was more by accident than by design, for he worked hard to pass as ordinary, but was always careful to disguise his effort. He had hoped to be of a piece with his perception of the other boys; a trifle arrogant, a twinge of the imp, a touch of the thug, a tilt toward academic nonchalance, and even, when he reached the senior forms, a token of the bully. At heart, however, he was none of these things. He was shy and serious, and above all compassionate, and never quite succeeded in wholly disguising these qualities. When he was made head boy everyone was surprised. But no one was as surprised as Nigel. His parents said it was the greatest and best surprise of their lives; Pamela was the only one who had said, 'Wonderful, Nogs! I'm not in the least surprised.'

'You're joking, of course,' Nigel said sadly.

'Not at all. Always knew you had it in you. I expected nothing less – '

'You can't mean that!'

'Just a minute, Nogs,' Pamela said. 'Just a minute. Am I right in thinking you think it's not only a surprise, but a mistake?'

'Some kind of unholy error, I'd say.'

'Poor old Nogs,' she said, hugging him. 'Try to have half the faith in yourself that others have in you, will you?'

Knowing that she knew he thought himself a fraud had helped him see through that year in the exemplary manner that had been predicted by everyone but himself.

For the truth was that though he was one of the most popular boys at the school, and later at university, he was friendless. His only confidante had been his sister; he had been born to the art of silence and was an authentic listener. The secret was that his genuinely wholehearted interest in other people far exceeded his interest in himself, he found the mysterious fascinating and believed he knew himself far too well: there was nothing left to compel him, and no mystery to unravel. His acute interest in others was therefore unrelated to his interest in himself which meant that he was as untouched by their problems as he was by their achievements. The result was that he was competitive but never envious, compassionate but never involved. In short, he could not have cared less about any of his friends, and if they mistook curiosity for concern that was not his fault.

So that Nigel, like his son Peter, had secrets.

Except that Caroline had always known. And perhaps Pogs?

And now there was Ilsa who knew nothing of this side of him. And what he felt for her was beyond friendship and outside humanity because it was not in the realm of anything he could define, because his need for her was as great, – and he thought as real – as his need for skin. She was his skin, for she had become his skin.

He was on the green for a birdie and sank the putt perfectly. He was playing immaculate golf, and it didn't seem to matter that no one was on hand to witness it. It occurred to him, though, that he could be playing so well simply because he was alone, and because his concentration was not absolute he was therefore more relaxed about his game.

Because his meeting with Pogs compelled him to question – but not to doubt – what he was doing. Damn it all – he knew what he was doing! Talking to Pamela, indeed, talking to anyone about his feelings for Ilsa, put him into the category of True Romance, or a letter in the agony columns. He felt somehow debased and resolved not to discuss things with his sister again.

What could Pamela, what could anyone know of *how* he felt, to say nothing of *what* he felt? Of course he had been happy with Caro – he had never sought to deny that – but what he experienced with Ilsa was beyond mere happiness and consequently more meaningful. It wasn't even excitement; after all Ilsa was now, so to speak, on tap and readily and constantly and ardently available, so it was – it had to be – more than that. He saw himself, he supposed, as essential, and more meaningfully still, as indispensable. He and he alone would not let Ilsa down. He and he alone had driven that look of heartbreakingly brave sadness from her features, her expression, her voice, her smile. He and he alone was responsible for her well-being. She had suffered loneliness and indignity all her life, and now he and he alone had the power to remove – as far as was humanly possible, as far as the Fates would allow, all forms of hardship from her. He could even supply her son with a father!

Caro had never been unhappy; accordingly she had never really needed his consolation.

And then of course – of course – there was bed. And with Ilsa each time was like the first time, not only with her, but with anyone – well, almost anyone. . . True, as he had admitted to Pamela, he had been happy with Caro – but what was happiness next to Paradise? Bed, with Ilsa, meant that bed and cradle and lullaby were all left behind, just as childhood and selfhood and even manhood were all left behind, too, as he reached for and struggled (and Ilsa knew – ah! how she knew – how to titillate, how to prolong the struggle) for that netherworld where all was sensation, where there was neither need nor space for anything else because neither breath nor death seemed to matter. That graceful rhythmical tempo to her golf-swing, that understanding intimacy with physical movement extended limitlessly, overflowing the confines of her own being to the point at which it embraced his. Besides, Ilsa was small; her shape, as much as her size, added infinite dimensions to his. . . This manner of thinking, however private, however silent, was none the less embarrassing, and Nigel felt foolish. But because it was all so high-flown and therefore so unlike him, it was also exhilarating.

A man, Nigel decided, is more than the sum of his responsibilities, his commitments, his ambitions, his conquests, if only because a man must do what he must. Which is why, he thought, as he sank yet another perfect putt, a man plays golf. Ilsa's golf – and she was a near-genius at the game – made her both man and woman which, in turn, made her everything.

After all, he *loved* Ilsa, and if he had not told Pamela that, it was only because that would have reduced them both to being no more and no less than star-struck lovers. And this banality Nigel could not – would not – accept. Besides, Pamela had hinted that it was all to do with his age, standard mid-life crisis was what she had had the nerve to imply. How could he explain to Pamela, or to anyone, except, of course, Ilsa, that Ilsa had presented him with the greatest miracle of all, because she had made him feel all his years, and be grateful for them. When he was with her he felt so authoritatively experienced that he respected the wisdom that, according to Ilsa, he had undoubtedly accumulated. Once Caro had said, 'But it is preposterous. Simply contemplating exchanging me for her is preposterous!' The tried, the tested, the true was what Caro had meant, whereas Nigel believed that not making that exchange would have been preposterous.

His drive on the ninth was as rare as it was perfect – the b ll left the club as a bullet leaves a revolver – and the sensation of rhythm combined with impact solved everything. For all that Nigel told himself that he was not really concentrating on his golf, he kept his score-card meticulously, and when he came to the end of his nine holes he was well pleased with himself – he had been out in 36, and had not three-putted once.

Nigel could not have said which he admired more – the consistently high standard of Ilsa's golf or her attitude to the game. He thought of Björn Borg and Jack Nicklaus, of their seemingly unconcealed nervousness before the game began, which nervousness, he believed, was vital to their success. And yet Ilsa played with a cool detachment. Nigel doubted whether she felt any anxiety – she reminded him of a seasoned player whose skill has been learned and then absorbed, and who now played with the ease of a practised champion. It was not that she was bored; she definitely enjoyed the game and was exhilarated by it, but it was almost in the same way that she enjoyed, and was exhilarated by, a shower. Nigel was no less astonished, now, by her control, than he had been from the first.

Without doubt, given time, Pamela would see things his way.

8

6th April

It's five weeks since we've been in *this* house. The other day I went to have a look at our old flat. I still have the key to the main door, I was going to go inside the building, but then I thought I might bump into the concierge who was one of Frederica's nosy friends, and so I didn't. I went across the road and looked at the swans, and wished I'd had some of the bread Frederica used to give me to feed them with. The *jet d'eau* was so high and bright – it's the tallest fountain in the world, and I used to see it from my bedroom window.

My Dad is looking for a new house, that will be better, I know. At least it won't be *her* house. . . I wish she'd go away. I wish her husband had not died.

Jean-Pierre is so babyish, he still wets his bed, sometimes! Dad had some tiny golf clubs flown in especially from the States for Jean-Pierre – my first clubs were nothing like those, but I don't care.

She knows I took that comfort blanket, but she can't prove it, and anyway my Dad knows I never lie. Mom thought getting rid of it would be a good idea, but she also thought that if I owned up to having disposed of it, it would be a very bad idea. Dad would get very very angry, she said; sometimes one had to be strict with little children, and Jean-Pierre was much too old to be sucking on a blanket, and one day Jean-Pierre would thank me for having got rid of it. Though of course he never would, because he would never know how it had disappeared.

My Mom thinks that it is sad that I had to lie to my Dad like that, it's sad but very understandable was what she actually said, because after all I had been forced to lie, even judges make allowances, sometimes, when people tell lies because of very special difficulties. She told me not to feel bad about that particular lie. But it would definitely *not* be a good idea to make that blanket suddenly reappear, my Mom said, because she could easily imagine the kind of

69

intensive search the Tick had made after it was missing. That's when I began to think it would be a good idea to get rid of it. I don't know what I'll do yet. Perhaps I'll burn it. Right now it's in my locker, and even the Tick can't get into the Men's Locker Room.

Jean-Pierre made such a fuss about the blanket that my Dad went out himself to get a new one, and when he gave it to Jean-Pierre he just screamed and flung it down. So I went upstairs and fetched my radio-controlled boat, but he got so angry that he threw it across the room and the window broke. So I called him a spoilt bastard, and my Dad sent me to my room! I don't understand my Dad – Jean-Pierre breaks a window, and I get sent upstairs. A little while after that had happened my Dad came to see me and told me that I must never be frightened to tell the truth, that no matter what I did he would always forgive me and understand, that even if I had lied about that blanket before and owned up now, he would not hold that against me, but he'd be proud of me for telling the truth. I wanted to tell the truth, I wanted him to be proud of me, I really did, but I couldn't take the chance of having him tell *her* – so I did not tell the truth. I feel bad about this, even now, although my Mom told me not to. I wish I could forget about it. Especially the part when my Dad asked me, man to man, to give him my word of honour that I had not taken it. He also said he knew that all this was hard on me, and though nothing could excuse lying, it could be understood nevertheless. I wish I had not taken that crappy blanket.

While my Dad was talking to me we could hear Jean-Pierre screaming. My Dad went downstairs and I heard him phoning for the doctor.

I want to go to London. I'd rather be with my Mom. But my Mom says I must have faith, in her, in myself, and even in my Dad. She knows I'm suffering, she says, but if I can last out then one day we'll all be together again. Meanwhile I must pretend that I'm at a boarding-school, and that the Tick is the matron, and that I have to be polite. Up until the matron gets the sack, and not a second longer.

All this is a secret, of course. I used to like secrets, they reminded me of surprises, like Christmas presents.

But now I hate secrets. Being secretive is like lying – you never know when you'll be found out.

I speak to my Mom almost every day. She's always there when I call. She says she doesn't care how much the calls cost – we can afford them she says.

The night they couldn't find the blanket Jean-Pierre had to sleep in the same bed as my Dad.

I only go in their room if I am forced to. The Tick never wears any clothes. It embarrasses me – I don't like it – it makes me feel sort of stupid. My Dad never wore pyjamas and I didn't either, but I wear them now.

9

'Peter sounds like a normal teenage when he laughs,' Ilsa said. She added a little giggle of her own, and went on, 'I'm not used to it.'

'He's always been a fairly serious sort of chap,' Nigel answered pensively, as if he were saying this for the first time. 'Jean-Pierre seems in seventh heaven. Just listen to *him.*'

Ilsa tilted her lips upward. Nigel, who always acknowledged her smallest movement at once, kissed her briefly, and then said again, 'Just listen to Jean-Pierre!'

'It's because of *you.*'

'I didn't give him the water-pistol. Peter did.'

'I used to get scared when he laughed, you know. It brought on an attack, sometimes.'

Nigel said kindly, 'Yes, I know.' Then, answering Ilsa's unspoken request, he called, 'Take it easy in there chaps. And, Peter, don't forget to mop up the water!'

'I'm pleased Caroline remembered his birthday,' Ilsa

said drily. 'I can't understand why she would have sent Peter's present to the school, though.'

'It fits. She said she wouldn't phone, and she hasn't. She usually does what she says.'

'But surely she worries about him?'

'No. Why should she? She knows he's being well cared for.'

'I've been thinking.'

They were seated side by side on the couch, her head on his shoulder, her hair streaming down his shirt. She hooked a miniature foot in its prim little moccasin about Nigel's substantial ankle. 'I've been thinking today,' she said again.

'What have you been thinking about, darling?'

'After all, it *is* his *birthday* – ' Ilsa's voice quivered. Bravely, however, she continued. 'He's so tidy, so organized – I can't begin to understand what Caro meant about a problem with discipline. I mean, his room is so tidy, and he's so polite – I mean, he's the best behaved kid I've ever seen!'

'Well?'

'I'm not criticizing him, of course. I'm just – worried. He's so disciplined, you see – almost too disciplined for his own good. So I can't say I go along with Caro's argument about Peter needing your discipline.'

'Of course he might not be quite as disciplined without me?'

'No – I don't believe that! She doesn't care, that's all, She simply does not care.'

'I wouldn't say that myself.'

'Wouldn't you? Though, I can understand that – it's too hard for a man to see the real truth about his son's mother. Not once, in almost two months, has she phoned or even written.' Ilsa winced, and shook her head. 'Poor Nigel,' she said sadly, 'poor, darling Nigel.' She rubbed her fingers along his cheek as if he were a child in need of resassurance.

'I can't say I follow you, darling. *I* think Nigel's a very lucky man myself.'

'It breaks my heart, I can tell you.' She unhooked her

foot, moved her head away, and sat upright on the edge of the couch. 'What a *heartless* woman – mothers like that make my blood boil! It's all very well sending an expensive microscope to your son's school on his birthday, but how in the hell a mother can neglect to phone her own son on his birthday, beats me!'

'*That*, I must admit, surprised me, too,' Nigel said thoughtfully.

Ilsa shook her head sadly. 'I find it hard to forgive heartlessness,' she said. 'I can't, for the life of me, understand Caro.'

'Well – you don't know her.'

Ilsa thought: Don't I? I know her down to the make of her toothpaste. She said: 'That's true. Of course I don't know her. But even so, you know, the funny thing is that the people who do know her also think she's heartless!'

'Who told you that?'

'The hairdresser.' Ilsa lied.

'I didn't know you went to the Continental for your hair.'

'I don't. One of their hairdressers left. He told me. A lot of his customers think the same thing, he says.'

Now the boys began to sound riotous.

'Better get Jean-Pierre off to bed,' Ilsa said, getting up. 'Wait for me, will you? Don't go away.'

Safely upstairs Ilsa wished, for the thousandth time, that she could have had a real woman friend. Most women have at least one confidante, but she had realized long since that this was the kind of luxury she could not afford. It was not that she had learned – through betrayal – to be secretive; her secrecy was the result, rather, of having had no alternative. When she had arrived as an *au pair* at the Pachouds, she had had no secrets, and gradually, as the secret between Maître Pachoud and herself had progressed in all its wanton terribleness, she had known – with the certainty that goes with the most innocent instinct for survival – that she must not tell. And she did not tell anyone, ever. Those who knew had been told by the Maître himself.

It was as well, Ilsa told herself, that Nigel believed she did not know Caroline, otherwise he might have guessed that she modelled her present style of living not so much on being different from Caroline, but on being as near to her opposite as was possible. Which was why she flatly refused to have domestic help more than once a week. This was, of course, in stark contrast to Caroline, who, even with the excellent help of Frederica, merely muddled through. Raffles's hairs clung to the upholstery, magazines and newspapers stayed where they had been left. Nigel had, at one time, found Caroline's careless disregard for possessions endearing, but now, compared with the sparkling order of Ilsa's rooms, Caroline (he remarked to Ilsa) had been merely slovenly. Because the bonus was that Ilsa's order provided privacy. At night, when the children were in bed, they could walk nude if they wanted to, they could make love in the kitchen, or anywhere they liked. They were spared the intrusion of the likes of a Frederica.

At first Nigel had protested that Peter and he would be too much for Ilsa to manage – she ought to have resident help – but Ilsa refused, and, to make her meaning abundantly clear, resorted – with absolute success – to vulgarity. 'I'd rather keep our fucking freedom,' was what she said. Meanwhile, she would send *all* their shirts, along with *all* their sheets, to the laundry. So it was that Madame Blanc, the *femme de ménage*, spent a whole day, now, instead of only the morning, every Wednesday.

Ilsa was convinced that Caroline would have been less of a presence in her own life, if she had not vanished, leaving Peter behind as a sort of live mascot. But for Peter's physical presence, Caroline and Peter would have been neatly filed away, to be brought out only on arranged or special occasions. Nigel believed that Caroline had bowed out gracefully and honourably, and logically, of course, he was quite right. Except that – well, Peter was a sort of rear guard, wasn't he? After all, there was no denying that Peter had been eavesdropping – that was why he'd brought them his gift of the microscope when he did.

Usually her quiet half hour with Jean-Pierre soothed – there is something pure and good about reading to a small boy – but now, having chosen a book that both knew almost by heart, she read mechanically, and even though from time to time Jean-Pierre lifted her hand to kiss it, as he often did, Ilsa failed to divert her mind from Caroline.

Because she knew she had not been able to penetrate the real reasons behind Caroline's decision to leave Peter with Nigel. There was nothing ulterior, Nigel assured her, but despite this she had formulated several theories, naturally, but (and this was almost unnatural for her) she had not come to any firm conclusions.

Caroline might have hoped to make things less idyllic for Nigel (an intruder or a spy in the love nest?) or perhaps Caroline was truly selfish after all, and knew that her own chances of making a new life would be greater without the burden of a teenage son? Maybe she was protecting Peter's future inheritance (a very substantial one, too) by plunging Peter deep inside his father's new life? And it may also have been that Caroline wanted Nigel to feel even sorrier for her, and even guiltier – the rupture had forced poor unselfish Caroline to lose not only her husband, but also her son.

But if Caroline honestly believed that mothers of the discarded wife variety cannot help turning their sons into homosexuals, Peter should have been at the same famous boarding-school as his father. And yet Nigel insisted that Caroline had always been terrified of the tendency towards homosexuality in all British public schools, which, as he readily admitted to Ilsa, was a reasonable fear.

True, Nigel and Peter were close – here Caroline could not be doubted. Whatever else Caroline might be, she was not a fool. But it was cruel of her to have abandoned Peter. Or was it selfless? It could not be both, though it might be.

It was confusing.

One thing, though, was *not* confusing: Peter snooped, eavesdropped, spied. *Proof was in the way he surprised us with his microscope while we were having that chat about his mother having forgotten his birthday. The way he said nothing, but placed that thing down on the table, like a detective exhibiting his evidence. . . Yes, that's what he is – a private eye. . .*

She was nearing the end of Jean-Pierre's book, when she was aware, suddenly, of being watched. Both she and Jean-Pierre looked up. They saw Nigel who made no attempt to conceal what an enthralled and delighted spectator he was. His expression leaned somewhere between adoration and awe, rather like the expressions on the faces of those good golfers when they thought they were exchanging a few words with a Gary Player or a Lee Trevino.

Ilsa let loose a giggle. She said, 'Darling, I thought you said you'd wait for me?'

'I got lonely without you!'

From Peter's room a cupboard door was heard to slam.

Ilsa pulled down her lips, raised her eyebrows, and inclined her eyes toward the direction of Peter's room.

'I'll be with you in a minute, my darling,' she said rather loudly. 'Go to bed. Wait for me. We'll have an early night. How does that suit you?'

In Peter's room, something crashed.

'Are you all right, Peter?' his father called.

'Dropped some books.'

'Good-night, then.'

'Good-night.' A pause. 'Dad.'

After about five minutes, Ilsa went down to the kitchen. She removed a tray she'd prepared and hidden in one of the cupboards. She was well satisfied. The champagne glasses, the silver champagne bucket, fairly sparkled on their bed of the finest *broderie anglaise* tray-cloth. She moved quickly to the fridge, and took out an opaque plastic box in which she'd placed small bowls of chopped egg, chopped onion, wedges of lemon, and the wafer thin toast she'd made herself earlier in the day. She opened the medium-sized pot of Romanoff caviare – medium, because it would not have done to have appeared too extravagant – and placed all these on the tray. Pleased with their arrangement, she turned to a drawer, opened it, and draped the matching napkins over her arm as well as a frilly apron. She inspected the tray once more, and frowned. She was a teaspoon short. She attended to that, then took off her tiny moccasins, and tiptoed up the stairs, balancing her equipment carefully. She did not go at once to their bedroom, but to the bathroom, which, though *en suite* with the bedroom, could be emtered separately as well. She locked both doors, and called, 'I'll be with you very soon, my darling.'

She proceeded to undress, then to cream (the sun-roughened triangle left by her golf shirt especially), then to perfume, then brushed her hair while she thought: 'Well, Mr Private Eye, if you're trying to outsmart *me* you won't succeed!'

Quite naked now, she began to dress again. First, she stepped into a pair of high-heeled satin slippers (which slightly modified bandiness, she would have preferred the fluffy pom-pom kind, but Jean-Pierre was allergic to fluff). Next she arranged her straight streaming hair around an Alice-in-Wonderland style of white bandeau, and finally tied the frilly apron around her waist. She unlocked the doors, draped a napkin over an arm, picked up the tray, knocked on the door that connected to the bedroom and said, in French, 'Room service. May I enter monsieur? Please – '

Nothing could have been more effective. Delighted, thrilled, charmed, Nigel bounded out of bed as forcefully as if he'd been given an electric shock. 'It's too heavy for you, that tray,' he almost howled as he grabbed it from her. He put it on her dressing-table.

'I thought we'd celebrate Peter's birthday,' Ilsa said shyly. 'Just you and me.'

In answer, Nigel crushed her to him. Urgently, he took her; he could not wait for the apron to be taken off, nor even, to take her to the bed. He lifted her muscular – but light – frame. She curled her legs about his back, his solid golfing legs supported both.

Spent, he yet carried her to their bed, to a new pair of Ilsa's recent collection of new sheets. It must have been fully ten minutes before either spoke. Ilsa waited for Nigel to speak first, and when he did, he said exhaustedly, 'Champagne. To celebrate.'

Now Ilsa jumped off the bed. 'I'll bring it to *you*,' she said. 'Let me wait on *you*.'

'If you insist.'

She brought the tray to the bed. He popped the cork, and then drank thirstily.

She said, 'I like to pretend I'm Peter's real mother you know – ' Her voice broke unexpectedly. 'Poor child,' she said, 'poor child.'

'This is a celebration, remember? The best celebration of *my* life. The best, ever!'

'Hey,' she giggled. 'Don't hog all that caviare. Give some to me. Good. Now turn over, put your back to me, and don't you dare turn round till I tell you to. O.K.?'

'Anything you say. Anything.'

She did not keep him waiting long. She removed her apron. She said, 'O.K. Turn round. More caviare for you.'

He turned. He saw. Caviare covered her nipples, filled her navel, about three teaspoons in all, but there, between her spreadeagled legs, lay at least a tablespoon. . .

'Eat, my darling, eat. It's gourmet stuff, I tell you. It's my *spécialité de maison*. Caviare on a bed of cunt, I call it – '

Nigel began. . .

'It must be eaten slowly, very slowly. Savoured, rather than eaten.'

And, while he savoured, she controlled. . . He ached, he said he ached, he begged not to ache, but she controlled. . . The dessert-spoon took the longest time, and finally, finally all her breath was sucked out, and she no longer controlled. He did not wait for her to recover either her control or anything else, but entered her at once.

He fell asleep with the light still on. The champagne bottle was three quarters full.

Near sleep, she thought of Jean-Pierre.

Because above all, and besides everything, there was Jean-Pierre. Who deserved Nigel, who was entitled to a father of calibre. Her very being was consecrated to Jean-Pierre, everything was subordinate to him. Jean-Pierre had been her inspiration, it was Jean-Pierre, fatherless at four, who had spurred her on, and who had compelled her to transcend herself. And his asthma was improving all the time.

Still, what *had* happened to that comfort blanket? *'You really should not snoop, Peter,'* she thought. *'Because snooping can be very dangerous. Very very dangerous.'*

That Caroline had remembered Peter's birthday was a pity. It was also annoying.

The next day Ilsa and Simone Morelli were to play in a friendly match with Katia Magnin and a friend of Katia, Suzanne Haig, who was visiting Geneva, and whose handicap was eight.

The first nine holes went well enough – Ilsa was out in 39, Suzanne in 38, which was two strokes below her handicap. She scarcely talked on the golf course, but made up for that when they broke for tea. It turned out that Suzanne, who took neat Scotch instead of tea, could be dismayingly frank.

'I knew I'd heard the name Ilsa du Four before, but I couldn't quite place where. Well, the penny's finally dropped – I used to live in Geneva you know,' she said with an unutterably large smile. 'I was quite friendly with Caroline Pritchett-Ward. She told me about you.'

'Oh, did she? How nice.'

'Hey, Ilsa don't go getting all uptight on me. I've been the O.W. myself in my time, you know.'

'O.W.?'

'Other Woman,' Suzanne roared loudly. It was the way in which some people – usually powerful people – laughed, and in Suzanne's case it was more than ordinarily unfortunate. Her manner and bearing – tough and masculine in aggressive contrast with her baby-pink silk shirt, her mischievous matching golf cap, the elegant make-up that only just missed making her small brown eyes appear lively instead of inquisitive – all this was somewhere an extension of that wrong-sounding laugh. 'I – ' she went on, 'saw my husband – I mean my ex-husband the other year. We were both with dates, both still wrangling over our no-contest divorce, so I sent over a bottle of champagne to his table and had the waiter take over this note. From Mrs Gerald Quinn and her date, to Mr Gerald Quinn and his date – we weren't divorced yet, see? He was furious. The next day I called him and said at least give me some competition – don't insult me with an old bag like the date you had last night – So –y'know what he did - ?'

'No.'

'He married a *seventeen*-year-old!'

That awful laugh-sound again.

A silence.

But Suzanne appeared not to have noticed the silence.

'You're different from what I thought you'd be. From what Caroline said – come to think of it she didn't say anything much about you – only asked if I'd ever played golf with you. I saw her the other week, you know, in Washington?'

As if she'd been asked an indiscreet question, Ilsa said, coldly, 'No. I didn't know.'

But in that raucous, eager, half-male voice the other continued: 'Sweet kid, Caro, but a bit too vulnerable for my tastes. Too sensitive for her own good, probably. Not into sophistication – wears her heart on her sleeve – I can deal with the heart – it's the sleeve I can't handle, you know?'

Ilsa, who had heard this talk about sleeves and hearts before, though in a different context, lapsed into her usual response to an awkward situation – she giggled.

Suzanne responded with her (equally humourless) roar. 'The kid's living with you – huh?'

'Yes.'

'She *mad* about him. I can't understand why she gave him up like that! Still, perhaps she's brighter than we think – I'm having hell with my fifteen-year-old male monster – I can tell you *that*. Amazing doll, Caroline – refuses to hear a bad word about that bastard. Ah – um – Excuse *me*. We'd best be getting back to the tenth – I talk too much, I guess – ' She got up, to Ilsa's relief – but only to take a second Scotch. 'I guess I shouldn't say this – and wouldn't if I hadn't been through it all myself – I just hope it's worth it to you – what you're doing to that doll. Hope you don't find out – like I did – that that little old truism's too true for speech – you know the one about you can't build your happiness on anyone else's unhappiness? My ex divorced her, married me, divorced me, married the seventeen-year-old, divorced her, and then remarried *her* again!'

Ilsa would have given a great deal not to respond, not to ask this creature *anything*, but the other two avidly listening women compelled her to make at least some comment. She said. '*Her*? Which of the hers do you mean?'

'Honeywell. His first ex-wife, that's the her I mean. Honeywell came to see me, you know, before I married that husband of hers. She wanted me to know that whatever Gerald – my ex – had said – that they had been happy for twenty years. . . 'Course I'm only telling you all this because Caro told me the same thing about her and Nigel. Well, in Gerald's case I really think it was his mid-life crisis – I was a mid-life crisis – get that?' And now she roared again. 'And d'you want to know what I am now? A lousy golfer!'

If Suzanne had hoped to put Ilsa off her game she was disappointed. Ilsa used golf as a means to combat upsets, and so her game almost never let her down. She handed in her card. Her score was 77.

Ilsa returned home. Some of Suzanne's remarks found their mark, and caught, and would not be shrugged off. She played with her Russian wedding-ring, but was more conscious of the callouses made by the club-grips than she was of the ring. Perhaps her grips needed renewing? Or perhaps she needed new clubs? This was not like her at all, puzzling idly over inconsequentials. Absently, she reached for her wallet – she would arrange it, order it. Instead she found herself handling, fondling, studying her credit cards, as if the magical powers in those new, small squares of plastic, whose magical computer numbering, raised, like the callouses on her hand, could somehow also solve the mystery that so preoccupied her and which with so much energy and accuracy – Suzanne had underlined: *Why had Caroline given up Peter?*

Very often it is the telling remark of a casual stranger that alerts us not so much to what we already know, but to the danger of it. And part of the magic of credit cards like

Ilsa's, which are backed as strongly by gold as the Swiss franc (which is also magic), is that they represent not only power, but safety. Safety in numbers, Ilsa thought. She giggled. A magical answer had been magically supplied by a magic card. She would have another child.

Ilsa felt peaceful.

Another child would be good for Jean-Pierre.

Which reminded her, she must fetch him from school, and if she did not hurry, she would be late.

It was before dinner, and Ilsa, carrying a tray of drinks, paused at the doorway, partly to take in the scene and partly to make Nigel aware of her quiet observation, of her calm appreciation of watching the three of them at play. Suddenly she wished again that Jean-Pierre could have a real brother, his own brother to play with. After all she was only thirty-eight. Though Nigel had indicated that the thought of babies – at this time of their lives – was not on. . . Anyway. . .Meanwhile, she willed Nigel to become conscious of her presence, to take her in as she was taking him in. In a moment she would admire his shirt – but not before he had looked up and seen the sharp creases on her pink and white striped Bermudas and the spanking white knee socks which, according to Nigel, drove men mad.

When, at last, he discovered her standing there in the doorway, his response was so spontaneous and so enthusiastic and so appreciative that holding that heavy tray had been well worth the effort. He was on his feet in an instant and the parts of the little car on which they had all been working so intently were strewn about the place.

'I'll take the tray,' he said. And he took it from her and placed it on the wrong table, and swooped her into his arms murmuring all the while 'knee socks knee socks – oh my God – they drive me mad. Mad, mad. Mad.'

But Jean-Pierre's little car was smashed, and he set up a wail, and Ilsa went at once to comfort him, and Nigel joined her, and they held him and hugged him and one another at the same time.

Peter was forgotten.

There were not too many bits to the car, and Peter collected them and set about the repair. The wheel was quickly back in place, the battery reconnected, and the little hooter was sounded before they remembered him.

'You got it to work,' his father said. 'That was clever of you. Good work.'

'It was easy,' Peter said.

Peter, for once, seemed pleased, Ilsa thought. She said, 'You are so clever with your hands Peter. I must congratulate you.' She offered her hand. 'Let me shake you by the hand.'

'Thank you, Madame du – '

'*Peter!*' his father said.

'I'm sorry, Ilsa,' Peter said shaking her hand very firmly. 'It was easy. Shall we take it apart and do it again, Jean-Pierre?' he said. 'When I was small like you, I broke all sorts of things. It made me cry a lot.'

'The wheel came off again,' Jean-Pirre said.

'O.K.,' Peter said easily. 'We'll fix it – '

'Are we not lucky?' Ilsa said softly. 'We are lucky, Nigel.'

'They get on well. Much better than I expected them to.'

'I knew they would,' Ilsa said. 'Didn't I?'

'You knew. You always know.'

'Trust me, Nigel?'

'I trust you. I trust in you, too.'

'So you like my new pants. You do. I can tell you do.'

'I most certainly do.'

'Well, I like your shirt,' Ilsa said. Suddenly she giggled.

'Hey – what's so funny?'

'I'm so happy,' she said seriously. 'I'm so happy darling. I can't help laughing.'

But it was her own remark about his shirt that had made her giggle. Because it was all going to plan, after all. Even though she had never reckoned on taking on an extra child. A full-time stepchild?

83

Perhaps she would tell Nigel about Suzanne Haig – perhaps not. She would see. It wasn't necessary, anyway.

10

20th April

Something very good happened today. It was like when I was very small, when sometimes my Auntie Pamela came with my Mom to the school to surprise me. The only thing is that this wasn't a surprise. Some things are much better than surprises. *I saw my Mom.* No one must know about it – it's a very very special secret.

Actually, she tried to arrange our meeting for my birthday, but it wasn't possible, after all.

My Mom and I planned the whole thing. She met me two stops away from my usual tram stop, and she had a hired car, a sports car, an Italian one, a convertible Alfa Romeo. That was my idea and my Mom thought it was a perfectly brilliant idea, and then we drove off into France. My Mom still has my passport – my Dad hasn't needed it yet, Mom said. My Mom looked quite different. Of course that was because she was in disguise. She did not want a single living soul to know she was in Geneva. She said she had special reasons, so special in fact, that I must not even think of what they could be. She wanted to be absolutely certain that I trusted her, the way she was trusting me. That's the really important thing, she said.

Anyway she was wearing this funny black wig, and dark glasses. She said it must look very strange to me, but she thought that was a lot of the fun. So did I! I was quite nervous at the *douane*, because she forgot to take off her disguise and she didn't look anything like her passport photograph. We must have had a whole lot of luck because the officers simply waved us through. As soon as we had crossed the border I told my Mom about it, and it was just as I thought – she'd forgotten about it. It was even worse than that, she thought, because the possibility of her not looking like her passport had not crossed her mind! It was O.K. because we had made it. But it was cool. Then I told her she would have to change when we went back. She said she felt a fool for not having even thought of that, but this really was turning out to be an adventure, wasn't it?

She had already been to see Raffles. She pretended she was inspecting the kennels because she wanted to leave four dogs with them. She said she was worried that Raffles might have given her away – she had to pretend not to know him, but he made such a fuss of her and was so excited that she had to think of a quick excuse. She told them that she'd just been with a bitch who was on heat.

She said she misses Raffles almost as much as she misses me.

And Dad.

That was when I asked why she couldn't stay in Geneva, why Raffles and me couldn't live in our old flat with her. And then she said it was because she was sure, she was certain, we would all live together again, not in our old flat, perhaps, but that one day not too far off, my Dad would live with us and not with Jean-Pierre and the Tick. She was convinced, she said, that we'd all be together again.

I must have looked doubtful because she asked me to try to have more faith in her. 'We'll all live together again, Peter, if you are sure that is what you want – ' I'm writing her words down exactly, because I could hardly believe my ears when she wanted to know if that was what I wanted. She knows I hate the Tick so much that I even hate Jean-Pierre, not only because he's her son, but because he calls my Dad, Dad. She knows all that now, but I told her again, because all that hating makes me feel bad, it makes me feel sick as if my stomach is stuffed with live, wriggling worms or snakes. . .

I try not to feel guilty because Dr Gaud told me not to – I don't really know what I feel, except that it feels bad.

And then my Mom suddenly stopped the car at the side of the road. She'd made a decision at that very moment, but if I did not agree she would change her mind. She told me to think about it for a few days before letting her know if I agreed.

This is what it is: if in six months' time we are not all living together again like we used to, then she will come back to Geneva and live in the old flat with me and Frederica and Raffles, or Raffles and Frederica and me will move to London. . .

She said she's thought about this whole thing a lot, so what she was going to say would probably sound madder than it actually was. She had met this wise old Armenian woman in London. This lady was very very clever and knew a lot about life because she was old and because she had helped lots and lots of mothers overcome the kind of problem our family was facing. My friend Guy is also an Armenian and he's just the brightest and the coolest – in our family we always talk about the way some people are different from others even though all of us would like to believe that everyone is the same.

My Mom said that she and Madame Sanossian had become friends, and that Madame Sanossian had given her some very sound and clever advice. She was like a teacher, as a matter of fact my Mom said she had become her teacher, now.

Anyway my Mom wanted to teach me something of what she had been taught.

The first lesson from Madame Sanossian had been about hope. There was this simple Armenian proverb which is like a kind of formula. Hope gives strength because hope is strength. I thought it sounded sort of complicated and Mom said she could only explain what she meant about why hope was so important to us if she told me another proverb, which we forgot about, because at that moment she suddenly said I must wait a minute because she wanted to look at me – she thought she had seen something.

She got very excited and started to laugh that her eyes had not deceived her – it was true – I was definitely growing a moustache. I didn't believe her, so she took out her magnifying mirror – the one that had belonged to Granny – and told me to look for myself. She was right, and I was pleased. I've looked at it a lot since then, my Dad hasn't seen it yet, you have to look very hard to see it of course. I might show it to him. I'll have to see. . . But anyway my Mom said it would be some time before I started shaving!

She thinks my voice is just beginning to break. It does sound funny, but only sometimes.

Well then she said she would tell me about that other proverb over lunch and wanted me to guess what we were going to eat. I was right first shot – *fondue chinoise* – my favourite. We went to a small bistro where it was unlikely we would see anyone who knew us. We each felt a bit like a spy, which was real fun.

The other proverb goes something like this: Encourage your enemy to believe you despair, so that hope may be your surprise weapon. Ilsa was our enemy, right? Now Ilsa probably thinks that her enemy, who is my Mom, has given up, surrendered, retreated to London. Ilsa probably believes that she has conquered her enemy. My Mom hopes that Ilsa does not know the enemy is lying low, waiting to attack. In a way, I was like a fifth column, a kind of Resistance. That's why Mom wants me to be so nice to Jean-Pierre and to everyone in that house so that they will never never guess that they have an enemy in their own territory. Ilsa had started it all. Ilsa, like Hitler, had been the one who wanted to rule the world, and as far as Mom and I and even Dad are concerned the Pritchett-Ward family is our whole world.

She knew it was complicated, but she and Madame Sanossian thought I would be intelligent enough to understand what she was saying. And, in a way, I do understand what my Mom means.

My Mom knows my Dad is innocent.

My Mom says none of this is really his fault because he is a victim. Kind people usually turn into victims – that's what makes all of this so sad, for her, because my Dad is certainly one of the kindest people she has ever met, which is why she hopes that I will not be too kind when I grow up.

Now my Mom believes that hope is the best weapon because hope is strength. She told me that scientists have proved that those patients who give up hope very often die, even when there are the right weapons, because when they give up hope they lose their strength, and when they lose their strength, they get weaker and weaker and weaker until they are destroyed.

I think all of this makes a lot of sense and I told her so. She was so happy when I said that, that I remembered how happy she used to be walking around our flat in long bright dresses without shoes and singing, and sometimes even dancing, to John Travolta's new record. And then all that changed and she started playing a song that I hate called I Will Survive, and even when she fetched me from school that horrible tape would be playing, but before she switched it off as soon as I got in the car, I had already heard the same words:

For as long as I know how to live I know
I'll stay alive – I will survive.

I must have looked sad because she asked at once what was wrong, so I told her. She was sad, too, but only for a moment because she said she had allowed herself to become weak then, when she was playing that song, because she had given up hope. She said she no longer listened to that horrible tape – she was sure I'd be pleased about that.

Wednesday

I got so tired yesterday, writing all that stuff about our adventure that I didn't write about what happened when I saw Raffles. I knew I'd remember all about Raffles, the other things were complicated so I had to write them down first.

My writing is changing – it's a good thing it's getting so illegible.

Of course my Mom couldn't take Raffles with us, because that might have given the game away, and our secret would have been out. She dropped me off at the kennels, and parked under some trees and waited for me.

Raffles looked O.K. to me – he *is* getting enough food,

that's one good thing. He was so happy to see me that I thought he cried with happiness. I felt – I don't know what I felt – almost as if I would prefer not to see him when I know I'll have to leave him. I half wish I hadn't seen him.

My Mom laughed when I told her what I did when I overheard the Tick telling my Dad that my Mom (Mrs Pritchett-Ward as the Tick called her that time) had even forgotten to send me a birthday present. I did not say one word – I simply put the whole microscope – case and all – on the kitchen table and of course they wanted to know where I got it, and I said, as if it was quite normal. 'My Mom sent it to school.'

The two of them just looked at one another then, and she said something about how thoughtful my mother was, and first my Dad kissed her so it was the longest time before he said that he thought it was a magnificent present and that it would keep me busy for hours, so I told him that my new camera that he gave me would keep me busy for hours, too, and then I looked at her and said that I was a lucky spoilt chap, wasn't I?

11

Of all the rooms in the house, the kitchen was the one that Ilsa found the most pleasing. It was not cosy, nor was it meant to be; all that gleaming black and white and silver was too stark for warmth, yet it somehow succeeded in being neither clinical nor sterile. Ilsa had intended it to be chic rather than elegant, and sophisticated rather than stylish. It was a large room which is perhaps why it was a comfortable and even a welcoming sort of room.

Nigel and Peter had been with her for eleven weeks or so, and during that time she had fallen into the habit of sitting at her round table covered with a black and white checked cloth (the checks were exaggeratedly large) as if she was contemplating her next move.

Her collection of recipe books was housed in glass shelves above that table, and she sat now with the *Larousse Encyclopaedia of Cooking* unopened. Being thus idle was still something of a difficult experience for Ilsa; she was a meticulous planner and during these past eleven weeks had been more than ordinarily efficient about things. She was a superb cook, planned the meals a week in advance, but still shopped every day, choosing each tomato with the kind of gravity that would not have let down a real Swiss. Nigel was fascinated by this habit of hers and found each supermarket excursion memorable. Caroline could no sooner have shopped every day than she could have – well, darned a sock, or, for that matter, tended a roast.

And so Nigel now – for the first time in his life – came home to the rich earthy smells of a kitchen which – as if by association – went so well with Ilsa, and where, at the end of a day, she was to be found. You don't need to be a genius, as Ilsa often laughed to herself, to know that men prefer kitchens to books.

Ilsa was determined not to slip, not to relax – not yet, anyway. She was a firm believer in the principle that a woman who wants to keep her man must work at it. She was all too well aware of the dangers inherent in the abrasions of day-to-day living, and perceived that she would have to expend more and more of her energy in preventing the kind of easy predictability that goes with familiarity, while still retaining the obvious advantages that go with comfort.

Because Nigel had found Caroline predictable.

Caroline was a source of endless interest to Ilsa, partly out of sheer curiosity, but Caroline's only real role for Ilsa was that she was a reliable informant of all the best ways of pleasing and fascinating and intriguing Nigel. Caroline did not like dining in the kitchen so Ilsa not only served almost all their meals in the kitchen but took the almost unprecedented step (in their club circle) of giving a dinner party in the kitchen. One-upmanship over an abandoned wife is – as Ilsa knew it would be – scarcely challenging, provided you are careful enough to uncover her failings, especially the smallest and seemingly insignificant ones that had irritated her husband, however imperceptibly. This kind of detective work meant that Ilsa had to be in a state of permanent alert. Nothing short of full-time vigilance would do.

It was exhausting.

And indeed Ilsa did feel tired, almost weary, but far from sleepy. She was aware, though, that this exhaustion was not entirely due to the strain of her constant vigilance. She was exhausted because of the quantity of sheer bodily energy that she had been expending lately. It was hard physical work. And Ilsa had, she believed, the highest motivation; it was all for her son, for Jean-Pierre. Husbands have an unfortunate proclivity, sometimes, of returning to a wife of long standing before the divorce is through and they are safely remarried. She could not, she would not risk this happening to Jean-Pierre. If Nigel were ever to leave them, Jean-Pierre would. . . But this was as far as she would allow herself to go. Which was, she chided herself, dangerous; no one got anywhere by failing to face up to facts.

Nigel would have to remain dazzled.

And it was up to her.

She would see to it that he kept his heart in the right place, well below waist level.

Keeping his heart in the right place may have been taxing and demanding, and even exhausting, but that it was all being done in the name of Jean-Pierre brought to it a dedication and a devotion she perceived as not only ennobling but also in a way, elating.

Shortly after Jean-Pierre's birth she had told herself over and over, *'Now I've made myself vulnerable again. Now I've made myself vulnerable again.'* And she had been almost grief-stricken, and altogether unprepared for this kind of reaction. But very soon her grief had turned to guilt; she had vowed she would make it up to him, and after that she could never kiss him enough nor hug him enough, nor love him enough, nor protect him enough. Her maternity flowed out of her which is why Nigel had remarked on this to Caroline all those months ago. Her maternity (as she saw it) may have been an obsession in the eyes of some, but she knew how to add it to her femininity and accordingly to her sexuality.

Jean-Pierre may have been an extension – as well as a proof – of his mother's soul. He was also his mother's greatest asset. But, all this notwithstanding, Ilsa recognized that he was a little person in his own right.

Which meant that, unlike his mother, Jean-Pierre was going to have a childhood, a real one, the proper, *memorable* kind Ilsa had heard about and read about and even seen, a correctly child-centred childhood. Slowly, far too slowly, Ilsa had come to believe the dimness (vague to the point of unimportance) of her own childhood memories was why André Pachoud had retained his dominance over all her thinking, all her actions: everything she did was strained through him. All was for his invisible inspection, including Jean-Pierre – especially Jean-Pierre. Unbelievably, though, Jean-Pierre had never seen Maître Pachoud, just as – equally unbelievably – the Maître had never seen Jean-Pierre. In fact, Jean-Pierre did not even know who the Maître was, and he never would.

Ilsa still thought of him as the Maître, and sitting now at her kitchen table, remembering him, if that is how an experience that is constantly at the forefront of the brain can be described, she picked up her squash ball and agitatedly began to exercise her palms and fingers. It seemed to her that that was when she had first begun – with the Maître – the first remembered pain of the soul is the real beginning of being, at any rate she could not recall the time that she had not known him, and though life without Jean-Pierre would be unthinkable, without the consciousness of the Maître who had been her example, her teacher, her benefactor and her destroyer, in short her childhood, her very source, there would be no life to think about. That is to say her life would have been that of the unlived kind of the unambitious, the dreamless, the lifeless. When she had come to Geneva as an *au pair* her sole objective had been to learn French so as to get a better sort of secretarial job. If she had not met the Maître, if she had not suffered as he had made her suffer, she would have obeyed all the precepts that had been set out for her – as they had been set out for her mother and her grandmother before her – and she would have been fat and serviceable by now, and very probably about to become a grandmother at the ripe old age of thirty-eight.

She must stop thinking like this, she told herself irritably, and knocked her squash ball off the table. If Peter had taken, that is stolen, Jean-Pierre's comfort blanket, as she suspected, then he was deliberately spoiling all her plans for Jean-Pierre's childhood. An idea was beginning to form – Nigel should adopt, legally adopt Jean-Pierre. Perhaps then, and only then, Maître André Pachoud's dominance would at least begin to lose some of its power?

But her restlessness, it seemed, would not let up.

She decided to go to Jean-Pierre's bedroom: she always turned to that perfectly constructed room as if both sight and smell of childhood's artefacts were enough to arrest doubt, irrationality, impatience. The very order of his toys satisfied and consoled – for the collections of miniature cars, of rocks, of water pistols, all displayed the right degree of precision and cleanliness, of affluence. He must have been playing with her binoculars (without permission? – her eyebrows rose). She took the binoculars out of their leather case, and moved to the balcony, the way she used to when she was studying then investigating Nigel's movements.

The balcony overlooked the golf course, and the binoculars were powerful enough to let her know who was on the eleventh tee or fairway.

It was a Monday, and so the course was closed to members, but open to the few waiters and caddies who chose to play. Not a very interesting viewing day, Ilsa thought, but still, it was pleasant, to bring the trees and greens right up on to her balcony. She swept the binoculars over the fairways, but from where she stood it was impossible to take in the patio which was behind the clubhouse. At the furthermost point were the greenhouses, the adjacent vegetable garden and flower beds which had always delighted her – the club was famous for its blooms and floral arrangements, and she angled the binoculars in that direction, casually, until her attention was captured by something unexpected enough to make her hold her breath. She thought she saw Peter, but could not quite make out if the figure moving about what she supposed was the compost heap, from which she could barely distinguish funnels of smoke, was in fact Peter. Either he was just too far away, or her binoculars were incorrectly focused – but whatever the cause, she could not be sure. She had never needed to look in that direction before. Perhaps she would command a better view from the attic? But by the time she got there the figure had vanished. She checked her binoculars – they functioned perfectly. In any case, Peter was at school, wasn't he?

Ilsa returned to her kitchen. She opened the *Larousse Encyclopaedia of Cooking*. They would start the week with onion soup – which looked so much more difficult to prepare than it really was.

She made her decisions quickly, and wrote them down nimbly. She got up to check her spice collection, and, stretching and bending, was made aware of her stiff aching muscles, a just reminder of all the hard work she was putting in so as to secure Nigel for Jean-Pierre's sake.

Not much could be done about the muscles. . . her bruised lips burned, and she applied the lip salve she had taken to carrying with her. She sighed. How long, she wondered, would this continue? Nigel was, after all, nearly fifty years old! She sighed again, for how could a child ever know of his mother's sacrifices? No matter, she would do all and even more – Nigel would stay. But what more, she asked herself, could she do? Yes, she would have to study his golf swing more carefully so as to see exactly where he was going wrong again. She thought she had detected something unorthodox in his grip. She would ask him to show it to her – no, she wouldn't – that might make him self-conscious, and she wouldn't get an accurate view that way. She would merely watch him practise. Ilsa enjoyed her golf – it was both satisfying and useful, and, in a way, challenging; Nigel however was passionate about the sport: obsessed, Ilsa sometimes thought. True, he was a good golfer, his handicap was four – but he wanted to be better still. Somehow Ilsa had to make Nigel's gratitude to her grow a little every single day.

It was late. She picked up her shopping backet and was about to leave when the door-bell rang. It was the postman with a large registered letter for Peter. The letter was from Caroline. Ilsa studied the envelope – she would have known those large uncomplicated characters at once, even if she had not seen Caroline's name at the back of the envelope, and even if the letter had not been addressed to Peter. About time, she thought, that Caroline wrote to her only son. . . It occurred to her, for the first time, that she was Peter's stepmother and she wondered why this bit of self-evident information had eluded her for so long. She found herself trembling. Peter's own mother was his step-mother for having abandoned him like that.

She would have to think about the letter. Meanwhile she would take it with her – she would take her time about deciding when and if she would give it to Peter. She rather thought she would read it first. This would not be the first letter that she had steamed open. . . She was reversing the car when she suddenly remembered that she had not looked at the postmark, so she did not even know where the letter had come from. She turned off the ignition. She took the envelope out of her shopping basket and saw that it had been posted in Washington. She knew that Nigel's sister, Pamela, lived there but so far she and Pamela had not met. For a moment she thought she would skip the shopping, but the thought of serving stale bread was distasteful; she would go to the *boulangerie*. She would do all her shopping there, they would have *croissants* filled with sausage, and *ramequins*, little cheese tartlets, and *éclairs* filled with cream, and *mille-feuilles* and, yes, the *boulangerie* also sold packaged soup which she would use and disguise. This would allow enough time to examine that letter.

She changed her mind: no, she would not go to the *boulangerie*. Instead, she would go at once to examine that compost heap. It yielded nothing, though it smouldered. What had made her think it could have been Peter – *what*? What on earth could he have wanted to destroy?

And then it came to her – the comfort blanket! But there was no clue, no trace. . . So, she could not be certain, so there was no more to be said. Except that she *was* certain, but had no proof, which left her with nothing more concrete than a suspicion. But suspicions are more useful, sometimes, than facts, the more so, of course, when one knows how to keep a secret.

Ilsa's timetable, meanwhile, was becoming more and more disordered – plans must be modified, there was no time, now, to shop. She frowned. She considered alternatives. She solved the most immediate problem. She would serve cheese fondue – it went better with near-stale bread.

12

1st May

My Mom's letter arrived, and of course I pretended to be surprised. I *think* Ilsa opened it before she gave it to me, but I am not absolutely certain. My Mom said she would put a little hair between the photographs, but it wasn't there. It may have dropped out when I opened the letter. The Tick gave it to me in my bedroom – I suppose she hoped I wouldn't show it to my Dad. That night I showed the photographs to my Dad while we were having supper – the Tick was serving cheese fondue even though it is summer. I didn't show my Dad the letter, I just said, 'Have a look at these photographs of Mom that arrived from Washington. You'll never guess who is standing beside her !'

My Dad stopped eating and we passed the photographs around and everyone was excited because my Mom was with President Reagan. He was grinning as usual, like a monkey, and my Mom was laughing. She looked nice – she's cut her hair, and she was wearing a sort of bright blue scarf which made her eyes look bluer than usual.

Jean-Pierre left his seat to look at the photograph my Dad was holding. He said, 'Who's that lady?' so I said, 'That's my Mom,' and he pointed to the Tick and said, 'That's my Mom,' and then he pointed to my Dad and said, 'That's my Daddy,' and I felt sick, and I could not help blushing which made me feel even worse, and I felt so angry at that moment that I was afraid I would cry, and I thought they were all looking at me waiting for me to say something like yes, that's your Dad, Jean-Pierre, but I would *not* say anything at all. So my Dad said, 'That's a very special photo, Peter. I'll see that it has a suitably beautiful frame.' And then Ilsa said she could give me one – wait a minute – and she left the table and came back with that frame she used to keep in the living-room the one that had that horrible photograph of Jean-Pierre's real father – how I wish that man had not died!

Then things happened too fast for me – I was holding the photo of my Mom – I was very proud that she had been photographed with the President of the United States, even if he is a punk, and even if it is only because my Auntie Pam's husband is a big campaign contributor, and when Jean-Pierre tried to pull the photograph out of my hand I held onto it very tight – and he pulled harder, and I let go suddenly, and he fell back, and the hot cheese fondue spilt over his legs and knees. The Tick began to scream, Jean-Pierre started howling, it looked as if he was about to start one of his asthma attacks – my Dad said he had better take Jean-Pierre to the *Hôpital cantonal* because it looked as if he might have third-degree burns, and then I left the table because I remembered about that emergency treatment for burns that my Mom had packed with all my things before she went away. It is called *Soffra Tulle*, and is a specially treated kind of gauze. Once, when I was small, I was about ten, I think, I tipped a cup of boiling hot tea over my chest – it was a hot day, and I was not wearing a shirt or anything to cover my chest – I've been frightened of burns ever since – but my Mom had my chest bandaged in that *Soffra Tulle* at once, and when I went to the *Hôpital cantonal* they said no other treatment was required.

Well, I raced upstairs and brought down my medical kit, and I could not possibly have been more calm or more organized, exactly like my Mom when that sort of emergency happens – and before anyone knew what was happening Jean-Pierre's burns were covered by that special medicine. He stopped crying, because I talked to him very softly while I was putting the stuff on him, and I was telling him at the same time that I had a surprise for him, that I had some magic balloons to show him, that he and I could make for ourselves. And all the time I heard the Tick and my Dad murmuring to one another, but I must say the Tick helped quite a lot by tearing the sealed packets open. I began wrapping the bandage. I wrapped the bandage around one leg, and she did the other – and Jean-Pierre stopped crying, and began asking me all about the magic balloon. So when we had finished I fetched it – it's a kind of substance in a tube and you put a blob of it at the bottom of a special straw, and blow, and then you get a very shiny balloon – you can make it round if you like, but it goes into all kinds of different shapes. The tube was sold in a package with a water pistol, so I gave that to Jean-Pierre as well.

When all that was over, and after we had eaten omelettes instead of fondue, my Dad took me aside and told me that he wanted to congratulate me on my behaviour – he said that both he and the Tick were sure I would be a very good doctor one day, the Tick was convinced that I'd become a brain surgeon. He knows I don't like her, but he pretends to think that I care what she thinks of me. He doesn't know that I overheard her telling him that she thought there was something not quite right about a thirteen-year-old boy keeping the *Penguin Medical Dictionary* at his bedside for bedside reading. I began doing that long before I'd ever heard of *her*, when I was about eleven. We had two in our flat – my Mom misplaced one, so she bought another. She often used to lose things. When the other one was found I took it – I didn't ever have to ask my Mom for things like that.

Of course I did not like the idea of putting my Mom's photo in the same frame that Jean-Pierre's dead father had been kept in, and so, when my Dad was telling me how proud he was of me, I told him. My Dad wasn't too pleased, he thought Ilsa would be hurt and said so, so I said I would like to take the photo to school because there were so many Americans there and I was sure my teacher would want to put it up on the class bulletin board.

And then the Tick came in and interrupted, and said she wanted to thank me, and to congratulate me, and to tell me how grateful she was, because she honestly believed that my quick and efficient attention had stopped Jean-Pierre from going into a serious asthma attack. She said that I seemed to know so much about medicine that she thought it would be a good idea for me to read about asthma too, so that I would understand why she was so often so anxious about Jean-Pierre. So I told her that I'd already read about it, and that it seemed likely that Jean-Pierre would grow out of it, and she said I was wise beyond my years, and that it was probably a good thing that the fondue had spilt over Jean-Pierre, because we now had a better understanding, and that that sort of emergency often brings people closer together.

I'll *never* be close to her – but I told her that I thought Jean-Pierre had been very very brave, much braver than I had been, even though when that had happened to me I had been older than Jean-Pierre. Yes, she said, it was true, Jean-Pierre had been brave, probably because he wanted to impress his elder brother. And then she asked me if I knew that Jean-Pierre thought of me as his elder brother, and had told his teacher that he now had an elder brother. I wanted to say that I was only a temporary elder brother, but instead I said I was sorry there had been an accident, but all's well that ends well.

She must know that I hate her – it is so hard for me to look at her in a direct sort of way – but they both pretend that I like her. I try to pretend too, but they are better at it. Hate is such a funny thing – it makes me shake inside – I would love to bash her – it gives me nightmares, too. I have this dream – or nightmare – I don't know what it is – but in it the Tick is lying down on the seventh green, the one that is near the little stream, and one of the small tractors that takes care of the grass is going over and over her head. No one is driving it, but the tractor goes forward, and the wheels go over her head, and then it reverses and the wheels go over her head again, and it does this again and again, but her head does not get crushed or even squashed – it is as tough as that squash ball of hers. I have had this dream a few times. She just lies there and then the tractor disappears and she gets up and calmly sinks a twelve-foot putt. She is a great golfer – my Dad says she could have been a professional player if she had wanted to be. She could be the World Champion and I would not stop hating her, that's for sure!

The longer I stay here the more I know that she has ruined my life. But my Mom's Madame Sanossian believes the three of us will all be happy and together again – I wish I could really believe this, too, I wish I had no doubts at all about it. . . That proverb is cool, real cool – I'll write it down again – HOPE GIVES STRENGTH BECAUSE HOPE IS STRENGTH. I must disguise my hate. I must force myself to look at her directly. She must never guess that she has a dangerous enemy in her own house.

But if my Mom and Madame Sanossian are wrong, if we don't win, I will definitely not live here next term. In fact I think I would like to leave Geneva, and live with my Mom and Frederica in London. Because if we don't win, I don't think I will want to see my Dad ever again, not as long as I live. I know he's my father, and I love him a lot – everybody loves him, but if he doesn't see me, he'll still have a son –

he'll have Jean-Pierre, won't he? I hope he doesn't have another child, with *her* – she's very old, she's thirty-eight – so I think I'm quite safe.

So when the Tick told me that Jean-Pierre thinks I'm his brother I asked her if I could take him to school with me on break-up day, when everyone is allowed to bring their little brothers or sisters to the end of term party. She said she'd never heard of such a thing, no Swiss school would allow that – but she thought it would be O.K.

So my Dad said he thought that Ilsa must really have a lot of faith in me, she must really love me a lot, because we all knew that Jean-Pierre was never allowed to play at his friends' houses, that they had to come and play with him at his own house, that Ilsa only trusted him with the school or with the woman who ran the *garderie des enfants* at the club, so that he felt I should feel honoured, and that he was very happy with the way our new family was going, and he kissed me on both cheeks, and then picked that little Tick up and hugged her, and swung her around as if she were a little baby, and I felt sicker than ever, and all that horrible omelette started to move to my chest, and I stood it as long as I could and then I had to rush to the bathroom.

They didn't seem to notice me leave.

And I made a special vow *never* to take Jean-Pierre to my school.

13

One of the main reasons why membership of the Mont Blanc golf club of Geneva is so coveted is that you can never tell who you will meet there, you might meet Sheikh Amman who is a member, or you could meet a former CIA director – the members' guests are no less interesting ranging from Frank Sinatra to the President of General

Motors as well as former prime ministers of major states. It is an eclectic collection of power: arms dealers mingle with judges, with ambassadors and bankers. Power – whatever its source – is respected and honoured. Of course an arms dealer has more power than say, even the French ambassador, but homage will be paid to both because while the one represents the tradition of power, the other is not power's representative, but power itself. For all that there are very few Middle Eastern members, and those are restricted to ambassadors, OPEC ministers and the like.

So it is perhaps not surprising that Ilsa du Four and Nigel Pritchett-Ward received their first dinner invitation from the Zellers. Franz Zeller was a Zurichois banker who had married an Egyptian girl called Zoreh. And the Zellers were among the very few foreigners who had won acceptance from the Genevois families. At any rate Zoreh and Franz were giving a dinner party at their lakeside home.

The invitation was addressed to Madame du Four and Monsieur Pritchett-Ward, and it was sent to Ilsa's home. She was aware that the party was only a week hence, which meant that they were rated as last minute and, therefore, lesser guests. Her training at the Pachoud household had not been in vain. She knew enough to know that the invitation ought to have been received at least three weeks earlier. The Zellers' parties were legendary. Zoreh brought the exoticism of Cairo to them – it was a form of rebellion for she had flatly refused to conform to the Swiss notion of elegance which meant that the food was as stolid and as heavy as the silver on which it was served, where caution was everything, which was why the beef was inevitably over-done, and where quantities were measured with exact precision second helpings having been taken into account – guests were expected to take two and not three roast potatoes, and as for sugar with the after dinner coffee the joke was '*Vous voulez un sucre ou pas du tout*?' – Will you have one sugar or none at all?'

They had been together for two and a half months now, about seventy days, according to Ilsa's reckoning, and in that time Nigel had gained six kilos. She smiled, thinking of the vanity that had made him go on the Ripper diet which meant that he would be home for lunch for the next twelve days. Today he would be lunching on cheese slices and spinach, tonight he was permitted shellfish, and Ilsa planned on serving oysters – she knew where they could be bought, even in June. Three days on, and already he had lost a kilo.

Jean-Pierre was home for lunch, too, and she told Nigel about the Zellers' invitation when Jean-Pierre had gone upstairs to take his usual short nap.

'Have you ever been to one of the Zellers' famous parties?'

'No,' he said. 'Why?'

'I couldn't remember,' she said. 'Were you ever invited?'

'Well, yes we were.'

'I suppose Caroline thought they weren't good enough for her.'

'No. Strangely, Caroline wanted to go. But we had information that Banque Zeller (he pronounced it exaggeratedly, Zellaire) was not playing the game. That was at the time when the Swiss authorities decreed negative interest rates on foreign accounts that exceeded one hundred thousand Swiss francs. You remember that time?'

'Not really. It made no difference to me, you see. I'm regarded as Swiss, remember?' She frowned and pushed the hair away from her face. 'An invitation from the Zellers came today. To both of us.' She moved closer toward him, and then touched his lips with her tongue. 'Of course we won't go if you don't think we should. But I won't pretend I wasn't thrilled to bits to get the invitation. Still, I won't mind, I really won't if you don't want to go.'

'Steady on, little one. Whatever made you think I said I did not want – '

'Oh, Nigel,' she interrupted. 'Don't you see? It's the very first social invitation we've received – as a couple – and they sent it to this house.' (Ilsa was always careful not to say 'my house'.) She hesitated. It was clear that she was about to be brave. She said, 'To tell the truth, respectable single women are usually excluded. You see, single women have a hard time, especially in Geneva.'

'Especially beautiful single women,' he said feelingly.

'That may be. I only know that it hurt. I felt so excluded, so isolated, so very insulted. Because I would not have looked at their husbands.'

She stopped suddenly, and blinked very fast. She was not given to tears, indeed he had only seen this sort of thing when she first told him of Jean-Pierre's asthma. He found himself unbearably moved. Because of those other times when the cries and tears were as uncontrolled as the rest of her, but that was a bodily thing for which he, and he alone, was responsible.

'Believe me,' she said, lying passionately, 'believe me, I did *not* know you were married when I first saw you. I only knew that just before it all began – when it was already too late.'

'I'm glad you didn't! You know that.' He took her cheeks in his hands. 'You know that,' he said again, 'and we both know how your scruples would have got in our way!'

'Ah, Nigel, you understand me so well.'

'Well enough to insist on going to the Zellers' party!'

Ilsa rarely entrusted a baby-sitter with the care of Jean-Pierre. She was reluctant, even, to leave him with Madame Blanc, the tried and trusted *femme-de-ménage* who came to her every Wednesday. Madame Blanc knew how to deal with an asthma attack and had coped very well when this had happened. Though Ilsa would not have settled for less, she congratulated herself on having found the likes of a Madame Blanc who satisfied the highest standards of competency. A French peasant woman from the Haute Savoie, Madame Blanc and her husband owned a small-holding, lived for hard work, and every Wednesday, whatever the weather, she cycled fifteen kilometres to get to Ilsa. Ilsa would not play golf on a Wednesday unless there was a competition. Wednesdays were reserved for Madame Blanc.

So when Madame Blanc's daughter had an inexplicable fever on the morning of the night of the Zeller party, it looked as if Ilsa and Nigel would miss the great event after all.

That Peter would baby-sit was Nigel's idea. 'Remember how Peter coped when the fondue spilt over Jean-Pierre?'

'Yes. I couldn't have done better myself.' She giggled brightly. Then waited. 'Still, I've *never* left him without Madame Blanc.'

'I know that. We'll do whatever you say. Pity you won't be wearing what we chose.' He put his lively dimple to good use. 'And what about the denim suit my tailor rushed through for me?' (The invitation had stipulated long dresses for women and jeans for men.) 'Besides,' he added solemnly, 'Peter would be honoured to take care of Jean-Pierre. Jean-Pierre could easily become a Mommie's boy, you know.'

'You're right as usual,' Ilsa said. 'We'll go.'

Delivery men could be forgiven for sometimes mistaking the Zellers' house, Laronde, for the Château Lavorel in which the former King of Bomania once lived, and which was only two houses away in the same quiet road. Laronde was an old house and the exterior walls were illuminated by the same sort of yellow light that is used in Geneva by museums and the like, and which made the place seem even older, even more solid, and somehow imparted an aura of eternal life. It was rumoured that when the attics were remodelled, an ancient cemented pipe was flung to the gravel driveway below, and the impact of the fall shattered the cement and released hundreds of old Florentine coins about Zoreh Zeller's waiting – and it was said perpetually lucky – feet.

Ilsa, who had heard this story, had always thought it entirely suited to Zoreh's golden background. Zoreh was the granddaughter, and the great-granddaughter of not one, but two Egyptian prime ministers before the fall of Farouk. Zoreh's own mother had been *demoiselle d' honneur* at Farouk's first marriage, and at the Cairo wedding of the Shah to his first bride.

Ilsa had often been told about Zoreh's mother's wedding, of how, during the contract signing ceremony the young bride had sat surrounded by handmaidens, while she stared at herself in the mirror so as to remember always how she had looked on this happiest of happy days, while she sucked a lump of sugar so that nothing but sweetness would pass her lips, while her feet rested in a bowl of rose water and rose petals, so that her life would be as smooth as running water, while a long candle glowed its symbol of the long and glowing life the bride had every reason to expect. And all this in 1952! It was this that Ilsa found the most exciting, because in 1952 she had been nine, which meant that all this was within her own lifetime, and was about to become part of her own life, too, now just as soon as she crossed the portals of Laronde. Merely being a guest at Zoreh Zeller's dinner table meant that the remnants of the fairy-tale glories of exotic and former kings and queens would touch, and, of course, elevate her own being.

Disappointingly, nothing of the spice of Cairo was immediately detectable as Ilsa and Nigel joined the guests around the pool. But then she caught sight of the giant silver candlesticks whose bases were made from finely crafted coiled silver serpents, and knew and finally believed that she was there, in the Zellers' perfect home from which she had so long been excluded. She looked up at Nigel and beamed him an openly grateful smile. She had allowed him to choose her dress, which could not, as she now saw, have been more appropriate to the occasion. She was where she most wanted to be, among the people who were known as the beautiful people, and who had chalets in Gstaad and villas in Villefranche, and houses on the lake or in the Old Town, close to Calvin's cathedral, and photographs in the French, in the Italian or in the German *Vogue*. And she was there purely because she had the necessary qualification – the right sort of man at her side. And this year she and Nigel and Jean-Pierre would rent a

Gstaad chalet, for surely Caroline would have Peter for Christmas? And next year . . . Well, she was pretty certain they would have bought one by then. Which was not bad for an *au pair* was it? Which thought brought a wicked gleam to her eye, which Nigel saw and responded to in that familiar way that was still so strange to him.

For his part Nigel, too, felt a certain nervousness, a delicious tension at being seen, publicly, with Ilsa. Of course they had faced this weeks ago at the club, but it was not the same as having been invited, so to speak, officially, as a couple. He and Caroline had avoided this sort of party; after all, he had had his reputation to think of, but that was established now and Nekker & Cie was in the first league of the private banks. His golf was improving and he believed his handicap would soon be cut to two. He realized that what he felt was akin to being on the first tee on the day of a club championship, when it was as if his whole world hinged on the tempo of his swing. He would carry that championship away this August; his determination was more acute than it had ever been and his optimism appeared to be boundless but well-founded. That move-ment of the wrists that Ilsa had taught him was already doing wonders. On Sunday he had gone round in 72, three strokes better than his handicap.

Because the chat around the pool was meaningless, it passed smoothly, if uneasily. When at last they were summoned to the dining-room a single long table awaited thirty guests. Zoreh appeared to have memorized her seating plan; she didn't as much as glance at the list on the board she held so elegantly, and her guests found them-selves seated besides well-chosen partners.

Ilsa was between a visiting Swedish surgeon and the Marquis de Lamartine, whose name meant that he wasn't required to be anything at all, though he was in fact an amateur historian. Nigel was placed between Yvette Eriksen who was a Dane who had married – as she laughingly put it – an ancient enemy because he was Swedish, and Barbara King, who was unmistakably and, as

107

Nigel was soon to think, unendurably American.

'Hi,' Barbara King said, 'I'm Barbara King. And you must be Nigel Pritchett-Ward.'

'Ah,' said Nigel, 'we've read our name plates, I see.'

'You're British?' she said triumphantly.

'Now how did you guess?'

'We're Caterpillar people. Been in Geneva for eight years. I'm trained to identify accents, see. I head up a workshop of fellow-Americans living abroad on how to get over their culture shock.'

'Oh yes. Of course. The bread isn't wrapped – that sort of thing.'

Nigel could not at first work out why the Kings had been invited – they were not, it was clear, members of the Mont Blanc golf club. Indeed, Caterpillar and Dupont were very poorly represented at the club. Surely no Caterpillar executive, whatever his seniority, would have had the imagination to bank with one of the smaller private banks? Like the Zeller Bank? But a glance at what he knew Barbara King would have termed her robe, and a further glance at her emeralds, made him known that though her husband was a company man there was plenty of private money in that family.

He attempted to listen to her prattle about how uprooted Americans were taken care of; from importing California wine to coming to terms with Switzerland's health laws which, compared to the States, were relatively non-existent. Ilsa was seated within eye-range, but there was no possibility of talking to her.

The dinner promised to be lengthy. The marquis, he noticed, had not removed the serviette from the centre of his plate, and the waiters appeared to pass him by. He longed for Ilsa to take her hair down. She had done it in a chignon, which was elegant, certainly, but which now reminded him of a hygienically wrapped doughnut. He attempted to speak with his Danish partner; it had been established that she was a fair golfer, but Yvette Eriksen obviously preferred her dinner partner, an elderly British chemist who was also a Nobel Laureate.

Then Barbara King said something that jerked him to attention.

'Say, are you by any chance related to that adorable little Peter Pritchett-Ward?'

Surprised, Nigel said, 'Yes, you could say we're related. I'm his father.'

'And I'm Wayne King's mother,' she said triumphantly, waving her fork. 'Of course Wayne and Peter are among the kids who've been longest at the International School. They've both been here since first grade which kinda makes me happy for them. Stability. Though it looks as if big Wayne'll be transferred back to Peoria. You know little Wayne?'

'I know Wayne of course,' Nigel said coldly. 'Rather large for his age, isn't he?'

'Oh – yes,' Barbara King said in that openly confidential way that Nigel found so distasteful. 'He's at least four inches taller than he ought to be. 'Course everyone expects him to be older than he is, so we've had one or two behavioural problems.'

'Difficult to handle, I imagine,' Nigel murmured politely. He would have liked to have told her what an objectionable and ill-mannered child she had managed to produce. Caroline and he had seriously considered having Peter removed to a different class.

'Say, that's a neat shot of your wife with our President.'

'You've seen it?'

'I was at the International School the day Peter brought it. Wayne told me about it and I made Peter show it to me. He's such a polite kid, but so withdrawn.'

'Withdrawn?'

'Sort of shy. You know.' She shook her head from side to side and her ear-rings tinkled. 'It's a tough age. Pubescent. Preadolescent.'

'You've been through it?'

'Wayne's our fourth son. We have six, and – wouldn't you know it – all boys.' She laughed proudly. 'Peter

109

promised to bring that photograph back to school. I wanted to have it xeroxed. Big Wayne's office has a colour machine, see?'

Nigel laughed. 'Well, he's your President,' he said.

'He is indeed.' She raised her glass. 'Oh Lord,' she said. 'It's empty.'

'I'll see to that,' Nigel said. He lifted her glass a little higher than was necessary and it was filled at once.

'Gee, thanks,' she said. 'You British have got class.' She tittered. 'I'm heading up the women's group of Americans abroad for Reagan.'

'You are?' he said somewhat mockingly inflecting his voice so as to mimic hers. 'You *are*?'

'It's demanding, but challenging work, I guess,' she said earnestly.

'You've had some training, some experience in committee work, I suppose.' Nigel smiled – about the only thing that Ilsa and Caro had in common was the fact that they both loathed ladies' committees.

'I guess you could say I've had some training,' she began in a teaching sort of voice. 'Previous experience includes what I just told you about, remember? Heading up our women's workshop on countering culture shock.'

'Indeed,' Nigel said politely. 'Interesting work, no doubt?'

'It certainly is challenging. Transferred wives customarily have to cope with more than a strange country where they encounter an inability to participate. I specialize in the empty nest syndrome.'

'Ah, yes, the empty nest syndrome.'

'You've heard all about that, I'm sure. You know, when the kids grow up, and leave the nest?'

'Oh, yes. Of course.'

'Well, to get back to what I was saying about the women's group of Americans abroad for Reagan. See, I wanted that shot of Reagan and the mother of a boy at the International School so that I could include it in our monthly bulletin.'

110

'I see.'

'I knew you would, I just knew it. Americans don't get to be photographed with their President so easily.'

'Well – '

'Wayne says Peter's aunt knows the President very well.'

'My brother-in-law is Bill Ridley, the political columnist.'

''Course we all know who he is. He's your wife's brother? Your wife is American?'

'No,' Nigel said abruptly. 'Bill Ridley is my British sister's husband.'

Nigel felt decidedly uncomfortable, and wanted to say that he and Caroline were separated, but, for Peter's sake decided – unaccountably, he thought – not to.

'Have you also met our President?'

'I've not yet had that privilege. I'm afraid.'

'You're expecting your wife back soon?'

She took his murmur for assent.

'That's good,' she said, again in that confiding tone. 'Peter appears to have a problem relating with the German cousin you and he are living with.'

'Problem?' Nigel said. 'Cousin?'

'The kids used to travel together when school got out. Wayne was often over at your house.'

'I know that, of course.'

'Well, between you and me, Peter seems to feel that your lady cousin is not ready to welcome his friends.'

'I wouldn't have thought so.' He smiled and flexed his dimple.

'Peter looks like you,' Barbara King said seriously. 'He has the same smile. 'Course your wife's a lovely-looking woman, isn't she?' Her ear-rings tinkled again. 'I'm sure our President thought so too,' she said archly.

'No doubt,' Nigel said coldly.

The first dish, *viande sèche*, had been served, and they were now on the second, turtle soup, which meant there were still three more courses to follow. Nigel glanced down the long table, and it seemed as if everyone raised and

111

lowered their spoons in unison, they looked like some sort of crazy brass band taking directions from the conductor, Franz Zeller, who sat at the head. Nigel stopped and watched for a while, caught Ilsa's eye and tried to signal her to watch the spoon orchestra too, but failed. He rested his soup spoon on the saucer. His indefatigable dinner partner laid her arm on his and turned her inquisitive eyes on him.

'You're disappointed in your soup, I see.'

This was too much for Nigel, who gave up. He turned away, making his dislike obvious.

Which slight was not taken lightly by Barbara King. Later, while Nigel was collecting Ilsa's wrap, a bony hand was laid on his arm. 'You're not living with any German cousin,' Barbara King hissed. 'You've got your own son living in sin with another woman. You make me sick to my stomach!'

'But not nearly as sick as your stomach deserves to be, I'm sure,' Nigel murmured. He slipped into French. '*Enchanté de faire votre connaissance. Bon soir, Madame.*'

Driving home Ilsa laughed about Barbara King's earrings. 'I could almost *hear* them,' she giggled.

'I missed you,' he said simply. 'D'you know I hadn't noticed you were wearing ear-rings, too. I simply didn't see them when we left. They suit you. Beautifully.'

Ilsa had not been wearing them when they left. She said, 'I only wear them when I put my hair up.'

He longed to know who had given them to her. They were delicate little rosettes of rubies and diamonds and were obviously very old. He supposed it was that American – whom she had refused to name – that American who had let her down so unforgivably. He, Nigel, never would.

'What did you think of those silver underplates?' Ilsa said. 'Did you know that they were engraved with the names of whoever had presented them? They were part of a wedding gift. Mine had been given by the Comtesse d'Evian.'

'Mine was from Sadruddin Khan.'

'I would love to have plates like those. I've never seen them before.'

'Haven't you? Caro and I have a whole set somewhere. She didn't care for them. I don't think she ever used them.'

Ilsa decided to see those plates, and for that matter, any other interesting possessions that might not have appealed to Caroline.

She said, 'I wonder how Jean-Pierre got on?'

Nigel wanted to tell her about his conversation with Barbara King. He decided not to, and his silence made him feel uncomfortable, almost dishonest.

Waiting for Ilsa, after what had certainly been a very long, very tense evening, Nigel reflected that he had never known her to look quite so well and happy. He smiled, thinking how trite a word happy could be, and how inadequate, too, but he had been very much struck by the effect she had of appearing to be smiling even when her entire face was in utter repose. Those heart-wrenchingly sad cheeks of hers had quite disappeared. It had been good for her, she had been so enthusiastic (almost to the point of childlike delight) about having been at the Zellers'. Whereas Caroline would have been slightly scornful, slightly mocking of the whole thing; she would have dismissed the place as Arabian renaissance or something like that, as indeed, Nigel admitted to himself, he would have done, too. It just shows you, he believed now, what a costly thing snobbery is, how much one misses. True, the Zellers were a trifle on the vulgar side, but then their pretensions lay among 'beautiful people' where there was no such thing as good or bad taste because it all rested on the right labels, *Gucci, Dior, Herms,* where nothing less than a *Cartier* cigarette lighter was acceptable.

Nigel remembered the story of how one of his associates had been invited to the Zellers' shortly after they had acquired four impressionist paintings – a Cézanne, a Sisley, a Monet and a Pissarro. The Zellers were proud of the reproductions of their acquisitions, and prouder still of the

Christies account which served as a book-mark. It was said that the Zellers found the bill and the fact that they were able to pay it far more beautiful than any of the paintings. Bill Anstey, who was something of an art connoisseur, declared the paintings to be the best example of the worst work of each artist. Ah well, whatever the Zellers lacked in taste was made up by their skilled hospitality. Oddly enough, all their guests had seemed very pleased to be there.

Ilsa, meanwhile, was preparing to join Nigel. She meant to see those silver plates. She meant to get that key, the key to Caroline's flat. Nigel had said it would not be fair for him to take her there, and she said she understood. But she would go there all the same. Nigel had a breakfast appointment in Lausanne, he would have to leave early the following morning. She would see to it that he would also have to leave in a great rush, he would be a little late, too – he would not have time to check his keys, he'd merely grab the bundle believing it to be exactly as it had been left. She knew how to arrange that sort of thing.

She kept him waiting, which – though she washed her underwear every night – was unusual, but which he did not in the least resent, and when she finally joined him he could not believe his luck. He thought, as she made her slow and dazzling approach, that she looked for all the world like a miniature dressed-up Lolita. She was wearing heels that were high, and black fishnet stockings, and no panties, though a suspender-belt, and a matching bra encasing the matching breasts she had never made any attempt to enlarge and did not, even now, and on her head she wore a blonde wig whose hair like her heels was higher than high, and in her hand she carried a switched-on tape-recorder playing The Second Time Around.

All that night she called him monsieur, and spoke nothing but French and urged him on to greater and greater heights, and he went higher than high and higher than that, and he managed all that three times and he could not believe his luck, could not believe anything at all, but knew only that he had not born in vain.

And in the morning Ilsa had her key, and while he was breakfasting in Lausanne she had already had a duplicate made.

14

5th May

The Tick was all dressed up when they went to that party, and as soon as their car had driven out of the gates that babyish Jean-Pierre began to scream for his mother. I don't know why he waited for her to leave, we were both watching television, and so I don't suppose he noticed her leave until it was over because he only started to cry when the programme ended. At first I told him to shut up; I said he was a big boy now, he'd already had his dinner, and that I would let him watch for extra long. Instead of being happy he lay on the floor and kicked and screamed, and he cried so much that even the carpet got wet because water poured from his nose as well. He just went on and on making these horrible noises, and I felt so angry with him, and when his face was bright red and sort of blotchy, and then I saw it begin to turn bluish I got more angry and frightened, too, and I don't know why I did this, but I thought I'd go mad if the noise didn't stop, and so I slapped him so hard that my palm tingled, and he got such a fright – I'm certain he'd never had a smack in his whole life – that he suddenly stopped crying. But that seemed to make things even worse, because he suddenly could not catch his breath, and he was wheezing, and it sounded like a blocked drain, and anyone could see that he was more than scared, and so I rushed for his spray – there is one in every room of the house – and I sprayed and sprayed – I may have given him too much which could have been just as dangerous as giving him none at all – but he began to breathe more calmly and sounded normal.

Then I decided to give him a piggy-back and carry him up the stairs to his room. I put him in his bed, and brought him my collection of tin soldiers, and started telling him stories. He can't play chess, can't even play snakes and ladders, or draughts, he is too stupid for that sort of thing, and then he got tired of the soldiers, so I brought some finger paints and we started making patterns. He liked that, and I thought he was happy because he was sort of humming and talking even more babyishly than usual, and then I told him that he had made a lovely ship – I was trying to be nice to him.

I was sitting on his bed at the time, and I thought everything was O.K. and he was quiet and I thought very busy when suddenly and without any warning he kicked me so hard that I fell off the bed and landed on my back. I was so angry that I couldn't say a single word. Before I could even stand up he threw one of his paint bottles at me, and because it came from something of a height it hit me with more force than that little weakling could have had, and actually hurt me. Then he jumped down from his bed and said that wasn't a ship it was a butterfly, over and over again he said that wasn't a ship it was a butterfly, and *I* was so scared he'd go into another attack that I said I was stupid, it was a beautiful butterfly, what a clever boy he was to have made one, and I started to laugh about the paint on my face, and he laughed too and then I went to the bathroom with him to wash it off, and he helped me and then we both wiped the paint from his carpet. We were lucky that it was washable, because the Tick is crazy about her carpets – I've always thought Raffles was sent away simply because of the hair he left on the carpets – I still don't believe that it was because of Jean-Pierre's allergy.

Anyway I thought everything was O.K. and that I could leave him and do some homework when he said, 'Your mother doesn't want you. Your mother is bad that's why you have to live with us,' and he went on and on repeating

116

it. I have *never* been so angry! I really wanted to punch him – I wanted to punch him so badly, but I was scared of one of those attacks. Instead of punching him I asked him to make me another butterfly – I've seen the Tick distract him that way, she calls it changing the subject.

It worked and he was quite peaceful after that, and when he had finished making what he called a butterfly, he put his head back on the pillows and fell asleep. Of course I had to tidy everything up.

When I was absolutely certain that he was asleep I went to phone my Mom. As soon as she heard my voice she asked me where I was and then said she'd phone me back at once just in case they would be able to tell that I had phoned her – it might show up on the bill. I told my Mom what had happened and she said I was absolutely right to have distracted Jean-Pierre like that, she thought that was very very clever of me. She also told me that Jean-Pierre had had an hysterical tantrum the way Frederica had sometimes had them, and she believed I had slapped Jean-Pierre because I had seen her do that to Frederica which is what one has to do when anyone is being hysterical. She was certain that Jean-Pierre's asthma was a kind of blackmail. She sounded so upset, it sounded as if she was almost crying herself. She said I would only have to be there for another six weeks, and then whether or not our plan had worked she would take me out of there. She misses me, she hates me having to undergo what she says is an ordeal by fire like this, but she's convinced we will win in the end.

She wanted to know where my Dad had gone and when I told her that it was to the Zellers she laughed because my Dad used to refuse to have anything to do with the Zellers. She reminded me that my Dad is ill, she said she knew it was hard for me, but you couldn't blame someone for catching a disease could you?

I had to agree, but I wonder if it really is a disease.

I wrote them a note. This is what I wrote:

117

Time 20 hours
Dear Dad and Ilsa,
    Jean-Pierre is asleep, now. He was a very good boy. He had a little attack of asthma, but I gave him the spray and he was O.K. at once.
    Over and out – Message Ends –
        Peter (your faithful baby-sitter).

I left the note beside my bed – I wanted to check whether my Dad would come in and check on me as well as on Jean-Pierre. As a matter of fact I was still awake when they came in, even though it was long after midnight. To tell the truth I was too worried about Jean-Pierre to fall asleep until they came home. They both went in to see Jean-Pierre – I heard them – and of course I pretended to be asleep in case my Dad would come and see me, too, but I guess he knew I was O.K. because he did not come to my room.

The next morning I told them about Jean-Pierre, and what I had done and my Dad asked me why I had not left him a note. I told him that I had – it was next to my bed of course, I said, and then I left him and went upstairs to fetch it, and when I gave it to him he read it, and then he said something about being sorry, old man, he should not have forgotten how responsible I was, you know, that sort of thing, but I had the feeling that he was more interested in showing Ilsa how responsible I was than he was in me. In other words, he was pleased with me, because of her. It's hard for me to work this out, because it seems to me that everything my Dad does or thinks or has (I guess he has me because I'm his son I'm a part of him) has been handed over to her to mark as if she were the teacher and I was one of my Dad's exams.

I wonder what she really thinks of me, what sort of marks she gives my Dad about me? I feel, all the time, as though I'm writing a public exam, as if I'm already one of the older kids at school, writing a public exam, the College boards say.

A very long time ago, before I was selected for the Swiss

Junior golf team last season when I was only twelve, I had to go for an interview, I still remember how nervous I felt because that is how I feel now, all the time. Sometimes it feels as if I'm being interviewed by my own Dad. I don't know why I feel like this, but I have the feeling that I've made a mistake, lots and lots of careless mistakes, and what is worse the mistakes are the same mistakes and I keep making these same careless mistakes, over and over again. And I don't know why, and I don't know what these mistakes are.

15

Caroline and Nigel's spacious lofty flat was in one of those fashionable late nineteenth-century apartment houses that face the lake. These buildings, rather gracious, rather solid, had always fascinated Ilsa for, though in the centre of the town, they were just across the road from the little harbour with its gay yachts and tinkling cowbells, and through the apartment's wide windows which opened inward instead of outward, you could see both shores of the lake, and in summer, the tallest man-made fountain in the world which the giant, beautiful and sometimes ominous Mont Blanc reduces in scale to the illusion of a single continuous tear. These houses did not represent the elegance of a bygone age, rather they appeared to stand still for gracious living. There were two or three blocks that had been prestige buildings from the moment their plans had been drawn, and were no less important now; these were the blocks that refused entry phones because their heavy, beautifully carved oak doors were securely bolted at nine o'clock each evening, and all day Sunday. If guests were expected, a butler or maid would be sent down to anticipate their knock. In the deep dungeon of the basement each apartment had its own wine cellar whose rough, splintery wooden doors were safely fastened with ancient and formidably ugly locks because the wine was frequently older than the locks. The texture and quality of the walls were sufficiently impregnable to have caused the authorities to have held them to be as safe as the lead-lined nuclear fall-out shelters that are obligatory in newer buildings. The attics which commanded what was widely held to be the best view in Europe were for the servants and other equally indispensable items, such as clothes, skis and of course the statutory hoard of foods – flour, sugar, oil and the like. Ilsa had known a banker who had shot himself in one of those attic rooms. His blood had seeped out along the stone corridor, which his family had found careless of him, so careless, in fact, that a brother had been despatched to scrub the concrete interstices himself to ensure that not a trace would be left: one was expected to die as tidily as one had been required to live.

Although the name *Plein de Soleil* had also been carved above its portals the building that Ilsa was most interested in was known simply as 22 quai du Rhône. Apart from that first time with Nigel she had been there once before when one of the committee members had invited her to what he termed a small champagne party. It turned out that her host had used the term accurately enough – each guest received exactly half an exquisitely small glass of an excellent champagne. Ilsa had gone onto the balcony and looked out at the lake, the *jet d'eau* was brilliantly illuminated, and she stared at the discreetly still reflection of the bright neon signs in the dark waters. Flashing lights were forbidden in Geneva, and Ilsa was grateful for that because it meant that even the bright primary colours were still and enduring. She listened to the tinkle of the cow-bells on the yachts, and decided that she would live there one day, and have a country house – a *maison d'été* – on the lake. She had scanned, that night, the names of the residents on the mail boxes in the foyer, and had come upon the unlikely name

M. et Mme Nigel Pritchett-Ward – unlikely because the rest of the names were all clearly and indisputably Swiss. She knew at once that M. Pritchett–Ward must be very important and very special to have been allowed to live among the venerable *Genevois*. That was when she decided to find out who he was.

And now, her duplicate key having successfully unlocked the heavy oak doors, she was walking nonchalantly up the stairs, her hair pressed under a scarf, her tiny feet tucked into her oldest gardening shoes, her slim body tucked under an enveloping heavy black coat. She resembled a serving woman, she could have been anyone's foreign *femme-de-ménage*. It would not have done to have been seen – it was an effective, if unimaginative disguise.

One key, she discovered, fitted all three locks on the front door; the first thing she would change, such carelessness was not to be tolerated. She passed through the entrance hall, and then found herself running along the passage, sidestepping her plan to inspect the reception rooms first and rushing instead to the bedroom that Caroline and Nigel had shared. She realized she was shaking and almost unendurably hot under that heavy black coat. When she had visited Nigel all those months ago Nigel had given her a Perrier in the drawing room before they had gone to the guest room where they had made love under Caroline's bridal photograph. But she had never seen the marital chamber. It was nothing like her expectations, although she understood that she had not quite known what to expect (satins and frills in pinks and mauves, perhaps?), but in that bedroom now, taking off her heavy coat, she perceived that she had not really got to know Caroline with anything like that accuracy she had given herself credit for. She had been wrong about everything except the four-poster bed. Somehow it was as if the room had caught her by surprise and she felt suddenly exhausted to the point of weakness. There was nothing else for it, she would have to lie down. She took off her shoes carefully, and lay down on the bed, on the patchwork quilt that was as gay as Joseph's coat of many colours must have been, and crossed her feet, and stared at herself in the large mirror that had probably been built into the wall when the house had been constructed, and, staring at herself, realized that she still wore that awful black head scarf. She took it off at once, but only after she had given way to one of her discomfiting twinges of superstition – the black scarf, black stockings, indeed all that black gave her the sensation of being a mourner at her own deathbed.

She recalled a long ago story of a mistress who had been let down by her lover and who had lain on his wife's bed and shot herself, after which the man and his wife happily continued to use that very bed. She had the feeling, then, that she was being watched, but was unable to move.

Looking for relief from her own funeral clothing, she took in the colours, the white shaggy carpet overlaid with Kashan rugs in gentle creams and golds. The walls were papered with blue and gold scrolls, which ought to have been garish, but which though far from chic gave off an undeniable warmth. The curtains were drawn. Ilsa would have had them made from a raw white silk but these had been fashioned from some sort of heavily woven blue linen. Ilsa had never seen anything like them. The large bedside tables were astonishingly practical, like cabinets with drawers and bookshelves. Four hundred books, Ilsa calculated, at the very least. An ancient military desk stood at an angle, and above it a bulletin board – made of the same blue stuff as the curtains – was crammed with photographs and all sorts of strange looking writings. She would examine those soon enough.

Presently something of the serenity of the room began to steal over Ilsa, and she found herself as relaxed and as calm as if someone had laid a reassuring hand over her forehead. Besides, she was remembering Nigel having told her that Caroline spent too much time in her bedroom. There was a study with two desks – one for each – but when he came home Caroline would inevitably be in her bedroom. Nigel said it was because Caroline saw their bedroom as the heart of the house – something like that. Though the large room was infinitely cosy and welcoming, yet, above all, private. She found herself giving way, unwillingly, but unavoidably, to all that peace, for had she not, she now argued with herself, been soothed by it, too? It was strange, almost eerie; she felt as if she had been overtaken by some sort of profoundly kindly spirit that hovered there, and in an effort to dispel this she lit a cigarette, puffed on it as if it were oxygen, and then glanced at the titles of the books. Which was as well, for this made her sit up and sift her own observations instead of merely absorbing them. The books that had so alerted her were called *The Joy of Sex* and *More Joy of Sex*.

Now she was alert enough to inspect Caroline's clothes, but to her amazement, the cupboards were locked. So already she had misjudged Caroline on two counts – she had been sure that the cupboards would be unlocked, and she had not even remotely considered the possibility that Caroline could be the sort who read books on sex. Well, well, well, she said aloud now, it's a case of who would have thought it. Her lips curved, and she smiled contemptuously for she had never needed this sort of book. A few moments ago she had felt the uncomfortable beginnings of some sort of stirrings of pity for Caroline, but those books changed all that. Which was a stroke of luck really, she could neither afford nor risk feelings of sympathy for anyone, leave alone Caroline. That she had even begun to feel the glimmering of compassion made her angry – who had ever shown her any sort of concrete sympathy and who, for that matter, had made any sort of allowances for her? Except Nigel, who had been sympathetic from the very start. But then the British are famous for their sympathy for the underdog. True, his sympathy now was for her, in her own name so to speak, in her own right. Because she worked for it, she earned it and what was earned was deserved.

Why should she have felt even the smallest hint of sympathy for Caroline? Anyone who entered this room could see what a smug and complacent woman she must be.

She deserved to lose her husband – after all if she was married to a banker what right did she have to an old-fashioned bedroom like this? It ought to have been glamorous, sexy, with a few provocative nudes on the walls. Instead Caroline had these abstract forms, these delicately shaded Hepworth lithographs. Although the room was in creams and blues it was a rosy sort of room. It even had a fireplace, and there were traces of it having been used, too, for comfort.

She returned to the night before, to the long and delicious night she had spent with Caroline's husband who was soon to be her husband. Whatever conscience she might have had about Caroline was now erased by the simple fact of being in her bedroom. Caroline and Nigel's bed seemed to be a good place for doing one's thinking – she could clarify things. Up until now all her concentration had been taken up with planning, scheming, arranging.

She gave herself a shrewd look across the way at the mirror that faced her, because of course he was mad about her, passionate, obsessed and delirious. The trouble was that she knew enough to know that this sort of delirium does not, cannot last, all enthusiasm given too much outlet has a way of dimming.

And now, for the first time, she asked herself the question whose answer Nigel was so certain of – and she asked herself this out loud: 'Do I love him?' she said. And then she knew that she valued him, she appreciated him, too, she was not bored by him, but love was for teenagers and for mothers – she had never had to ask herself whether or not she loved Jean-Pierre, for example, or Maître Pachoud. It was necessary as well as pleasurable to love Jean-Pierre just as it was necessary as well as pleasurable to care for Nigel – but caring for Nigel was more in the way of doing a job well enough to facilitate her real calling which was Jean-Pierre. That she did *not* actually love Nigel was, she was convinced, in his best interest; the imitation is often so much more carefully made than the real thing, and because she did not love him she would be more controlled,

124

and capable therefore of demanding extra-vigilant loving from herself to ensure that her counterfeit would never be detected. But then again, perhaps she was wrong because there was no doubt that she loved Nigel for the way he handled Jean-Pierre, and for this she knew that she could never pay enough, nor do enough.

She turned her thoughts at once to other mothers who had healthy children, other mothers like Caroline who actually abandoned healthy children, all those more fortunate mothers, all of them more fortunate than she because they had healthy children and did not know what they had, did not know how lucky they were! How she hated them, all of them, how much more she hated Caroline who had taken all of her many blessings for granted all these years and who had compounded it all by foisting her own only child. Peter, on her!

True, Peter was good for Jean-Pierre, or had been so far – but she did not trust him yet, which hardly mattered because there was no way in which she would have Peter living with them permanently. If Caroline didn't want him there were plenty of boarding-schools who did.

Well, she had dallied too long. She would now inspect the desk. Its military aspect was remarkably odd, Ilsa thought, it was a strange sort of bureau, very old, with a flap that slid out from the underbelly of the working space. She opened this, scornfully noting that her prediction had been right, Caroline was the arrogant sort who would lock up her clothes, yet leave the really important things unlocked. After all, only one key to unlock all those locks on the front door. This sort of woman enraged her; she couldn't possibly count the number of Parisienne wives' bedrooms she had entered while the wives were away when she had been passed along Maître Pachoud's circle. These women who had so much that whatever she had taken had never been missed. And her snuff box collection was one of the most interesting around, she was sure. Well, all that was over, this would be the last bedroom of the last wife that she would ever wish to inspect. The sliding drawer was crammed with all manner of ill-assorted cottons and wools and ribbons and combs and hairbrushes and all of these were in a tangle of hair. Almost bored now, Ilsa thought: *what a slut!*

But wait, the sliding drawer, it seemed, slid further still. Ilsa pushed it out as far as it could go, at which point a hidden shelf slid upwards, on which stood a small fireproof filing cabinet. The drawers were slender, of the type jewellers keep their watches in, three of them were labelled N's letters, two P's school records, and the last and bottom drawer, C's rubbish. But these drawers were locked. Ilsa was furious and felt irrationally as if Caroline had deliberately tricked her. She stood up to calm down, and studied the photographs – nothing interesting, all family shots randomly displayed. She would do the same thing, she decided, she would put up a bulletin board of Nigel and Nigel and Nigel, Nigel and Ilsa, Nigel and Ilsa, Nigel and Peter, Nigel and Jean-Pierre, Nigel and Peter and Jean-Pierre, Nigel and Peter and Jean-Pierre. She arranged them like this in her mind as she would arrange them in appropriate order on the board. Caroline had written out two sayings and pinned them above some photographs. Ilsa read them. The first said NOTHING IN LIFE IS SO BAD THAT IT CANNOT BE MADE WORSE BY HOW YOU TAKE IT and the second, which Ilsa thought was ridiculous (she approved of the first) BRAINS TO THE LAZY ARE LIKE A TORCH TO THE BLIND AND JUST AS USELESS.

She very much wanted to get into that filing cabinet. She thought a heavy blow from the heavy silver mirror she had seen would do the trick, and was just about to do that when something made her look up and into the frightened eyes of Peter Pritchett-Ward. Then Ilsa did something she had not done since she had been a very little girl. She screamed and screamed and screamed.

16

I got the most horrible fright when I caught the Tick in my Mom's bedroom. She was the last person I'd expected to see, although I had not expected to see anyone at all. For a moment I thought it was a nightmare, and that I was nightmaring the whole thing. I have that dream about her very often, so often now that I don't bother to write it down. It's the one about me driving wheels over her and reversing and going forward, squashing and crushing her head over and over again because no blood ever runs out of her head, and so she can't be crushed, can't be broken. But it was true, and I was awake after all. She screamed for the longest time, and when that stopped, for a moment neither of us said anything at all. I don't suppose either of us could speak. Then she shook her head and said something about having been frightened, though it was a surprise to see me, she didn't know that I ever went there, and wasn't I supposed to be at school? So I mumbled something about needing a book and said I'd come to fetch it. All this happened while I was still standing at the doorway and she said I should come in and sit down which I did. She'd been smoking, I saw the ashtray by my Mom's bed, and the quilt was all wrinkled so I'm pretty certain she'd actually been lying down on my Mom's bed. I saw her see me notice that, and I don't know why, but I felt very very frightened.

I didn't know what to do, so I sat on the edge of the bed and began to re-tie my shoelaces, because that way I didn't have to look at her. She said she supposed I wondered why she was there, what she had come for. I think I spoke too loudly when I answered yes, I do, I do wonder what you are doing in my Mom's bedroom. She gave her usual sort of stupid giggle and told me that it was going to be a secret, her visit there, and that it was all spoilt now, the secret, she meant, because I had come and taken her by surprise. She said she was going to tell me what the secret was, and that when I knew I could decide whether or not to let it stay a secret between the two of us. She said something about it being up to me, and then asked me if I agreed. I had to say yes.

This is what she said. Of course I guessed she was lying and when I phoned my Mom later, my Mom said that she most definitely was lying. Anyway she told me that she was planning on having a huge montage of family photographs made for Nigel's (she hardly ever calls him your Daddy or your father when she speaks to me about him) birthday in five months' time. She walked over to me, to show me what she had chosen. It was a photograph of my Dad winning the President's cup. She said she'd been silly, she ought to have told me about it, because I probably had hundreds of photographs she could have chosen from. She asked me if I would co-operate now that I knew, in fact she was pleased that I knew, because she believed we could work on this together. Because there could be no doubt that I would want to help her prepare this lovely surprise for Nigel. I couldn't bear that, so I said, a surprise for my father you mean? And then she said that of course that is what she meant, and she giggled in her normal way and told me that she had got used to thinking of him as Nigel the way he thought of her as Ilsa rather than as Jean-Pierre's mother, though she understood that Jean-Pierre and I probably thought that a bit strange. I didn't say anything, I stared at her although I knew that was rude, too, because I have already heard her tell Jean-Pierre to take this glass to Daddy.

It was so hard for me not to call her a liar, I had to bite my lips together to keep my mouth shut – spies often have to do this when they don't want anyone to know who they are. The Tick knows who I am, but she does not know that I am her enemy. She probably doesn't care if she's my enemy or not. I couldn't think of anything to say, so I started on my shoelaces again. I was dying to tell her that I have never called my own Dad *Daddy*, the way Jean-Pierre does, and that I do not think that that is fair, and I just could not bear

128

the thought of her knowing that I was really thinking. She pretended that she hadn't noticed my silence and went on and on about parents having identities of their own, she understood how I felt because when she was young she had believed that her parents were only parents; she had only discovered that they were also people when she was already quite old, about sixteen or so. (When I told my Mom this she laughed that new laugh of hers that I don't like because it sounds like sandpaper being grated against more sandpaper and said that it was hard for her to believe that a creature like the Tick had ever had parents.)

Ilsa said she hated adults talking to her the way she was talking to me, but thought I would understand all of this a lot better if I stopped and thought that I would also be a father one day, and that I would then understand what it was like because although I wasn't a father yet I was already a person, and when I became a father that would not mean that the person part of me would suddenly vanish. I started to swing my foot, and to watch it as if I were studying the second hand on a clock. I was so embarrassed about all this talk about becoming a father, and I hated hearing about it because I am thirteen years old and I don't think I even want to become a father myself. But then she went on about what a wonderful father I had, how lucky I was because not all fathers were as interested in their sons as my father was in me – very few fathers play golf with their young sons, and above all had I ever thought how lucky I was to have a father at all, had I ever thought how unlucky Jean-Pierre had been because his father had died. She certainly hoped I knew what a lucky young man I was, she certainly hoped I was grateful. Then she ended up by saying that Jean-Pierre knows how lucky *he* is even to have only a stepfather because Nigel is such a wonderful man.

And then I began to say to myself, you will never be my stepmother, you will never be my stepmother and I said it over and over again, never, never. *Never*! I was screaming inside, and I felt my face getting hotter and hotter, and I was afraid I might start to cry. Perhaps my feelings showed,

129

because she suddenly said she would have to go very soon, she had stayed longer than she had planned to, and was I certain that I was going to keep this a secret, and not say a word about it to anyone even after we had given my Dad the montage which she knew he would be so pleased with? She asked me to promise her that I would keep it a secret with a capital S. Then she promised not to call my Dad Nigel to me again, and that in case she forgot she was apologizing in advance, because she had not guessed that that had upset me, so would I please make allowances for her, and would I forgive her for having been so thoughtless in the past. She thought that our meeting there the way we had, by chance, by accident, was a stroke of luck actually, or else it was the hand of destiny, because if we had not met the way we had met then she would never have known that calling my Dad Nigel had been offending me, and because I was polite and good-looking and kind, she liked me very much, and believed that I could become a champion golfer in time if I worked at it, because she would gladly help me the way she had helped my Dad whose swing had already improved so much, as I must have noticed, and she really very much wanted to be my friend if only I would allow her to become my friend, and she had been wanting to tell me this for a very long time but had not because she had not thought I was ready, so she had taken the bull by the horns and decided not to wait any longer, and what did I think of all this, that the two of us now had a special secret with a capital S, which meant that we could also now have a special friendship, and would I now shake the hand that she was holding out to me?

I shook her hand of course.

I could not stop her from kissing me on both cheeks.

My cheeks burned as if they had been scratched.

The Tick left then. I told her that I would be leaving, too, just as soon as I had collected the books I had come to fetch. She did not even clean up the ashtray, because she pretended she had not used it. But I knew she had. I tested it, and it was slightly warm.

I waited a few moments and then when I was sure she had left the building I put the latch down so that I would get no more surprises like that.

Checking the lock was the first thing that I did after she had left. The next thing was to check on my hiding place. I've already filled four of my diary notebooks, and I bring the completed ones here now – in case my Dad ever needs to use my locker – to my room, to the place I have made for them. It is underneath the carpet. I was able to lift the carpet and the underfelt and then get to the floor. The flooring is laid in squares, so it was easy to lift two squares out. I prised them out, actually. This part of the carpet is against the wall, under the curtains that reach the floor. My Mom and I chose these curtains together, we decorated the whole room together. The curtains are orange, and so is the wallpaper and the carpet is brown. I always thought of the curtains as the sunset, and the carpet as chocolate. The curtains sort of drift over the carpet, they actually cover that part of the carpet, and since the curtains are not directly against the wall, no one could possibly tell that that part of the carpet had been lifted. I always lay some hairs over the flooring blocks before I put the carpet back as a kind of protection. I read about this in a book of mine called *How to be a Spy*. Well, I checked and she had not discovered my hiding place. I was so happy when I found that out!

After that I phoned my Mom to tell her how I had caught Ilsa going through her desk.

I was going to tell my Mom about Wayne King and the terrible things he said about my Dad. All because his Mom met my Dad and the Tick at a dinner party last night. Wayne King will tell *everyone* that we are living in my Dad's German girlfriend's house – I just know he will! But in one way Wayne did me a favour. I cut class because of him, and if I had been at school I wouldn't have caught the Tick red-handed the way I did. The funny thing is that my Mom didn't ask me why I wasn't at school – I suppose she thought I'd caught the Tick during our lunch break.

I was thirsty, and so for the first time since my Mom went to London, I opened the fridge. It seems stupid, now, but I really thought it would be stuffed with all sorts of things – especially with Cokes – the way it always was. The Tick's fridge is usually half-empty – not that I open it unless I'm asked to! Our fridge was totally empty – that is, there was no food. But sitting all alone on a shelf was that funny ugly voodoo doll of Frederica's. I don't know why, but I picked it up and flung it into the cupboard under the kitchen sink. I suppose it was because the fridge had that awful sour smell.

One day I'll tell my Dad about the way I caught her. I promise I will. I swear I will! Meanwhile the whole thing will stay a secret as long as *I* want it to.

I'm getting very good at keeping secrets.

17

Ilsa had grown more and more fond of her diary. A particular shade of maroon, unmistakable and therefore immediately identifiable as *Hermès*. A gift from Nigel, its inordinate expense meant that it was just right for club use. Neat and slim, because each month clipped in separately, it held pages for a summary of the year's events as well as a miniature address book. It was superbly efficient, and the more you used it, and the more worn it became, the more important you felt. At least that was what Ilsa was thinking as she thumbed her way through it. Because for the first time in her life there were no gaps in her diary. Now, when she said, 'Just let me check in my little book,' she really meant it. She had always said this of course, even when she knew the pages were clear of social engagements. Her diary, though, had never been empty, each asthmatic attack had been assiduously noted, the onset, the duration, the medication, scrupulously recorded. So that, even better than all the engagements in the world was the miraculous fact that she had made fewer and fewer references to asthma. Which was, she told herself, all due to Nigel.

Ilsa fondled the diary as lovingly as if she were fondling a puppy. She read, for the hundredth time, today's engagement. *Lunch – Pamela Ridley – M.B.G. 12 o'clock.* For Pamela, or Nigel's adored sister, Pog had telephoned an invitation from Washington. Ilsa accepted at once, though it meant cancelling a golf date, and, what was more, arranging for Jean-Pierre to lunch with Zoreh Zeller's children who went to the same school as Jean-Pierre. The two women had become friends, and Ilsa found, to her continuing astonishment, that she actually enjoyed having a woman friend. Living with Nigel had clearly brought more bonuses than even her most optimistic calculations had calibrated. It was odd the way random though connected thoughts slipped about her mind, she had reached out so avidly, and for so long, and now there was so much that was good that it was impossible to order her mind. For she was thinking of André Pachoud again, of what he had taught, which was at least a change from how he had taught her, which made her giggle out loud. Even so, she still half dreaded and half hoped to see him, she still searched for him wherever she went, still dressed the way he had liked her to dress, just in case.

Well, finally, circumstances had allowed her to avail herself of the advice he had given his daughters: 'Marry the life you love, and not the man you love,' was what he had counselled. But it seemed to her that the life you loved became the man you loved, because if you loved the life then surely it followed that – in time – you loved the man? It seemed that she could hear herself listening to her own thoughts – why else would she be thinking that she was in love with her own life?

Because Jean-Pierre was much better. He would grow out of his asthma; her faith would be justified.

Lunch with Pamela Ridley at the club – there was no

better method of drawing attention, of attracting respectability than via Nigel's illustrious sister. Ilsa had not met her, but had seen photographs, and when Pamela had telephoned, and after speaking to Nigel had asked to speak to her, and had then invited her to lunch, she had very quickly suggested the club; perhaps she had imagined a moment's hesitation before Pamela agreed? No, there would be no need for Ilsa to collect her, she had one or two errands, and she could not be sure when she would be through, though she would try to get there as close to twelve as possible. Ilsa knew that Pamela had visited Geneva about two months ago, and knew (though Nigel had barely hinted) that Pamela had not wanted to meet her. Nigel had hoped, during that visit, that the three of them would dine together, and when this had not happened Ilsa had known better than to have made any reference to it.

Six days had elapsed since Pamela's phone call. Ilsa knew, even as the invitation was being proffered, exactly what she would wear. It was a little Dior suit that Nigel had brought home for her. He'd taken one of her skirts into the little boutique, to make sure that the length would be right, because he knew that everything Ilsa bought had to be shortened. It was made of the softest silk, but textured to look like wool, it was cut severely, and the lines were somehow serious and uncompromising. It was shaded in blues, like her eyes Nigel insisted, for though her eyes were brown this was Nigel's kind of humour; anyway, Ilsa had softened the lines with the gentle folds of a simple *Hermès* scarf. Of course she had checked the suit at once, for wrinkles, and she had tested the zip, neither of which had been necessary – Ilsa was not the sort who suddenly discovered a stain on a dress at the last moment. She kept her clothes the way a super-efficient secretary keeps her files. Her shoes at the club were the neatest there; the clothes she kept in her locker were protected under a calico wrap, and she had nothing but contempt for the casual way in which some women handled their clothes – no wonder they were such indifferent golfers – they scarcely deserved to play well.

Her fingers traced the indentations her pencil had made in the diary lovingly, as if it were a much loved face, and then she shut it, and placed it in her handbag. Zoreh Zeller thought her handbags were too large for her, but how else could she fit in all the things she needed? She took out the scarf and thought grimly that even the wearing of a scarf had not come easily to her – she had been compelled to study magazines in order to learn how to knot, or tie, or drape a scarf. There had been no one to teach her.

Ilsa arrived at the club too early, and looked around as if for an emergency exit. Philipe bore down on her in all his maître d'hotel pomposity, and, waiting, irritation accumulated like silence. She found herself irretrievably nervous, and was almost unable to draw courage from the memory of that day at this club thirteen weeks ago when Nigel had told her Caroline would be leaving. She said what had to be said to Philipe dismissively, then busied herself in her handbag. Drawing out her cigarettes and her diary, she tightened her lips in her old way, the way they had not been tightened for many weeks now. These simple movements, and this small activity, strengthened her, and for further reassurance she took out a recent photograph of Jean-Pierre and studied it as if for the first time. Once, she had counted how many photographs she had of her child. Five hundred. She gave an interior happy laugh at herself and smiled into the photograph.

Which was how Pamela Ridley found her.

'Ilsa!' she said.

Ilsa stood up at once, and in her haste dashed a glass off the table. Philipe was there at once. Ilsa was confused.

'I'm not late?' Pamela asked politely.

'Oh, no. Not at all.' Ilsa fumbled. 'It was sweet of you to suggest this lunch,' she said.

'I had to come to Geneva, anyway, and I thought it would be a good idea for us to meet.' Pamela's voice glanced away. 'I'm famished,' she declared sharply.

'Famished. Starving. *J'ai faim.* I love the way the French say I have hunger – it always rather reminds me of the way we say I have a cold.' She seemed unable to stop herself from babbling and went on. 'I can't for the life of me think why I'm so hungry. How do you say you're hungry in German, I wonder?'

Frantically Ilsa looked around for the ubiquitous Philipe who was for once nowhere to be seen.

'Let's look at the menu,' Ilsa said firmly, and added, 'I'm hungry myself.'

'Good idea,' Pamela said stoutly. 'What do you suggest? What do you recommend? How about the Rhineland special?'

'I wouldn't know what that's like. I never order German food here. I don't suppose you know that I left Germany many years ago?'

'No. I didn't know that. Of course Geneva is alleged to be French. I *am* a naughty girl, I always forget that.'

Ilsa decided to giggle. 'The Genevois wouldn't easily forgive you for that,' she said. 'Better not say anything like that within their hearing.'

'I see you're almost one of them. You have their accent, anyway.'

Ilsa attended to her photographs. She began to put them in her handbag. Seeing that, Pamela swept on. 'Is that your little boy? But he is pretty, isn't he? What's his name?'

'Jean-Pierre.'

'How odd. That's similar to Nog's little chap isn't it? John Peter? Peter was named after our eccentric grandfather whom everyone alleges me to take after.'

'And your twins are called Romulus and Remus. *Très amusant.*'

'*Très,*' Pamela said slightingly.

'Well, I know what I'm going to order – something very simple like smoked salmon followed by *paillarde de veau* – they do that very well here. What about you? Will you have the same?'

'O.K.'

'All the food is excellent here.'

'Have you been a member for long?'

'About three years.'

'Really? And you're the reigning club champion, I'm told?'

'For the moment, anyway.' Ilsa attempted to laugh. 'The ladies' championship is only ten days away. I suppose you heard that Nigel won the Captain's Cup for the first time in his life.'

'Did I not hear!' Pamela thumped her chest. 'He phoned me to tell me. He wasn't half as proud when he was made head prefect. That game – I sometimes think it's his whole life. And to think I was the one who introduced him to golf. He was only eleven at the time, and I took him out for fun. Had I but known . . .' Her voice trailed away.

'Do you still play?' asked Ilsa who knew perfectly well that she did not. 'I can't remember.'

'No,' said Pamela, who was pretty certain Ilsa knew. 'No, I don't play. Years ago Caro and I threatened to take it up, but he positively forbade it.'

Busily now, and carefully, Ilsa replaced the photograph in her handbag and, rather pointedly, rather resoundingly, slammed it shut. She was altogether unprepared for Pamela's attitude, and still smarted from the way Pamela had called Jean-Pierre pretty. Pamela would pay for this, and she would pay for every arrogant syllable she had uttered so far, and would no doubt continue to do. But not before Ilsa du Four was Ilsa Pritchett-Ward. For the moment, she, Ilsa, would, whatever the provocation, remain the perfect lady Nigel believed her to be.

The food was brought, and nimbly served, and Ilsa knew she was saved.

'Thank God,' Pamela said. 'Bless all the powers that be. I'm sure my blood sugar had dropped dangerously low. I always feel so irritable, and I get so mean when I'm hungry.'

Ilsa was nonplussed. All this talk about hunger was, she thought, unseemly. One could admit that one was starving, one could mention it once, perhaps twice, but one did not labour the point. She wondered what Maître Pachoud would have said about Pamela. He was such an infallible judge of character.

She sighed.

'Are you all right?' Pamela asked, sounding alarmed.

'Yes. Thank you. Why?'

'You sighed.'

'Oh, did I?' Ilsa smiled. 'It's the good food, I suppose.'

'What a pretty suit. Nogs get it for you?'

And now Ilsa focused her fullest beam on Pamela. 'Yes, Nigel bought it. He simply brought it home. He even had the skirt altered to the right length. I thought that was *so* clever. How did you guess he'd bought it?' Ilsa said, and immediately regretted having asked.

'Because he's got such good taste. He used to love giving us all pleasant surprises. I suppose you know he bought most of Caro's clothes for her. He's one of the few men I've ever met who actually enjoys shopping. Matter of fact, he's the only man I've heard of who likes that sort of thing.' And Pamela took her turn, and beamed at Ilsa. 'I know a lot of people thought poor old Caro dowdy. True, she didn't like shopping, but truer still is the fact that she dressed only to please Nogs.' She fluttered a bracelet and said, 'But of course you knew that.'

'I didn't know that. No.'

'Oh, I'm sorry. Hope I haven't trodden on your tiny toes.'

'Of course you haven't.'

'Caro told me that you and she had met only once.'

'Yes.'

'It was at the very beginning, Caro said. She also said that she knew Nigel was involved with someone, because she had found that photograph. You know, the one that had been taken so long ago that even when Caro met you at close range, she could not recognize you. She *was* mad with herself, I can tell you. She thought she was so stupid. She could barely forgive herself.'

'Well – '

'Of course,' Pamela rushed on, 'I told her that it wasn't a case of her being stupid, but of you being so clever! I suppose you think I'm being deliberately unkind?'

'You must say what you must. It's a free world!'

'Caroline tells me that she never came to see you, never.'

'No. She didn't. Nigel and I thought she would, though. I used to tell him that I'd bolt all my doors and windows if she did come.'

'How clever of you. You implied that she'd come through the windows like a witch on a broom-stick.'

'Nothing like that, you're quite wrong if you think so. It was scarcely easy – or pleasant – for *either* of us.'

'I can just imagine.'

'You are making things very difficult for me, Pamela,' Ilsa said, a distinct finality to her tone. 'You *are* Nigel's sister, and I had hoped we might be friends.' She frowned, and went on, 'I know you and Nigel are very very close, and I would hate even to try to come between you, and you probably don't realize that putting me through the mill like this will not change anything between Nigel and me, but it may well change things between your brother and you.'

'Perhaps,' Pamela said, speaking very gently, 'perhaps you'll hear me out and reserve judgement until then. O.K.?'

Ilsa shrugged, then said grandly, 'O.K.'

'Good. I believe in being perfectly frank, and you obviously believe in the same thing. So you see we have something in common – besides Nigel – already. Agreed?'

'Agreed.'

'I suppose you know that the same thing has happened to me that is now happening to Caro? Only there is this one great difference. Nico and I had only been married for five years when that woman came along, and although we were not unhappy, we were not ecstatic either. But Caro and Nogs had been the happiest married couple anyone had ever met for twenty years. Twenty years.'

'Caroline was happy. Nigel was not.'

'But Nigel was happy. Everyone knew that. We'd often

discussed it, he and I. They were best friends. Good God, even when he decided to destroy his home they were still talking to one another. And talking for hours and hours on end.'

'I know that. Like brother and sister.'

'*No*. It wasn't like that at all.'

'You reckon?'

'Yes. I do. I do reckon.' Pamela leaned forward and touched Ilsa's arm. 'I know it seems as if I'm putting you through the third degree. Maliciously, too. But I'm not that sort of person. I really am not. I want you to know that.' She withdrew her hand. 'You see, I feel I have to tell you that until you came along, until you entered his life, my brother was the happiest married man I know. Of course he fell for you. Who could blame him?' Pamela smiled disarmingly. 'Who can blame him?' she said again. 'He was at that crucial age, he was out of his own environment, too. I always was opposed to their living in Geneva. Neither of them have ever really belonged here, you know.'

Ilsa decided not to interrupt. Let the woman have her say, let her rave, she thought, she'll feel better for it, if only because she'll know she has had the satisfaction of having given me a piece of her mind.

'I wanted you to know what you are doing,' Pamela went on 'Marriages are not to be changed, like wardrobes, simply because one's taste changes. Good marriages like good clothes last forever. Oh, you're happy now, now, while Nigel is still in the first flush of his mid-life sexual excesses, but, mark my words, he'll be miserable in two or three years. He is a man with a conscience, you know, and then *your* child will have to face what Peter is facing now.'

'Of course,' Ilsa said appeasingly, 'you are entitled to your opinion on that. You want to have your say, and so you should, and I can understand that, I'm sure.' And now, she in her turn leaned over and touched Pamela's arm, the irony of which was not lost on Pamela. 'But I'm not sure why you are telling me all these things. I *am* sure, though, about Nigel . . . . I can understand your having no sympathy

140

for *me*, of course, but why don't you think a little more carefully about your brother, instead of your friend Caroline?'

'But – '

'I was going to say – oh, never mind!'

'What were you going to say?'

'It's not important.' Ilsa again laid her hand on Pamela's arm. 'You want to do your best, and you are doing your best. But don't you see, nothing you can say or do will change things . . . Except, perhaps – '

'Perhaps?'

'That's not important either . . . I respect you for what you are trying to do, and because you are Nigel's sister. But right now, if you don't mind, I'd prefer to change the subject.'

Once again, Ilsa opened her handbag, this time to take out and use her lip salve. Pamela watched. She understood precisely what Ilsa meant the lip salve to convey, and was silent.

Their lunch, needless to say, terminated sooner than either had expected, though it had gone on for too long.

Pamela declined Ilsa's offer of a lift: she was going the other way, she said. Each invented urgent appointments.

At an unaccustomed loose end, Ilsa, though behind her steering wheel, deliberated . . . It was only fifteen minutes before two, and she had expected the lunch to go on until three, if not longer. She was clear about one thing, and only one thing: she did not know where she was driving to. And yet she drove with an unusual and angry speed. She drew up at the customs barrier – where she found herself unintentionally – and felt amazed, even dazed, worse still foolish. She had no passport and was compelled to turn around. Still, she had no idea where to head. She thought of dropping in on Zoreh, unannounced, as Zoreh had taken to doing, and because Zoreh lived close to the border, but once outside Zoreh's tall imposing gates, she drove on. She might drive to town, might park in that wonderful under-lake garage – it excited her, somehow, driving safely under water, but only when she was with Jean-Pierre, because she found his excitement exciting. She decided against that, too.

She longed for Jean-Pierre, ached for him, and thought briefly of fabricating some excuse and getting him out of school earlier, but she rejected that as well. She really needed to hit a few golf balls – in Ilsa's experience nothing absorbed rage quite as successfully as the force she brought to the club-head when it sent the ball soaring. But that was out, too – she had said she had an appointment, and could not, therefore, be seen at the club.

In the end she headed home, back to Ripaille and Madame Blanc.

And then your child will have to face what Peter is facing now. Pamela should *not* have brought Jean-Pierre into things – but she had dared to do just that, and that had been a bad mistake. She had gone too far for her own good. Because she, Ilsa, would make sure to turn Pamela's mistake to Jean-Pierre's permanent advantage.

All the same, Ilsa hated Pamela Ridley – Nigel's sister – and in the grip of all that spreading, uncontrollable hate, struggled for sense. Driving helped. Hate wastes the hater, as Ilsa had learned too well. And yet her heart raced. She must be strong enough, now surely, to lay hate aside, to view Pamela through the eyes of logic instead of the eyes of hate? She was a *winner* – she reminded herself – everyone on the golf course knew she had nerves of steel. Ilsa du Four would *not* be defeated by the likes of a Pamela Ridley who happened also to be Nigel's sister. Especially not by Nigel's sister! Because, looked at coldly, looked at clearly, Pamela Ridley simply was not worth it. Nigel's sister was uncivilized, that was all, which was unforgivable! Besides, her lack of manners meant that she was a lesser being after all.

But when Nigel would ask her about the lunch, at first she would be openly brave. She would concentrate on Pamela's elegance, Pamela's jewelry, and then she'd allow, finally, Nigel to wring some of the tearful truth from her. But not a single condemnatory word about his sister would pass her lips, and if that was what Pamela had hoped for, it was another of her mistakes.

Madame Blanc was pleased to see her. She was ironing a pair of Peter's trousers and held them up and said, 'Beautiful cut, Madame. Where did you get them?'

'I didn't get them.'

'But they are brand new.'

'Are they? Well, of course, his mother bought him a whole lot of things before she dumped him. It was the least she could do!'

'Poor child. He's so sad. I see that whenever I see him. So sad and so quiet. It's not natural.'

'What do you mean?' Ilsa said seriously, making it obvious that she would pay very serious attention. 'I think I've been thinking the same thing.'

'What do I mean? Well, it's not right for a young boy to be so quiet. It looks wrong to me.'

'Wrong?'

'Well, haven't you noticed how he walks?'

Ilsa considered this. She shook her head slowly. 'No,' she said. 'No, I haven't noticed anything special about the way he walks.'

Madame Blanc clucked. 'The poor child. The poor child stoops like an old man. It's like he's trying to hide something all the time. Poor child, he's probably trying to hide himself!'

'He certainly is a very secretive young man, I must say. You're quite right, though, Madame Blanc.'

'Secretive, yes. But shy, I'd say. Yes, shy. Too timid. Poor child. My heart breaks for him.' Madame Blanc indulged a not unpleasurable sigh. 'Of course he is a strange one.'

'Of course? But why d'you say of course?'

'With a mother like that, how can he not be strange?' Now Madame Blanc clucked disapprovingly. 'A mother like that – it's not natural. He takes after her, of course.

You know we say a selfish mother makes a suffering son. And, *voilà*, Madame, Peter suffers. As we see.'

The drift of the conversation did not please Ilsa, but because she wanted to please Madame Blanc, and at the same time display her own largesse, she said, 'Peter's a very clever boy. He'll be a doctor one day, I'm sure. You heard what happened when the fondue spilt over Jean–Pierre?'

The tactic worked.

Madame Blanc clucked again, this time with delight.

'I'll make you a coffee?' Ilsa said.

'I will not say no. Thank you.'

It was good to be with Madame Blanc. A sturdy woman, tall, Amazonian even, a woman who knew her own mind about everything, who was never plagued by doubt, things were right or wrong, good or evil, black or white, people came from good stock or from bad stock, bad stock could explain but never excuse, good stock, however, was its own justification. Scrubbing, like ironing, was virtuous, which is why she enjoyed it, because she was paid, her enjoyment was more virtuous still, and consequently more enjoyable.

Madame Blanc chatted on about her nieces and her apples, her roses and her sons with equal interest. Watching Madame Blanc's large practical-as-formica hands with their wide serviceable fingers so strangely graceful when they were still, while Ilsa's small childlike hands tirelessly exercised their squash ball, her rage began to recede. Pamela lived in Washington, after all – a bitch like that scarcely counted anyway. Really, that was all she was – a bitch. Thoroughbred or mongrel, it made no difference, Pamela Ridley was a bitch . . . All at once Ilsa felt happier – odd, how this simple label made the whole matter easier to handle.

Which was as well, for as it turned out, Pamela had very cleverly given Nigel an entirely different account of the lunch. It seemed Pamela had been enchanted by Ilsa, was disappointed not to have spent more time with her, though understood how disruptive urgent errands could be. Pamela would have dearly loved to have joined them all for dinner, but had spoken to Bill who was in London and needed her to go to some boringly important dinner. Nigel had assured his sister that of course Ilsa would understand.

Ilsa, who understood too well, even though she had not known anything about the dinner that was now being cancelled, decided to leave things as they stood. She'd deal with Pamela, though, but in her own time – that bitch to end all bitches would have to try much much harder if she ever hoped to outwit Ilsa du Four!

Meanwhile, rage returned. It stayed with her all through dinner with the children, even while she read to Jean-Pierre, indeed accelerated and later when everyone was in bed and she was rinsing her underwear, and nude, the rage gathered more momentum, and she marched into the bedroom, and to Nigel's unyielding astonishment picked up her golf club, a seven iron, and silently set about effecting a few savage but expert swings.

Something in her manner made Nigel hold silent. Finally, after about the tenth swing, he said, 'You would have hooked that one.'

The sweat ran down her arms.

She felt the beginnings of a truce with her rage.

'I know,' she said. 'I know.'

She began to giggle.

Emboldened, Nigel said, 'Your little tits produce a pretty good swing themselves. You should have seen them waggle. Perfect tempo, perfect. Sexy sexy *sexy* rhythm!'

Her giggle expanded.

Emboldened further, Nigel bounded out of bed. 'Look,' he said, 'look at my own unique home-grown club – look!'

Ilsa could not but grip his manhood, so boastfully erect. 'How about sinking that putt?' she said.

Acting the whore in her own bedroom felt glorious. She felt nothing otherwise – nothing at all. Except that is, for the sensation of power that goes with the giving of pleasure.

Afterwards, because Pamela's enmity still rankled, and because towards the end of the lunch she had come too

145

perilously close to telling Pamela that her hostility had further strengthened her ambition to have Jean-Pierre du Four become Jean-Pierre Pritchett-Ward, but mainly because she judged it the right moment to begin her negotiations, she said, 'I'm a bit worried about Peter, you know.'

'Peter? Why?'

'He's developed a stoop.'

Nigel laughed. 'Is that all? You had me worried.'

'Well, Madame Blanc noticed it, too. She mentioned it today.'

'Shouldn't have thought it very serious myself.'

'Of course it's not serious. But it ought to be corrected, don't you think? Perhaps you should say something to him?'

'I'll mention it. Good idea, darling. You see things I don't see, and you see them so clearly.'

'Oh, well, he's such a sweet boy!'

'I'm rather partial to him myself, I must say.'

Ilsa giggled. She said, 'You know, darling, I heard Jean-Pierre say he was Jean-Pierre Pritchett-Ward. It sounded so funny, the way he said it – verrreee verrreee French, you know? Like *je vous en prie*? Prrreeetchettt Wurrrd.' She giggled again, explosively, then more explosively still – it went on and on, until the sounds changed, and Nigel heard weeping instead.

'What is it?' he said. 'You're not like this, you never cry like this. What's happened? What have I done?'

It seemed the sounds would never let up, but, as if there were no alternative, went from loud to louder to loudest. In desperation, then, Nigel cradled her in his arms, lifted her off the bed and carried her as he would a little girl. And like a little girl, the calm came before the explanation.

'It's so sad,' again and again she whispered, 'so sad, so sad, so sad . . .' Then she explained, 'Jean-Pierre wants to be your son even more than he wants to be my son. He needs to have *your* name, he needs *you* to be his father.

Oh, my God, what have we done to him? What have we done?'

'*You've* done nothing – nothing at all. You're a fantastic mother – everyone knows that! It's my fault,' Nigel said decisively, 'I've been insensitive. Criminally insensitive. Of course I must adopt him, legally. I should have understood that before. I'll see about it tomorrow. First thing in the morning. O.K.'

'You can't just do that. Adoption's not as simple as deciding whether to buy or to sell, you know.'

'Of course I know that. I don't have to think about it. It's part of loving you isn't it?'

Eventually, about two hours later, when it was safe enough, Ilsa gave way to Nigel's persuasion, and agreed to the adoption.

At dawn, still awake and too alert, Ilsa reached for her squash ball. This was almost too good to be true, frighteningly good, even. Because an adopted child cannot also be a stepchild. An adopted child, Swiss law decrees, is a full and equal child, and cannot be disinherited. For it is written that a parent may not disinherit a child. Ilsa received her thoughts with something close to anguish, because all this was better than good: *Oh, my God, Peter will be compelled to share everything with Jean-Pierre!* Peter, of course, will have a stepmother, a distant part-time stepmother perhaps – ah, but what did that matter?

A thin gentle snore whistled from Nigel's throat, and Ilsa listened to it gratefully. There was no possibility of sleep for her, nor did she wish for it. She had pulled it off, and she blessed her success just as she blessed her son. For she had once again provided him with a legal father.

She spared a thought for Caroline. One day, perhaps, she would tell Caroline what she was now telling herself. She would say, '*You see, Caroline, if you had not left Peter with me – and you alone know the true reason for that – the thought of having Jean-Pierre adopted would never have occurred to me.*' Then, just as suddenly, she undertook to say nothing at all to Caroline about this, because even

imagining such a future conversation might – just might –
be pushing her luck too far for safety.

18

May 25th

I don't know how long I can last out. I thought spying was
adventurous, but it is not. It's not that it is the opposite of
adventure, because it is not boring, it's just that you have to
wait, and you have to act *all* the time, you have pretend.
Because no one must be allowed to guess what you really
think, what you really feel, and it is very very hard. It's like
playing chess all the time, in a way it is as if you are playing
against yourself, because the others don't know that they
are even players. I want to go away from here, I want to live
with my Mom and my Dad, but if I can't live with both of
them I'd rather be with my Mom. Only I can't tell her that I
want to run away, because that would make her decide to
drop our plan before the six months are up. We have got
exactly 150 days to go, before we might have to (I don't like
to say this) surrender. If we lose and the Tick wins (I don't
like to say this, either) I don't think I will ever want to see
my Dad again. At least I'll be able to tell him how much I
hate her. If only he knew how I really feel!

I wonder what he would do if I told him the truth? He
always told me never to be afraid of him, and I'm not afraid
of him, even now, it's her I'm afraid of. I don't know what
has happened to his mind, all I know is that if he has caught
a disease she is the disease. She is not even nice to him all
the time. I heard him ask her something, and she answered
that she had already told him what he wanted to know, and
she wasn't going to tell him again. He looked quite upset,
sort of sad, but I think he knew it was because she was mad
with worry because her precious little Jean-Pierre was ten

148

minutes late. She had allowed Mrs Zeller to take them to the circus, and he was supposed to be home at six o'clock, and it was already quarter past, or ten past, I can't remember, and she had already phoned the Zellers' house, and been to the bottom of the driveway I don't know how many times, and by the time Jean-Pierre came home, it was exactly half past six, I remember, she was already blaming my Dad, saying she would never have let him go if he had not said that it was a good idea for Jean-Pierre to go out with other children, that it was his fault that she even knew the Zellers in the first place. She had already forced my Dad to phone the police, and the hospital, and she was pulling that horrible witch-black hair of hers, and saying that my Dad couldn't possibly understand, because he had never been unlucky enough to have had an asthmatic child, the way she had, because he had always been privileged, and that how on earth could she even expect him to understand when he thought it was perfectly normal for a mother to have left her child, had (and these are her exact words) pushed the responsibility for another child onto another woman who had a sick child of her own to care for. She would never have left Jean-Pierre, never, never, never, even if he had never had a sick day in his life. She thought that Caroline knew what she was doing, Caroline had all the luck and didn't even know it – mothers who did not deserve to have children who were well and strong always had children who were well and strong.

And then she started to cry and to sob, and she was just like Jean-Pierre when he can't get his own way (which is almost never – I really mean that she was just like Jean-Pierre until he gets his own way) and my father put her head against his chest and smoothed her hair, and she let him do this for a little while and then she looked up and saw me, and told me to go to the driveway at once to look for the Zellers' car, and then she said (and again these are her *exact* words) 'What are you doing here anyway? Are you too selfish to go and stand at the gate so

that you can run in and tell me when you see them coming –
if you see them coming? Oh, God, dear God – '

Of course I ran out at once. I was relieved and happy to
get out of there! When I saw their car, I almost did not race
back to the house to tell her at once, but I did, and then she
started laughing and told my Dad to fetch her a comb,
quick, quick, and when the Zeller family came in, she was
smiling, and looking very different, and very tidy, and
started to tell me to fetch ice, she was sure Zoreh could do
with a stiff strong drink the way she could, because she was
a silly nervous sort of mother, it was idiotic of her because
she had been in a blind panic. My Dad gave the Zeller kids
Cokes, and I brought the ice. She hardly ever asks Jean-
Pierre to do a single chore when I'm around, it's always *me*.

Lately she has started calling me Peter dear. She had
even begun calling me Peterkins, which made me feel sick,
so I told my Mom about it, and she suggested I ask her not
to, but only when she said it. My Mom said I should be very
very polite, and explain that I thought it was a bit babyish,
now that I was a teenager.

I felt angry and sad and sick and shaky when I heard her
say that my mother had *abandoned* me. I still feel angry and
sad and shaky about that. I wish I could get her back
somehow, even before we win, even more if we don't win. I
won't even think of losing.

Only I wonder if my Dad believes her when she tells him
that my Mom abandoned me?

I hope he is not *that* stupid! He's gone soft in the brain,
though: Wayne was right when he said his mother told him
my father had lost his head, but my Mom says that hope is
strength, and I still have hope.

When we win I hope we will all live somewhere else,
where no one will ever know what happened.

My Mom says she prays a lot now, and feels more and
more strong. She says faith is as important as hope. She
says I should pray, too, if I can. I don't know why, but I
don't want to tell her that I started praying long long ago,
the very first night that I moved in here, and that I still

kneel and pray every single night. Perhaps I'm not telling her because I don't want her to know that it hasn't worked yet, not even after all this time. It may be because God knows that other boys have far more serious problems. Frederica is always praying and crossing herself, so that we have three people praying on our side. I hope the Tick does not pray. I don't think she does – she only goes to church at Easter and at Christmas. We used not to go even then.

We never went to church. Sometimes I'm afraid this has been a sort of punishment. Maybe I should include asking for forgiveness in my prayers. This is what I say when I pray: 'Dear God, Thank you for the things we eat.

Please bless my mother and my father and Raffles and Frederica.

Please let me live with my mother and my father in the same house at the same time.

Please send Ilsa and Jean-Pierre away.

Amen.'

But I am going to change my prayer. After I say thank you for the things we eat. I am going to say: 'Please God forgive us for not going to Your House. I promise to go every Sunday when my parents and I are all together again.'

I should have thought of that before.

I hope it is not too late.

It may be a sin, but in a way, I think praying is almost exactly like wishing. When you pray you speak to God, and when you wish you speak to the sky. I speak to the sky quite a lot, often I don't even realize that I am speaking to the sky. But whenever I pass under a bridge and a train passes, or if I lose an eyelash and I put the eyelash on my hand I always make a wish before I blow it away. I know it's babyish, and I had stopped doing it ages ago, of course, but I started again when I started to pray.

The praying and the wishing are secrets. I never

151

thought, I never dreamt I would have so many secrets to write down when I got my first diary-book. I have already used four of these books.

I have too many secrets, I think.

I might not have kept all these secrets so secret if I had not been able to tell everything to my Diary. Writing is like talking, sometimes. When I do my school writing it is not at all like talking, because I have to write so neatly, and think of the spelling and try not to cross anything out. All the same it might have been easier to have talked into a tape recorder, but I think I prefer talking with a pencil.

19

All envelopes marked 'private' or 'confidential' or 'private and confidential' that were addressed to Nigel were opened by him. None of these was private, though all were confidential. These envelopes had long ceased to excite even the mildest curiosity in Nigel – they all related to numbered bank accounts. So when two genuinely private letters arrived in the same mail Nigel was altogether unprepared.

He had first read and then re-read the mysterious letter from Caroline's lawyer, and at the third reading had still not divined quite what it was that her lawyers must have wanted him not to understand. The second letter was from the office of the Director of Studies of the International School, Dr Stephen Bowen. Even before he read the contents he found himself irritated by the logo. This was his sixth reading of the letter, and as he read he formed the words with his lips as if this would help him connect the words with his mind.

Dear Mr Pritchett-Ward,
I would not be taking the liberty of sending this communi-

cation to you via registered mail if there had been any response to my two previous communications. However, it occurs to me that although we have found the Swiss mail system to be highly efficient, some members of my staff are sufficiently ungrateful to call it fanatically efficient, it seems likely that my earlier missives have gone astray.

As you no doubt are aware from your son's mid-term report, there has been a marked deterioration in every subject. I must confess that – along with my staff – I am nonplussed. Peter had been widely, indeed unanimously nominated for the Merit List for which a Grade A is required for each subject. As you will see from the enclosed additional report card the lone 'C' for Mathematics represents Peter's highest achievement this term.

Whilst we take his age into consideration, the (notorious) onset of adolescence seems scarcely enough to account for a deterioration of these dimensions.

It is my sad duty to report a general decline in his behaviour as well. He is sullen, uncommunicative and passive in the classroom, and somewhat belligerent on the playground. These behavioural changes would not in themselves be any cause for serious alarm, but over the last two weeks his school attendance has been fitful.

> Yours faithfully,
> Stephen Bowen

'I am pretty well stunned,' Nigel said out aloud. 'Stunned. Stoned. Bombed. Or, as Peter would say, mentally done out.'

After a while he asked his secretary for a line. He would dial this number for himself. He had told the school not to send the mail to 22 – he had been foolish enough to have left all that to Caro. Idiot, he castigated himself, idiot. Nor had he seen a half-term report. For God's sake when had half-term *been*? And what the hell had happened to those earlier missives?

But when he finally got through to the school he was told that Dr Stephen Bowen was in conference.

I need to think, thought Nigel.

He buzzed his secretary.

'No calls, please,' he said firmly. 'None.'

'Madame du Four?'

'I said no calls. None. Oh, except for a Dr Stephen Bowen. Put him through at once. Tell him that I'm in a meeting but that you have instructions to interrupt.'

But he could not think.

That much – at least – was clear.

As if for distraction he read Caroline's lawyer's letter and again mouthed the words.

Monsieur,

I am instructed by the London firm of Garratt, Hartley and Williams to act for your wife, Mrs Caroline Pritchett-Ward, in Geneva.

My client does not authorize me to institute any action whatever. My client wishes to know that you are entirely free to take whatever action whenever and wherever you may so desire, and to institute proceedings whenever and wherever you may so wish.

My client wishes me to convey to you her belief that you will do your best and not your worst. She has instructed me to communicate her very best wishes to you.

My client insists that you be informed that she has retained a Swiss lawyer such as myself in order to facilitate matters for yourself.

I remain, dear Sir, your distingusihed servant,
André Pachoud.

Facilitate matters, indeed!

He was grateful but unsympathetic to Caro's obvious need to exile herself from his life; she had wanted nothing so much as she had wanted to please him, and he felt a gathering sense of contempt, for in her desire to please him she had spared no one, and not even Peter.

What on earth did this letter mean? Did it mean institute proceedings and Caro will co-operate or institute proceedings and Caro will not co-operate? Where the hell was she anyway? And when did he last speak to her?

It occurred to him that he had not spoken to her since she had left. And then he knew what it was that had been preventing him from taking a decision over the proposed merger with Langham Holdings – he had not discussed it with Caro. And he understood, suddenly, how much he had discussed with Caro – he had invested heavily in a new insurance venture in Australia because Caro, who knew the directors, had pronounced them unscrupulous enough to make millions, had gone heavily into gold at $40 because Caro had overheard a conversation at a swimming pool and had reported it to him along with her comment that her source – whom she named – was a man whose sense of danger was acute enough to have sent him into the air during the Cuban missile crisis. He'd been on one plane or another between New York and Geneva for six days because he'd believed air was the safest place – he was a survivor as well as a millionaire and if he trusted gold, then. . . And so Nigel had gone into gold for his own as well as for (now adoring) clients' portfolios. That little venture, based on such a seemingly flimsy premise, had netted him personally something in the order of $6½ million. Caro sat at that pool in 1972 – Caro urged him to buy 8,000 ounces of gold at $40. He sold at $800 in 1979. $320,000 became $6,400,000! Which was real money, all right. In anyone's language. There was something startling – almost frightening – about accumulating $6½ million for so little effort. That sort of thing could make a man lose his bearings, he thought.

And yet, unlike Ilsa, Caro was definitively unbusiness-like in all respects. It was, he admitted, one of those curious paradoxes. She had an intuitive sixth sense, and Nigel only regretted things when he failed to take her advice.

Anyway, he had long since concluded that Caro and Ilsa were not to be compared – they might have been of separate species. Caro was a creature of instinct and Ilsa was a creature of fact.

Ilsa was a woman of muscle and bone, whose skin, he believed, he had grown for her – for she had been without protection until he had found her and (he could put it no other way) taken her unto himself. Caro was a woman of tissue and sinew and, because she had always been protected, she had her own – and known – skin, which, though not thick was nevertheless resilient and would survive with or without him, as by going away she had demonstrably proved. Yes, Caro took things on her stride. There was about her a slow contentment while about Ilsa there was a running wildness, and at the same time, a contradictory attentiveness to the tamer joys of life – like lunching with friends in a restaurant.

He ought to tell Caro about Dr Stephen Bowen's letter. Shamed, he shook his head. How Caro had neglected Peter! Neglected, abandoned, discarded was what Ilsa so rightly said. Because Caro saw Peter as an encumbrance because she thought another man would find a thirteen-year-old a liability. It didn't bear thinking about. No wonder he hardly ever thought about Caro. But, no matter. . . He would phone her. He would be diplomatic. He would read her the letter. . . She ought to know what had happened to her son, what her neglect had done to him.

Astonished because he was compelled to look up the number of the Belgravia *pied-à-terre* in his address book, he dialled London. A woman's voice responded with the number.

'Caro,' he said automatically.

'Are you looking for Mrs Nigel Pritchett-Ward?'

'I am.'

'Mrs Pritchett-Ward is not at this moment available, but if you would care to – '

'Are you an answer service?'

'We – '

'So you are an answer service!'

'Speak up please. I did not get your communication – '

Nigel slammed down the receiver. He trembled, which was not in the least like him. He had just discovered that he hated Caroline for the way in which she had let Peter down, and, for that matter, for the way in which she was letting him down, now, too, by having an answer service, by being unavailable when he most needed to talk to her. He still shook, and what was worse, perceived himself to be in a cold sweat. To think that he had been naive enough to believe that Caro had committed the supreme act of self-lessness by leaving Peter with him. Ilsa was right about her – Caro was unnatural. Ilsa knew the true meaning of motherhood; but for Jean-Pierre she could have been another Nancy Lopez, or a Patty Berg! Ilsa's was the true sacrifice, Caro's was phoney.

What about that lawyer of Caro's then? He'd heard of the firm, but he could not remember what he had heard. He tried again and was told that Maître Pachoud was in conference.

Well, then, he'd have to phone Pogs. Lord, it was only 6 a.m. in Washington. Too bad, whatever else Pogs was doing, she was not in conference. He smiled. To her sleepy hello he said, 'Pogs? Have I woken you?'

'No. Of course you haven't woken me! I've usually had my bloody breakfast by four in the morning.'

'It's not four. It's six.'

'So you *do* know the time over here. What's up?'

'Where's Caro?'

'Caro?'

'Caro. Yes, Caro.'

'Caro?'

'You know who I mean; Caro. My wife. Caro.'

'I wasn't sure about that bit.'

'It's about Peter.'

'Peter. What's happened?'

'Letter from the headmaster.'

'That's *all*. He's *well*?'

'Behavioural problems. Low grades etc. Truancy.'

'My goodness I can't tell you how relieved I am. He looked pale, I thought, when I last saw him.'

'You saw him? He didn't tell me.'

'Took him to lunch the way I used to take you, remember?'

157

'I remember.' Nigel laughed and felt better. 'Peter didn't say.'

'Should think there's quite a lot he doesn't, as you say, say.'

'This is not the time for a lecture.'

'Sorry,' she said, and he knew at once that she meant it. 'Tell me what the problem is.'

Nigel told her.

'I'll get hold of Caro.'

'Her answer service, you mean.'

'I know where she is.'

'Some mother, I must say. What if Peter were ill?'

'Did you leave a message with the answer service?'

'Of course I didn't.'

'Silly boy. They'd be in touch with her in two minutes flat. You should know Caro.' She sighed, and across the Atlantic he heard the whistle of her exhaling breath. 'Caro's not silver,' she said. 'Don't sell her short!'

'Whose side are you on anyway?'

'Yours, of course.' And then, very gently, she let him know that he was rather preoccupied with Ilsa, and with Jean-Pierre, and above all his misplaced, misdirected, but no doubt over-worked – for the sake of a euphemism and of diplomacy – *heart* – so that perhaps Peter felt his father's heart was not quite with him. She ended by saying, 'Much as I hate to talke in clichés, Peter's behaviour is a desperate plea for help. Peter has as much right to you as Jean-Pierre – '

'Save your irony,' Nigel interrupted.

'You know what I mean Nogs. It's not Peter's fault that Jean-Pierre's father is dead.'

'Hold on. Hold on,' Nigel said. 'You've made your point, and what's worse, you're right. I've been trying to be a real father to Jean-Pierre, and I suppose I took the fact that I'm Peter's real father for granted.'

'Nogs darling, how I hate having to be so cruel to you.'

'Thanks. I'm glad I called you.'

Dear old Pogs would win Ilsa over soon enough, even

though she probably had been even more insulting than Ilsa had said. Pogs had charmed her way out of worse situations; even her worst victims ended up with some feeling of affection for her, if she wanted them to.

Pogs had the annoying habit – at crucial moments – of being irritatingly accurate. *It can't have been easy for Peter*, she had said – and it was all too true that in making room for Jean-Pierre, he had somehow forgotten to include Peter. It was not that Peter had not featured in his father's thoughts; on the contrary he had thought of him, though primarily in connection with Ilsa and Jean-Pierre. Caro had sworn that Peter's real security rested with his father. And his father now realized – and with more than a twinge of guilt – that he had taken Caro literally, believing that his mere presence was enough for Peter. He had not stopped to think the thing through, and indeed now found this sort of thinking through decidedly uncomfortable; the top of his head felt as if it were being bored in several places by a multi-headed corkscrew. He must do something at once, he was used to putting things right. What was needed was action, and instant action at that. He began by doing what most businessmen in any sort of crisis do – he buzzed his secretary. 'Cancel my lunch with Tyler Bank,' he ordered. 'Tell them – I'll leave it to you what to tell them.'

He would take Peter out to lunch – the Palais des Anglais gave an excellent English meal. Besides, it would be best to quiz Peter before tackling Dr Stephen Bowen. As he was leaving he heard his secretary speaking to André Pachoud. He shook his head – there was no point in even trying to understand either Caro or her best wishes.

Waiting for Peter and watching the gum-chewing, sneakered and jeaned children Nigel reflected on the quality of freedom, of independence this kind of international children had. Within the confines of the school eighty-three nationalities became one world, even if, listening to the accents, it was an American world. He had waited for Peter at this time many times before – the school

159

had a two-hour lunch break. He caught sight of Peter, and was shocked, even from a distance, by the way the boy had grown. He saw Peter stop to fondle a cocker-spaniel. The boy put his face against the dog's face, his eyes closed and then, abruptly, he left the dog and continued walking. Parting with Raffles must have been terrible, Nigel thought, and suddenly understood that he had not been nearly sympathetic enough. As Peter drew nearer it seemed he had glimpsed his father, too, but he gave no sign. And when he drew alongside his father his expression gave no evidence of having noted anything out of the ordinary.

'Hello, Peter?'

'Hi, Dad?' Only the slightest inflection.

'How does the idea of an English meal strike you?'

'At the Palais des Anglais?'

'Right on.'

Peter was silent for a while, and then he said, 'Is Jean-Pierre coming too?'

'Just the two of us, my boy. Just the two of us.'

'Good,' Peter said. 'I'm pleased about that.'

But the lunch did not go well. Nigel placed Peter on the red velvet banquette, but the boy leaned back, while Nigel, seated opposite him in the less comfortable chair leaned forward with all his weight on his elbow as if he were trying to sell a dicey deal to a banker. Peter was enthusiastic (yes, real mint sauce was a treat, and yes, the roast lamb was very good) polite and devastatingly respectful; Nigel did not approach the subject of Dr Bowen's letter, electing to wait until the boy's stomach – at least – would be more relaxed. The man at the next table was pronouncing, very loudly, in English 'Where there's good snail there's good wine,' and Peter, catching his father's eye, smiled at him for the first time. Nigel winked back at him.

'I thought we might have nine holes tomorrow,' he said. 'Ilsa says she's still some work to do on your grip.'

The merest hint of a wince scraped Peter's features. His

left eye twitched for a moment. *The boy's nervous*, Nigel thought, shocked.

He was casting about for something to say, when Peter said unexpectedly, 'I hope you don't mind, Dad, but I'm not so keen on golf any more.' Then, as if by way of a suggestion, and to help his father over the growing silence, he added, 'I suppose it's what you would call one of my phases – I've been thinking of judo.'

'Judo? Have you been having trouble with Wayne King? Is he at it again?'

'Yes,' Peter said, and blushed.

'Care to tell me about it?'

'His usual,' Peter said casually. His attention appeared to be diverted to something in his back pocket.

'I see.' Nigel leaned further forward. 'I met Mrs King at a dinner, you know. Did I tell you?'

'No,' Peter said bitterly. '*You* didn't.'

'I see,' Nigel said again. He leaned even further forward. 'Well, Peter, we'll arrange for judo.'

'Thanks, Dad,' Peter said, 'that's very nice of you.'

Peter had always thanked him for the smallest things, Nigel remembered. Once, when he'd been given a remote-control boat the boy had thanked him over and over again, saying, 'I can't get over it, Dad, your giving me a boat like this. . .' But this time, though Peter's thanks were harmless enough on the surface, something – deep inside his tone – jarred. Which was why Nigel, who had not planned on mentioning this yet, said: 'I've had a letter from Stephen Bowen.'

'I see,' Peter said, exactly imitating the way, a few moments before, his father had said the same thing.

'Do you, Peter?' Nigel said. 'Do you see?'

'Well, I haven't read the letter.'

'It was about your grades. About truancy. What do you have to say about this?' He swept his face with his hands. 'For God's sake, Peter, stop fidgeting with that pocket of yours!'

Peter stopped and looked down. He appeared to be

holding his breath. Nigel thought, *he's close to tears.*

'Peter,' he said, 'this isn't like you at all. I'd like to help – ' He broke off. Seeing Peter bite his lip Nigel said something he had not known he was thinking. He said: 'Would you like to see your mother?'

'Yes, Dad, yes I would.'

Used, as Nigel was, to putting things right, or turning things round, an idea took shape and evolved into a strategy. He would urge Ilsa to accept the Zellers' invitation to go off for a golfing week in Chamonix. He half-suspected that she longed to go anyway, and that but for Jean-Pierre, would have urged him to take a week off from Banque Nekker. They would go away, with the Zellers, without Jean-Pierre who needed to be weaned – at least for a little while – from his mother – and without Peter who clearly needed his mother. And he would say nothing to Ilsa about Dr Stephen Bowen's letter or his lunch with Peter.

He said now, to Peter, 'Let's keep this lunch secret. O.K.?'

Nigel thought he detected a flicker of distaste behind his son's concentrated eyes.

'If you like, Dad,' Peter said.

Going away would be good, Nigel decided, and more than good. It would be a relief. For the first time in his life he openly welcomed the idea of being without children – anybody's children – at all.

When Nigel returned to his office his secretary told him that Maître André Pachoud and Dr Stephen Bowen had returned his calls.

First things first, Nigel decided, and less than three minutes after he had spoken to Dr Bowen he was in his car, driving back to the International School, to have a meeting with him. He drove his Mercedes with his usual competence, and reflected – as always – on the splendours of the absence of London traffic.

It was early afternoon, the lake glinted in the pale sun, and the brightly coloured sails on some of the little yachts

162

made delicate little movements in time with the light breeze. Everything about Geneva was restrained, Nigel thought, and it was this quality of restraint (or moderation?) that some foreigners (mostly Anglo-Saxons?) found despairingly dull, and which was so deeply pleasing to him. Because no motorist expected another to be helpful enough to allow an unauthorized change in lane the traffic flowed without niceties and with all due precision.

Dr Stephen Bowen's office – high fees notwithstanding – was particularly uninspiring. All was steel – cabinets, bookcases, desk – even the chair on which Nigel sat. Had the steel been more substantial it would have resembled nothing so much as a bank vault, Nigel thought. The two men exchanged the usual formula endemic to foreigners living in Geneva (how long they had been there, how they felt about the place) before they settled to serious conversation. Nigel thought Dr Bowen seemed rather young for the job – Nigel assessed him at around thirty-five and would have preferred him to have been a little older. His soft but well enunciated voice made Nigel categorize him as 'your typical East Coast academic snob' – Dartmouth or Brown followed by Harvard for the PhD, and not in the least like any British headmaster he had ever known and been intimidated by. His eyes fastened on the slim gold bracelet around Dr Bowen's wrist – severe as a wedding band – it was hardly the sort of thing one expected to see on the wrist of a headmaster, even if he was known as Director of Studies. Franz Zeller wore a similar bracelet, Nigel remembered. It was more in Zeller's style, anyway; it was of a piece with the flashy silk suits and flashing chains and it did not go with shabby cuffs and even shabbier tweeds. Nigel found the bracelet somehow offensive; almost as if Dr Stephen Bowen wore it expressly to irritate and confuse.

Nigel believed that – unlike Americans – he had no penchant for discussing personal details of his private life and although Dr Bowen probed very gently it was clear

163

that he wanted to know 'Nigel's thinking on the basic causations of Peter's problem'.

For his part, Stephen Bowen believed that he was behaving somewhat unprofessionally. It was not that he liked seeing Nigel squirm, it was just that he thought he deserved to. Stephen Bowen felt uncomfortable himself, making value judgements was worse than unprofessional, it was unethical. He must have allowed Mrs Pritchett-Ward to influence him too deeply, indeed, he could not get her out of his mind.

He had elected to go along with Caroline Pritchett-Ward's startegy, which was as unorthodox as it was untested. But then Stephen Bowen prided himself on being something of an innovative risk-taker; and if he was to follow her theories he was required to dissemble. (Disinformation she had called it.) He had agreed partly because he knew himself to be a good judge of character and she had shown him she was the sort he could trust and respect, partly because he thought her rather beautiful, and partly too because her deviationist theory made innovative sense.

The main thrust of the strategy was that Nigel had to understand that for a short while – about four to five months or so – the responsibility for Peter would be entirely his. This was an emergency measure which would correct Nigel's temporary defection. The keeping of the family together was, Caroline held, a female biological imperative. Stephen Bowen had been deeply moved, for she had spoken so lovingly of the man, so warmly of his relationship with his son, and above all, she had spoken honestly. Where she might have expressed bitterness she expressed compassion; it was this quality of worldliness that set her apart from those other discarded, conformist and therefore vengeful wives who had so often faced him across his desk in the past. It became more and more important to him to have her take it for granted that he was a like-minded kindred spirit who inhabited the same classy world as she.

Her husband was, she insisted, honourable, and she was

convinced that she owed it to him to do all that was possible to help restore him to his senses. After all, she had asked reasonably enough, if Nigel had lost his health would not everyone expect her to do everything she could to help him recover? If only she could be strong enough and courageous enough, wise enough and controlled enough, then, in time perhaps, both she and Nigel would come to look upon this as something like a viral infection. This way even the past need not be contaminated. The overriding difficulty, she explained, was in not letting her hurt outweigh her love, because she hurt beyond all telling of it. . . But then she loved beyond all telling of it, too. 'Because you see, Dr Bowen, I know all that we have been, all that he has been, and all that I have been. A marriage – a real marriage – is more than the subtraction of its parts – ' She had broken off then and he had leaned forward and, as if his entire world depended on her answer, asked, 'What is it then?' 'It is not to be measured, because it is also space or, if you like, indivisible territory. . .' These last were the words that had convinced him, that were now as firmly committed to memory as were the opening lines of Jane Austen's *Emma*. Caroline Pritchett-Ward had, until now, been an Emma Woodhouse – she had as good as said so.

But she had come to see Dr Bowen because it was vital for Nigel to believe that she had abdicated her responsibilities, too, and would he therefore not disclose the fact that the two of them had been in any sort of contact? It was unorthodox, iconoclastic perhaps, but would he – *could* he – co-operate?

Even if he had been seduced into it (only in a manner of speaking, of course) he was co-operating now, wasn't he?

'I thought,' Nigel was saying miserably, 'I thought Peter's mother had informed you of the domestic circumstances.'

'Ah – she'll be returning very soon, then?'

'No.'

'I see. But Peter of course is in her care?'

'Not at the moment. Peter is in my care.'

165

'Ah – Well – Of course that explains it then.'

'Explains what?'

'If Peter is in your care then his mother would very logically – and, if I might say so, quite properly – have assumed that you would have taken it on yourself to have apprised the school of all relevant details.'

'I take your point, sir,' Nigel said irritably. 'I take your point.'

Dr Bowen fiddled with his braclet for a moment. Then he said, 'Don't you think Peter has been rather low these past weeks?'

'I shouldn't have thought so, actually,' Nigel said seriously. 'I've just taken him to lunch. . . He's always been an exceptionally polite young man. But – yes – he is withdrawn. He would like to see his mother. I'm about to arrange that.'

'I must have misunderstood you – I had not realized that Peter's mother had not been informed of his current difficulties.'

'Oh no, you were right. She doesn't know.'

Stephen Bowen frowned, fingered his bracelet, and seemingly at a loss, said nothing.

As if to fill in the silence Nigel said, 'Peter's mother believes that mothers can't bring up sons. She thinks that from ten afterwards they need their fathers.'

'Ah – does she? I can't say I altogether disagree with her. The Swiss courts seem to see things her way. Sons – from the age of fourteen – are awarded to their fathers.'

'Interesting. I didn't know that.'

'Strangely enough, it does make some sense. Though don't quote me, please, in this egalitarian world – this is heresy!' Dr Bowen laughed.

Nigel thought: If Bowen was trying to make him think he was a man's man he was mistaken. Pretentious prick! Nigel said: 'Well Peter has always been close to both of us.'

Dr Bowen felt he had dissembled for long enough. Accordingly he conducted the rest of the interview via standard procedures. It was one of his less successful interviews. He suggested a consultation with the school psychologist, and was turned down. Nigel, in turn, suggested they wait. Meanwhile they would keep a watching brief on Peter and they would liaise.

Later, in his minute handwriting Dr Bowen wrote: Though NPW's response to my communication was as immediate as a reflex his paternal instincts appear somewhat impaired.

Dr Bowen could think of no good reason for having noted anything at all. He crumpled the paper and flung it away. 'What,' he said out loud, 'What the fucking hell do I think I'm doing?'

He was not given to the use of expletives, but this case – for all its iconoclasm – disturbed him. He was sure of only one thing – the outcome of all this was not to be predicted. When you can't formulate a prediction you have a premonition. Dr Bowen shuddered. He began to consider what it would be like to return to the real academic world, the world of his beloved Jane Austen, where all predictions were safe.

It had been an unsatisfactory and trying day, Nigel felt. The best thing he could possibly do for himself would be a vigorous hour or so on the practice range. A golf ball machine dispensed two buckets of twenty-five practice balls for two Swiss francs. There were five balls left in the second bucket which meant that Nigel was about to strike his forty-fifth ball. Practising usually helped him sort things out, but today it seemed his swing went more wrong with each shot. He told himself he was not confused, but irritated, and perhaps angry. He disliked Dr Bowen who certainly was not Nigel's idea of a 'man's man', and as for that Maître André Pachoud – well, he'd be dealt with in due course. But both Pachoud and Bowen were trivia, really, and Nigel knew he was not the sort who let petty details and pettier people get him down. His talk with Pamela had not actually made things much better either.

He hit a particularly savage hook and the ball flew at least forty-five degrees off line. He was hitting the ball like

167

a beginner! What the hell was going on? There had to be *some* explanation. Yes, well, he was troubled. He had to face it, Peter troubled him. . . Not Peter – he was a good boy, a fine boy – but Peter's attitude. Peter had become remote and strange and somehow – secretive. . . Yes, it was this secretiveness that Nigel found so – well – distasteful, so distressing: there was something sneaky about it, too. . .But above all it was the sort of secretiveness that could be dangerous.

Nigel could not give a name to whatever it was that he felt, rather than thought. 'Don't think of what you will be losing,' Caro had said, 'think of what you will be giving up.' Nor could he have said why Caro's words kept returning to him like a newly developed bad habit, repetitively, like a faulty right-hand grip. He must have hit too many balls – there was always the risk of becoming over-golfed.

He peeled off his glove, and left the last four balls untouched.

He could not decide what he wanted to do, or where he wanted to go. All he knew was that he despised indecisiveness.

If Caro was, as usual, so irritatingly right, then everything that he was not losing, but merely giving up, meant that the end result was that all his losses would be borne by Peter.

Because, effectively, Peter had lost Caroline. Peter had lost his mother. Which was quite a thought.

He was pleased – if only because it made him feel better – that he had given way to impulse and suggested that Peter spend some time with his mother. Besides, Caro had an uncanny way of smoothing things, of salvaging feelings, of solving problems. And yet, for all that, she could be way off beam: she had said she would not speak to him for six months, and she had not spoken to him, and her silence had solved nothing at all, and he could not understand her reasoning. Unless, of course, she had reckoned on him missing her. Still, it would have been helpful to have been able to discuss Peter. His decision was in line with the way he did things: whenever he wrote company reports – at which he was uncommonly skilled – he always composed the conclusion before the first sentence was even begun.

20

May 28th

I think that maybe praying does help after all.

My Dad took me out for an English meal. We had a secret lunch. No one knows about it, not even my Mom. It's another one of my secrets. A man next to us was talking about snails, and my Dad winked at me when we heard that. I'm going to have judo lessons, and my Dad didn't say anything about giving up golf.

It was nice when my Dad said just the two of us. He often used to say that.

I don't think he knows what to do about Stephen Bowen's letter. I think he's going to leave that to my Mom.

I don't even know what he really thinks about the letter. I know he's not pleased. Sometimes I think I'm going mad because I was pleased about that letter. It was like a ticket in a way, or if not a ticket then a permit, or perhaps an invitation. Because I know that if Stephen Bowen had not sent him that letter my Dad would not have taken me to lunch. Of course that is just another one of my secrets.

When I think of that lunch now I think of snails. I don't know sometimes, what I think. I don't like thinking about things. But I wonder, is praying different from thinking? Praying seems easier – because when you pray you hope, and when you think you worry.

I've begun to pray more and more, lately. Sometimes it's as if I'm praying all the time – non-stop. I heard them talking about adopting Jean-Pierre – even when I don't want to hear what they are saying I hear her voice. That machine-voice of hers never switches the volume low enough. *I don't want my Dad to adopt Jean-Pierre!* So I pray and pray and pray.

MyMom certainly was definite about what I must do if my Dad ever mentions this to me. She hopes he won't – in fact, she's 99% certain that he won't. She made me promise, though, that if my Dad does say anything to me about this – which she doubts anyway – that I must say nothing at all. Not a word. Not yes, not no, nothing at all. But if the Tick says anything I must say, 'That's nice.' Nothing else. If I am pressed to say more I must say, 'I said that's nice.' If they tell me about it together, I must do the same thing. But my Mom begged me not to worry about this and to try very very hard not to even think about it, because she said it will never happen. *'Not over my dead body, Peter – it will never happen. This I promise you.'*

So I'm not thinking, I'm praying.

21

Leaving Jean-Pierre with the Zeller children and their nurse, Nicole, was, Ilsa believed, probably the most momentous decision of her life. Perhaps it was because this decision carried a component of high terror that all those other decisions – however important – had not. When she had decided, with the proper degree of detachment, to cut herself off from her family to move to Geneva, to embark on an affair with her *patron*, Maître André Pachoud (yes, even *that* – as only recently she had admitted to herself – had been her decision) and then to leave the Pachouds to take on the position of assistant to the matron at the English School of Leman, and after that to marry Luc du Four, and later to become a member of the Mont Blanc golf club of Geneva, and later still, to live with Nigel, there had been little to lose.

And now she had decided to take a week's break up in the French Alps close to the Mont Blanc, without Jean-Pierre, but with Nigel and the Zellers. That she could actually do this both amazed and angered her. She was angry because she had managed to convince herself that – but for that brat, Peter – she need not have been obliged to take such a decision, and she was amazed to find that she had been able to bring herself to take such a radical step.

Ilsa understood that successful decisions are altogether dependent on timing. And she was about to decide that she could not – and would not – include Peter Pritchett-Ward in her family for very much longer. She knew all the things the boy was not – he was not impolite, not untidy, not demanding, not nearly as spoiled as she had expected him to be – she knew also that he did not like her, although patient and dedicated and determined effort could, in the end, win him over. But knowing what he was not told her little or nothing of what he was. He was as helpful and as unobtrusive as the most perfect house guest, but she could not tolerate a permanent house guest. Nor should she be expected to – she who found even the presence of a resident maid an imposition. And then she understood that what she most objected to was the fact that Peter was a stranger, and wanted to remain a stranger. And, as everyone knows, one should never trust a stranger.

A moment of fear like a premonition assailed her, and she would have woken Nigel, but something stopped her. She could not take the risk of exposing her real feelings for his son.

Unusually sleepless, she reached for her squash ball, but merely rocked it to and fro in her clenched fist. The distance between herself and Jean-Pierre grew and grew; the three and a half hour drive that separated them became irrelevant – what if there was a summer storm up in these mountains? This had happened – people had been stranded. At least no harm could come to Jean-Pierre from

171

Peter, because Peter, thank God, was with his own mother, where he belonged. Ilsa supposed Peter would tell his mother, now, about having caught her in their flat, in Caroline's bedroom. Tell-tale.

And yet, if anything, Ilsa resented him for keeping it secret. He was stuffed with secrets, that Peter, over-stocked she suspected, because he hoarded them like a miser and guarded them like a sentry. He was one big secret, that's what he was, he even held himself like a secret, bent and coiled, as if he were forever listening, forever straining for whispers that came from a secret source. Oh, why the insistence on driving herself mad like this? No harm could come to Jean-Pierre from Peter – she reminded herself – Peter was with his own mother – where he belonged.

She tried to make sense of her thoughts. But her mind struck only one thought, and there it stuck: *Peter was unnatural, like his mother. . .* The night dwindled, but there was no end to the thought which stuck tighter, and tighter still. *The boy is unnatural, like his mother. Peter is unnatural, like his mother. . .* She began to whisper the words to herself, and then, as happens, the words suddenly changed: *He must go. Peter must go. The boy must go.* Relief came in a long, airy sigh, and when sleep finally met her it was as feckless as the dream which accompanied it.

She dreamed in English, dreamed she sliced off steak-sized chunks from Raffles's face. These she gave to Peter, who fried them, carefully and perfectly, in her new non-stick pan. Strange, but the kitchen she'd been in was Caroline's. She knew she would never forgive Peter for having come upon her in his mother's bedroom like that. As a result of which she'd been unable to inspect Caroline's lovely things, after all.

At breakfast the next morning Ilsa seemed bleak, tenta-tive, sad. She spoke effortfully, bravely – she had not been able to get through to Geneva – she did not know, she could not be altogether certain how Jean-Pierre was getting on without her. Her concern, though excessive, was rather touching, rather impressive amd the conversation centred on it, and rather kindly, rather patiently, the Zellers and Nigel humoured her.

Nigel, after a while, excused himself, and when he returned it was to say, 'I got through to Geneva. Jean-Pierre is fine. *All* the children are fine. I spoke to Jean-Pierre and he said I must tell you that he's having – and now wait for his exact words – he's having a real fun time!'

Ilsa began to giggle. 'Jean-Pierre is starting to speak English to Nigel,' she explained. 'Darling, thanks for calling for me. You're so thoughtful.'

'Good. Now we can all relax,' Nigel said, somewhat unnecessarily, the Zellers thought.

A business meeting had been arranged. It was the real reason for the Zellers' suggestion that Ilsa and Nigel take this break with them. A new and highly innovative resort development was to be discussed – Franz Zeller was putting the deal together and Nigel's bank was thinking of recommending it to a few of their clients, amongst whom pieces of the deal would be apportioned. There is never a scarcity of venture capital in Switzerland. Zoreh was deeply interested in every aspect of the deal, but Franz thought it best for her to accompany Ilsa on a small shopping spree. Zoreh understood perfectly – business and friendship made successful partners.

So the two women strolled through the little village, inspected the boutiques, but made no purchases, Ilsa was looking for a toy shop – there wasn't one, so, lured by the strong coffee aroma emanating from a small bistro they went in, sat down, and ordered two coffees, and, enticed at the same time by the sight of golden chilled wine, though it was only 10 o'clock in the morning, they decided to drink wine as well. The clientele in the bistro were workers, mostly; of course everyone was welcome at those standard tobacco-coloured formica tables, with their standard tri-angular ashtrays, at those standard well-worn benches, but the harsh, and basically cold furniture drew warmth from the thick pungent smoke, and from the sound of real laughter and natural voices. Ilsa and Zoreh were out of place, and, in the way of a couple of matching oddities everywhere a certain commonness of purpose, or, if you like, of identity, emerged, and was given more prominence, more meaning. At any rate an extra intimacy arose between the two women. Up until now they had gone in for the usual sort of unimportant but vital small talk, as if it was only life's lighter difficulties that permitted mention.

'That man's besotted over you,' Zoreh began boldly. 'I've never seen a man quite as besotted over a woman as Nigel is over you.'

Ilsa merely lowered her eyes, but allowed a grateful smile.

'I mean, I thought true romance was dead until I saw the two of you together!' Zoreh went on. 'Take this morning, for example. The way Nigel went to phone Jean-Pierre.'

'Oh, yes,' Ilsa said fervently, 'Nigel adores Jean-Pierre.'

'So I saw.' After the briefest hesitation, 'I didn't see him phone his own son.'

'But Peter is with his mother.'

'Are you pleased about that?'

'Of course. Delighted.' Ilsa quickly amended, 'For Peter's sake.'

'Poor kid – I can't understand how any mother – '

'Nor can I!' Ilsa interrupted.

'What's she like?'

'Peter's mother?'

'Yes.' Zoreh wanted to say 'Nigel's wife', but controlled herself.

'Well, Peter's a very secretive sort of child, but his manners are excellent, so I suppose she must have been a good mother.'

'But what sort of woman is she? What does she look like?'

'You've never seen her?'

'Franz assures me I have met her. But, for the life of me, I can't remember what she looks like – and, even if I say so myself, I'm unusually good with faces,' Zoreh said,

174

sounding very frank. Zoreh could not say she had never met Caroline – that would have been too obviously untrue. But in confessing to having met her she communicated, wordlessly, a great deal more: Ilsa would understand that Zoreh felt free enough to own to having been curious enough to discuss Ilsa with Franz. Besides, hinting that Caroline had been eminently forgettable could not fail to further their relationship.

'She's not bad looking,' Ilsa offered. 'Average height. Good figure. Tinted blonde. Tailored clothes. Elegant, in a sort of British way, I suppose.'

'She sounds very dull to me.'

'Well – in a way – yes, you could be right.'

Now Zoreh judged it timely to move in for the kill. 'How do you feel about her?' she asked quietly.

The other, taken unawares, answered, 'If it weren't for Peter, she'd have no place in my life.'

Zoreh appeared to consider that. 'I can understand your saying so,' she said, managing to sound ponderous as well as sympathetic. 'But even if she has no place in your life – in either of your lives – you probably can't help feeling *for* her?'

'No,' Ilsa said firmly. 'I don't understand her, that's all.'

Now Zoreh chose silence.

Her choice was not without effect, for it obliged Ilsa to proceed. 'She gave up her child. Pushed her responsibilities on to *me*. So what can I feel for a woman like that?' Ilsa tendered a dismissive shrug.

Which was not taken up by Zoreh, who persisted. 'But if she had not done that, if she had taken Peter, would you have felt for her then?' She took an exaggeratedly long sip from her glass, leaned over, and touched Ilsa's arm. 'Please don't think I'm being bitchy. Please.' She spoke urgently, and therefore disarmingly. 'It's just that I really want to know. It fascinates me, you see, because I can't help admiring and respecting a woman like you. I mean, it's not easy, on your own, with a child, to get a man to leave his wife.' Zoreh seemed very moved. Sincerity blazed when

175

she said sadly, her voice dwindling, 'I can't help wondering what Nigel left behind, and how you feel about it, in case it ever happens to me, I suppose.'

'We all worry about that,' Ilsa said kindly. 'We all do. You want to know how I feel about Caroline? Well, since we are being honest, I'll be *very* honest. The truth is that I don't feel very much. What's the point in spoiling what Nigel and I have with pointless guilt? I don't honestly *feel* guilty. There's nothing on my conscience. My own life hasn't been all that easy, by the way. Jean-Pierre without a father. His asthma's really improved since Nigel's been with us.'

'That *is* wonderful, I agree.'

Ilsa acknowledged Zoreh's response with a smile – again that brave and grateful smile – and swept on, unretreatingly. 'Nigel has made very generous – enormously generous – arrangements for Caroline. At *my* insistence, I want you to know. I suppose that says something to you?' Ilsa shrugged again. 'He didn't have to be that generous, you know.'

'Yes, that does say a lot,' Zoreh agreed – though what, she could not guess.

A silence. This time, intimate.

Zoreh gave an inner shudder. As if to conceal it she tinkled her collection of gold neck-chains thoughtfully. She had learned nothing new about Caroline, but a great deal about Ilsa. She concluded that Ilsa had been entirely truthful – there was no room for Caroline in Ilsa's life, there was some, but not too much, room for Nigel who would – too late – find himself cramped – for Ilsa's life was already overcrowded with Jean-Pierre. Ilsa was neither quite as clever or quite as ruthless as Zoreh had thought. It was clear that Ilsa was besotted, dedicated, absorbed, taken over – owned and possessed, lock stock and barrel – by her small, sickly son. It seemed it was more than a matter of having exchanged her life for her son's – in favour of his life she had given up her own. And Nigel's only true relevance was what and how much he could offer the boy.

(Zoreh thought in these financial terms because this was the language she would use when she reported her findings to Franz.) Zoreh saw she'd been wrong a few seconds ago, for during this brief conversation she had learned, through Ilsa, a great deal, not only about, but also from Caroline. It came to her that Caroline must have divined Ilsa's only – though limitless – weakness and known where to strike. So – the rather bookish, rather pale, rather striking Caroline she remembered was really rather more than clever – she was both cunning and logical – devastatingly logical. Very sensibly, and, as Zoreh saw it, very naturally, Caroline had planted Peter as her own intelligence agent within the inner sanctum. Zoreh approved, for her own precepts held that guile and guts separate the women from the girls. It was simple: Ilsa was a girl, Caroline was a woman.

Zoreh's mind had long since been trained to perform mental acrobatics of this sort with an almost indelicate speed, just as she had been trained to disguise whatever it was that she might be thinking. (Already her ten-year-old daughter had displayed evidence of natural aptitude in this area.) And so, during the few moments that it took to form these deductions, and while she was still under Ilsa's eye, she had been playing with, and seemingly studying, the interior of her coffee cup. Now that she had penetrated Caroline's secret, she smiled.

Whereupon Ilsa interrupted the silence.

'Why do you smile?' she said.

'Because I'm telling my fortune.' Zoreh turned the empty coffee cup towards Ilsa. 'I learnt this from an elderly dowager in Cairo, and whenever a brown coffee cup of mine has a white lining, I tilt it, look at the designs made by the coffee dregs, and analyse the shapes.'

'I've never seen that done before,' Ilsa said enthusiastically. 'You're pleased with what you see?'

'Tall dark strangers always please me.' Zoreh made to lift Ilsa's cup. 'Would you like me to read yours?'

'I'd love you to.'

'O.K. But I must concentrate.'

A sudden sympathy for Ilsa mingled with a sudden contempt. What an improbable innocent she had turned out to be, Zoreh thought, warming to her. . . She said, 'You've suffered in your life. This is the pattern that tells of unrequited love. . . and this little squiggle shows turns, as you can see, for the better. You are a very proud person, and very organized, and you are going to be very lucky. . . Wait a minute. Something's been worrying you. You wanted something very much. And then you changed your mind – and now – well, it will not happen after all.'

'My God, you are fantastic, fantastic. . . I was worried, I was even *very* worried. But after breakfast – '

'Jean-Pierre – I was at breakfast, too, remember?'

'I always worry about him. No – it was something else.' Ilsa stopped suddenly, to interrupt herself. 'You didn't see anything in that cup about Jean-Pierre, did you?'

'No. Nothing.'

'Thank God for that. I'll tell you what was worrying me.' She paused, then, rather shyly, added, 'I feel I *can* tell you – now.'

'Of course you can. You always could.'

'I thought I was pregnant. . . I'd wanted to be. . . I only discovered after breakfast that I wasn't. . .'

'Disappointed?'

'Oh no – I'd changed my mind. I'm a very happy woman this morning.'

'Nigel wasn't pleased?'

'I don't know. I didn't tell him. I wasn't too worried about how he'd feel, though I know he's not too keen on having more children. It was Jean-Pierre I was worried about. A new baby would mean a real rival – it would upset him terribly. It might have made him ill.'

'I suppose you're being careful?'

Skilfully, Zoreh steered their conversation in the direction of less dangerous intimacies such as contraception and frequency.

When they left the bistro, Ilsa glowed with more than wine. She had a friend – she had, at last, made a suitable woman friend.

22

June 18th

It is exactly three weeks since I last wrote anything in my diary. I hardly know where to begin, so I think I'll begin with the best part. The best part has only just ended, but even though I am now back at the Tick's house again, I still feel good because the week I spent with my Mom was like being on holiday, only better, because it was like going away and taking your whole house with you. Sleeping in my own bed, among my own things, was pretty special. But it is being with my Mom I like – I like that more than my own things, more than my own bed, even – I suppose I'd nearly forgotten what a nice lady she is although I don't know how I can say that because I don't think I really knew how nice she was when we were all living together, and you can't really remember what you don't know.

When my Dad told me that he had something to tell me I thought it would be more of all that hassle about Dr Bowen's letter. Instead he asked me if I would feel comfortable with the idea of spending a week with my Mom at 22? I honestly did not have the faintest idea what he was talking about, so I asked him what he meant. He said that it had all been settled and that my mother would be coming back to Geneva for a week so that I could stay with her.

'Mommy'll probably fetch you from school tomorrow.'

'Tomorrow?'

'That's what I said.'

'I'll go and pack at once.'

'Ilsa's already done that for you.'

'I know how to pack.'

'Have you ever packed? We thought Frederica did all that for you.'

'Even so I know how to pack.'

'It was very kind of Ilsa to do your packing for you. I'm sure I don't have to tell you to say thank you to her. Come now Peter, admit that it was nice of her.'

'Of course I'll say thank you. Naturally I'll say thank you.'

Then my father sighed very loudly and said, 'You'll understand more about things when you're older – '

I wrote out all those things because I repeated the whole conversation to my Mom later. I nearly left something out, and this is the part my Mom thought was the most important. I asked my Dad if he had spoken to my Mom. He answered that he hadn't, he'd left a message with that fancy new answering service of hers, and then her lawyer had called him to ask what he wanted and then the lawyer had called him back after he'd spoken to my Mom. 'Mommy won't speak to me,' he said, and I thought he sounded as if he could not quite believe that she won't speak to him. 'She will not speak to me. She will not. She refuses to speak to me until six months have passed. She told me that when she left us.'

I told him that in fifty-six days, six months will have passed.

I asked my Mom why she wouldn't speak to him. She says that it's because if she does speak to him he won't miss her. She said that her silence was a sort of weapon. She laughed about that because she had the feeling that the weapon might be working. Anyway she said that when you go to war you have to have spies and espionage, and guns and bombs, and all sorts of things if you even hope to destroy the enemy. She wanted to know if – as her chief of staff – I understood all that.

I do.

At least I think I do.

But I'm getting ahead of myself. I'm not saying anything

about the day she picked me up from school. It was so like old times. She often used to fetch me before she went away. She's got an old beat-up yellow Fiat – the back wheels are higher than the front ones, and so it looks askew. Anyway that car of hers always reminds me of the illustrations in nursery rhyme books of the house the old woman who lived in a shoe lived in. It's a cosy comfy sort of car, and you feel good in it because it does not matter if you drop one of those bright glittery purple silver papers that wrap my favourite candy.

The Tick also has a Fiat – what am I saying – she *used* to have a Fiat – my Dad just bought her a brand new *Lancia*! Anyway that Fiat of hers was snow white, and inside it was as tidy as a bank. My Mom's car is untidy and even a bit scruffy, but *it is not dirty*! Since I've lived with the Tick I have got to understand the difference between disorder and dirt, if only because the Tick sees no difference between disorder and dirt. To her, even untidiness means dirt. All I know is that disorder can be good and dirt can be bad. I think the disorder in my Mom's car is good. I suppose you can be very comfortable in disorder, but you can never be comfortable in dirt.

'I've discovered that my diary is a very good place for working things out as well as for keeping secrets. Now I think I know why I'm talking about dirt and disorder. Things seem to depend on my thoughts – I think my Mom's untidiness is good because I think she is good and I think Ilsa's cleanliness is bad because I think she is bad. She can't complain about the way I keep my room, though, it is just as tidy as hers – it is so neat that it is uncomfortable to be in that room. I'm like a disturbance!

I guessed Raffles would be in the car with my Mom and I was right. He ran all over me and barked and yelped and cried. I swore I saw real tears in his eyes. It's funny how such a little dog – he's only forty-six centimetres (I know because I measured him this time) could cause so much trouble. And he is so sweet, he's like a four-legged teddy bear. We took him everywhere with us. We hired a little

181

motor boat and went on the lake – we had done that a few times before, my Mom and I, only we had never taken Raffles, and my mother had trouble lighting her cigarette in the wind the way she always does, and her hat flew off into the lake, and for a terrible second both of us thought Raffles was going to jump in after it.

We had what I've called ever since I was very young A Fun Time.

When we went to the barber we all laughed like anything. The barber, Albert, decided that Raffles would have to have a shampoo as well as me. Albert does my Dad's hair, or used to, until *she* stopped him, and his salon is in the basement of the same hotel whose swimming pool my Mom and I use. The Tick won't go there – she says it's not hygienic because of all those Arabs who use the pool and the coiffure. Albert was in such a good mood because one of those unhygienic Arabs had just given him a thousand franc tip (in a single note!) and he was waving it around. All the other barbers and manicurists were drinking champagne – unhygienic champagne, too. My Mom looked so happy, sort of gay, and her eyes had the same old merry glint in them, especially when Albert said that I looked just like my Dad. Even my hair is like my Dad's – very, very thick, he said. My Dad took Jean-Pierre and me there once, and Albert had some funny things to say about Jean-Pierre. He thinks Jean-Pierre not only looks like an owl, but blinks like one, because he also seems so sleepy. When I told Albert that Jean-Pierre wants to become an *avocat*, Albert hooted like an owl himself. Poor Jean-Pierre! It's true – he is a bit slow.

Raffles really enjoyed his *coiffure*. Albert actually shaped his hair, and then because it was his first haircut, put the cuttings into a special envelope which does up with a golden tassel, exactly the same one that he gives to mothers when their sons first have their hair cut. My Mom still has the envelope he gave her.

And then what made me laugh even more was meeting the son of one of my parents' friends who was also having his hair cut, even though anyone could see that he didn't really need a haircut. It turned out that Brad's father gives Brad's pocket money to Albert to give to Brad each week. No haircut no pocket money. Poor old Brad. But I don't think he really minds – I think he just pretends to be embarrassed. Everyone at the salon knows about the joke, and they tease him about the kind of magazines he likes to read over there. It's a friendly sort of place for Geneva, and for some reason they were all especially friendly to me that day. The unhygienic champagne, I guess. My Mom laughed so much that tears poured down her cheeks. Which made me remember how much she *used* to laugh. Remembering that I felt sad for a bit.

I like the sound of my Mom's laugh – it's a sort of chuckle, but it's hard to say exactly what it sounds like, though it sounds as if it begins deep inside her tummy and has to travel a long way to get out – it's not the sort of laugh that can be acted, that's for sure. The Tick has the kind that comes from no further than the throat or tongue, it's a giggle that she brings out whenever she thinks it's necessary. I always have the feeling that she trips a switch or presses a button and the giggle comes out, like the steam from an electric kettle.

Even the manicurist came over to have a look at Raffles's nails. She said they were too long, and said it looked as though Raffles was not getting enough exercise, and that she thought that was not exactly *comme il faut*, and that she was sorry to see I was not really looking after the dog as he deserved. She sounded so strict. So my Mom told her that Raffles had been in a kennel for many weeks. I was happy when my Mom said that because I did not want that manicurist to think Raffles's condition was my fault.

That was when my Mom decided to take him to the vet. Dr Michelin also thought that it was a terrible pity that such a dog had to live in a kennel.

All our days were busy like that, fitting everything in.

And then of course we were doing something we had never done before – spending time in the kitchen – just the two of us. It *was* fun, tremendous fun, but how I wished my Dad could have been there! I don't know why, but when he's around the place sounds much noisier, much livelier.

Well, he wasn't there, and it seemed to me that there was nothing I could do about that. And I thought, if he had died it would have been worse, but then Jean-Pierre would not have had him. . . And I began to hate what I was thinking so much that I thought I had better take Raffles for a walk along the lake. My Mom came too, and we fed the ducks, and though we didn't talk much, I felt much better after that.

All that time I tried not to think of the week coming to an end.

My Mom says she's not very good in the kitchen, but the meals were wonderful, at least that's what I thought. She said that she was better at cooking than she had thought she could be, and she just could not seem to be able to do anything in a tidy organized fashion, so I didn't in the least mind helping her with the cleaning-up. I had to teach her how to use the dishwasher anyway. It was when I was looking for more dishwashing detergent in the closet under the sink that I found that awful ugly voodoo doll Frederica had got hold of. I'd thrown it in the closet myself on the day I'd caught the Tick, I remember. It looked more like a pin-cushion than anything else. My Mom tried to laugh about it, but the laugh didn't really work. Anyway she said that Frederica's tricks hadn't really worked yet, because we were still *out* and the Tick was still *in*.

Then she said something about not allowing ourselves to spoil our time together by getting maudlin, and when I asked her what that meant she told me it was a sort of mixture of bitterness and depression, and then laughed sharply and said what a way to improve my vocabulary! But she quickly rushed out of the kitchen saying she'd remembered something she'd found for Raffles; she'd bought him some presents. She came back with some plastic bones and plastic strips which were meat and chocolate flavoured. And they really did taste like that – I know because I tasted them. Raffles went crazy, chewing and biting, and yapping and barking, and even dancing. My Mom thought it was a miracle what science could do – who would have dreamed of inventing chocolate-tasting plastic bones for dogs?

Then she told me this amazing story she'd heard from an American psychiatrist she'd met in London. The psychiatrist is called Dr Westmoreland, and he's more of a scientist than Dr Gaud, because he works in laboratories. He's a research doctor. An experience – that happened almost by mistake – with his own son turned him into a kind of specialist in asthmatic children. One day Dr Westmoreland took his son and his whole family to spend an afternoon in the country with some friends who had a horse called Lucky. The rest of the family were all very excited about meeting this horse, but the son who had the asthma (my Mom doesn't know his name, she only knows that he's about ten or eleven) was unhappy all the way there because he is allergic to horses' and cats' and dogs' dander (that means hair or feathers, my Mom taught me) and before they had even got to the house, while they were still on their way, the boy started to say that his chest felt tight, already, so they gave him the inhalator spray, which helped for a bit, but as soon as they arrived he began a bad attack. Of course his father knew what to do, because he is a doctor, and he stayed with his son while the others were having tea, and then the whole Westmoreland family were given the most unbelievable surprise – the horse called Lucky turned out to be a *wooden* horse! So it was the *word* horse that had caused the attack.

My Mom found it difficult to understand exactly what the doctor meant, so he explained that although the attack had been caused by his son's imagination, his son had not faked the attack. I didn't understand this at all well, so my Mom explained that it was almost as if the boy, hearing the word horse, saw a film in his mind, a film of his own past attacks, and of his own terror. Sometimes, my Mom said, you remember a dream, and even though you are not even remembering anything that actually happened, the

185

remembering can trigger off feelings of happiness or sadness, or joy or even terror. Because the mind is a strange thing, stranger, even, than the brain, and scientists still have lots and lots of work to do. My Mom always tells me that maybe one day when I grow up I will be a scientist, and, who knows, I might make a highly important medical discovery.

After that experience with Lucky, the wooden horse, Dr Westmoreland experimented with his own son. He put fur and hair and feathers under his son's pillow, and nothing happened. Dr Westmoreland was still carrying out this experiment on his own son when he read a medical paper about some new experimental work that was going on in England. This new work proved that asthmatics who were allergic to cats and dogs and horses were not allergic to dander, but to the urine of the animal. So Dr Westmoreland exposed his own son to animal urine as well, and again, nothing happened – not one attack. Then – and this is about the most amazing part of the whole experiment – Dr Westmoreland told his son about all these experiments, and that is how he cured his son. My Mom wondered if Jean-Pierre wouldn't benefit from the same sort of thing? It would be wonderful if Jean-Pierre could be cured, too, it would be wonderful for everyone, for Raffles especially.

I asked her about Madame Sanossian, and she suggested that we go to the little American church that is in the same building as the American library. Or rather, the other way round, the library is in the church. She'd got her priorities right now, she said, she believes in God. I didn't tell her about my own prayers, I only said I would like to go to that church. So it was decided that we would go on Sunday, and that after services my mother would take me to Evian and walk around with me. She said she hoped I'd understand that she wasn't up to going to the Mont Blanc golf club. I sure do understand!

To tell the truth I don't like golf any more. I only realized that when my Mom suggested we go to Evian. All of a sudden I got to know that I *hate* golf. I hate the game. I hate the slowness of it, the ball only moves if you make it move, it's a stupid game, and I can't understand why golf was once the most exciting thing in my life. It must have been a phase. There and then I decided that I was going to stop playing – that way I won't have to be seen with *them*. They can play with Jean-Pierre who hasn't got the first idea of a golf swing – his swing looks like he thinks the club is a broom-stick!

So I told my Mom I didn't want to go to Evian – we could go there of course if she wanted to, for lunch, but I wasn't madly keen on playing. And then I told her that I would not be playing golf again. And she rumpled my hair and told me that she understood how I felt, but was certain that I would play again, and play very well, too, when we won.

She was right, of course. She knows me so well. Just being with her made me understand how lonely I had been, strange, like Raffles must be with all those whippets.

Report cards and Dr Bowen. . . I guess I hoped we would not talk about this, and my Mom waited quite a few days before she mentioned it. She said she wasn't too concerned with my poor grades, because she understood that it was because I was preoccupied and abstracted, and that the grades are a sort of mirror reflection of my unhappiness with my present situation. But she said she was forced to admit that she was very worried indeed about my poor attendance. Put more bluntly we were talking about *truancy*. She said that was *really heavy* (using American to make her point) for her, the thought that her son was a *truant*. Though she was convinced that something must have happened at school, another kid perhaps, who was being cruel or making me miserable? She'd been afraid of that happening, that was one of the things that had been upsetting her all the time she'd been away in London.

As usual she guessed right! So I told her all the things Wayne King had said about my Dad being a bird-chaser and a liar who thought he was the only man in the world who had a prick (and I blushed when I told her that) and even that he'd said my Dad's prick was more important than his family. My Mom certainly knew how deeply hurtful that must have been to me, even though she also knew that I knew that as well as being a thug and a hooligan Wayne was also stupid – but it was so hard, impossibly hard, even, to take things from whence they came. She too, has been hurt by the same sort of malice even though she is supposed to know better because she is an adult after all, so she believes she really understands very well, perhaps too well, how dangerous it is to allow this sort of thing to almost destroy one.

But she had a secret to tell me, a secret she'd known for a long time, and she would disclose it to me now, so that I would understand more about Wayne, but she had to have my most sacred promise that I would never betray her confidence, because she was betraying someone only because it was every mother's duty to help her son. I promised. She knew she could trust me she said. *Wayne's father beats his mother*! He beats up the whole family! He gets drunk. Wayne is an unhappy child, a distraught child, and that is why he is so cruel. He doesn't know what kindness means because he never sees kindness. He mistakes cruelty for strength and so he thinks he's being strong when he's being cruel. He hopes by hurting others that he'll hurt less, and perhaps he does hurt less, for a while, but then it doesn't last long enough and he gets angrier each time, and then looks for someone else to hurt, like a smaller brother, or a cat, or, as in my case, someone else who is already down in the dumps so that it is easier to push them down even further. Wayne's Dad was probably beaten by his Dad, and Wayne will probably beat his son. All people have weaknesses, and all children find their parents' weaknesses very hard to forgive. Wayne's Dad has a weakness, and so does my own Dad – for the moment – but my Dad's weakness is the kind from which it is possible to recover more easily, she thought, than can Wayne's Dad. And then she laughed and said a funny thing. The difference between my Dad and Wayne's Dad is that Wayne's

Dad is a bastard because he intends to hurt, and my Dad is a rascal because he hurts without intending to. Not a real rascal, of course, only a temporary one, and she had a feeling that very soon, now, I'd find that out for myself. I hope she's right!

She was sad about disillusioning me, but hoped I would find it in myself to feel sorrow rather than hatred for Wayne, but even if I could not do that, I should not allow a miserable unhappy and probably mentally disturbed hooligan like Wayne King to keep me away from school, or to turn such a fine sensitive intelligent chap like me into a truant. My Mom often says nice things about me, and even if she does say them only because I'm her son, I like to hear them.

My Mom wants to see my teacher, Mrs Robinson, as well as Dr Bowen, but not without my permission, she said. I said I didn't mind.

After that we played Scrabble, and then we went in for some vocabulary games. When I was about eight, my Mom wrote to America for this huge book called *How to Prepare for College Entrance* in which there is a large section called Building Your Vocabulary with words like 'opprobrious' and 'asseverate' and 'tergiversation' – all sorts of crazy interesting words no one would ever dream of using, but words my Mom and I like to play with. My Mom believes she must have one of the largest funds of useless words all wrapped up and tightly tied in case she would ever be tempted to use them. But just in case we do decide to try for Harvard I'll have a high verbal ability score.

When I was very very little – about three or so – and people used to remark on my vocabulary, she taught me to ask them what sort of words they would like me to say – purely irrelevant words, or words germane to the subject. It was showing off, I suppose, but we all had fun with words, my Dad, too.

I hated saying good-bye to my Mom, but not nearly as much as I hate being back with the Tick. It's even worse, now that she's taken to coaching me with my German.

189

23

The effect of Ilsa and Nigel's brief sojourn in Chamonix seemed to her to be entirely disproportionate to the length of their stay. Everyone appeared to have benefited. What was more, Jean-Pierre and Peter were taking judo lessons together. At first it was feared that the dust might have an adverse effect on Jean-Pierre's asthma, but fortunately, so far he had not had a single attack. The boys' instructor was certain that judo would increase Jean-Pierre's self-confidence, and that it would at the same time bring about an emotional release. Ilsa understood that all this had something to do with being grounded – a concept, in judo, that was related to a way of standing, but what was of far greater significance to her was the fact that the instructor recommended the boys do this together, without parental supervision. So Ilsa found herself agreeing to the boys meeting after school and taking the tram together. This in turn promoted another level of friendship between the boys; it was not something altogether tangible though there was an alteration in the atmosphere at Ripaille.

Ilsa was pleased about this because Jean-Pierre began to look stronger, his complexion lost something of its pallor, and while he had not yet, thank God, grown away from her – they were still very close – he had she thought – developed. Jean-Pierre also spent more time with the Zeller children. Often they would lunch together, and Ilsa and Zoreh would take time off to scour the boutiques, to visit the coiffeuse or the masseuse. All of which required just enough organization of her time to allow her not to feel idle.

She had flatly refused to hire the all but statutory Portuguese couple but Zoreh had persuaded her to employ a housekeeper, and Ilsa was in the throes of considering several applicants. Nor did she pretend that it would be easy to work for her.

And then of course, there was golf. Nigel scored consistently in the low seventies and Ilsa remained with him. His handicap was lowered to two while Ilsa's stayed at six. But though Nigel's golf had improved, he had more than improved, he had changed.

Which change, Ilse supposed, was responsible for the alteration in the atmosphere of her household. Something had happened that very first day in Chamonix; Nigel had changed his attitude.

They had stayed at a wondrously luxurious hotel. She thought now that perhaps the change had been brought about by the very suite Nigel had reserved for them. It was called, very simply, in English, 'The British Suite' because the hotel had used an English interior decorator. It was a harmony in grey; grey carpet, grey couches, grey walls – even the paintings were surrounded by grey mounts – and yet the grey leaned towards blue, so perhaps the grey was almost blue – though it most certainly was not a grey-blue. Ilsa could not, even now, make up her mind as to how to define that colour; she intended duplicating it in their new bedroom. To say it was dove-grey would give no hint of its luminosity. Hyacinth-grey, on the other hand, would veer too strongly toward blue: Again and again her mind would return to that indefinable shade, for the walls, the carpet, even the towels were made of it. And then again, it may have been the lighting, and not the colours, that had, in the bedroom especially, brought out all those wonders. For, when she had caught sight of herself, unexpectedly, on the afternoon they arrived, she had been stunned by her own beauty. Somehow the greys or whatever they were flattered unbelievably; her eyes, her hair, her very complexion reflected and radiated this flattering light, which was softer and infinately more flattering even than candlelight.

That Nigel had taken this suite she found unexpectedly moving, almost spectacularly kind: it was said to be the most expensive hotel suite in Europe. But perhaps, Ilsa wondered, she had been so moved and thought Nigel so kind, because she had – for the first time in her life – found

191

herself beautiful, and so thought everyone and everything else beautiful, too. She could not be sure.

When they arrived that afternoon she had not begun to unpack, to organize, to arrange, but had sat instead on one of those sinky-soft grey couches in the drawing room, and leaned back, and raised her arms, and played with the long rope of pearls which Nigel had just given her, and which hung from her neck, and listened to the Chopin which came from the sparkling chrome hi-fi which as soon as the porter left them Nigel had snapped on, when Nigel had called, 'Ilsa, where are you?'

'Waiting for you – here.'

'I'm in the bedroom.'

'I thought you'd gone to the bathroom.'

But, though he usually came to wherever she was, she went to join him. When she reached the bedroom she could say nothing but 'Oh'. For Nigel had drawn back the covers, and now lay, naked, with his head propped up on one of the large square lace pillows, his perfect body stretched to its fullest height, with one arm stretched behind his head, while the other acted as a leaf-like covering, legs stretched and ankles crossed, he looked for all the world like a Renoir nude. A male nude in a female pose, Ilsa thought, and a long unfamiliar excitement of the kind she had only known with Maître Pachoud all but wrenched her apart. 'Oh', she said again, and took off her pearls, and threw off her clothes, and, exceptionally, left them wherever they lay.

Nigel said nothing at all.

She took him at once, in her mouth, but he moved away, and he turned her over on her side, with her back to him, and in a moment he was inside her, and she felt that neither he nor any man had ever entered her before, and Nigel who all the while was half-seated turned her head towards him, and commanded her to look at him, and she saw that he was smiling. And in that smile she thought she saw herself – she thought she saw him know her every secret, her every evil.

And then he stopped, and moved away.

And she moved towards him, and kissed his lips, and drew his breath.

'No,' he said, 'not like that. Little kisses, Like this. I'll show you.'

In short, Nigel took charge. He commanded her body to move this way, and that, to stretch, to flex, to aim, to swing. Dimly she heard sound issuing from her, from unknown places, dimly she thought she heard flesh tear and bones crack. Then she forgot herself and didn't care, because nothing mattered, not even memory, all she cared about was that she had ceased to be. Nigel had sloughed off all her skins, and now she slithered and rolled, and sucked, like a snake.

Soon she lost count of her climaxes, and even of Nigel's. Even now she did not know, and could not ask.

Afterwards, other than saying 'the sheets are full of come', Nigel said nothing. He left her to make a phone call. Once again, and again uncharacteristically, she followed him, this time to the drawing-room; she paused only long enough to grab a huge towel for – almost unprecedently for her – she found her nakedness embarrassing. He opened his brief case and spread out his papers and made more phone calls. He looked at her only once.

He said, 'I think you'll find a small cupboard in that kitchen. You could make some coffee.'

'Instant coffee?'

'O.K.'

He returned to his calls.

She made the coffee and sat down beside him. When he had done with one of his calls, she could not help it, she touched him again.

'More?' he said.

'Yes.'

'O.K. But on the carpet.'

To protect the carpet she laid the great towel down.

'Nigel,' she said. 'Oh, Nigel.'

'What?' he said. 'What?'

'Oh Nigel – what are you doing to me?'

'What? What am I doing to you? Tell me what I am doing to you.'

'You're killing me.'

His movements went faster.

'But what am I doing to you? *What?*'

Breathing from her dry, wide, throat, straining as she had in childbirth, she said. 'You're fucking me.'

'Tell me again.'

'You're fucking me. You're fucking me. You're fucking me.'

Which is what Nigel must have needed to know. Or so Ilsa believed now, because there could be no other explanation for the all-round improvement that had taken place everywhere, with everyone and everything.

Unless, perhaps, she had been changed by that afternoon, too? Because that afternoon among those luminously unidentifiable colours she had wanted Nigel with something close to the intensity – the burning stomach-splitting intensity – with which she had once wanted Maître André Pachoud. She had wanted Nigel for himself – as it were, gratuitously – not for what he could, or would, or might do for her. That need had not – since that afternoon, thank God – been repeated; it was the kind of need that could, if it persisted, overwhelm all else, and then control would pass from her to Nigel, and that would not do. Ilsa considered sex to be, above all, a mechanism for control. It was something husbands thought they needed – or were owed – by wives who – in order not to be husbandless – complied. Because the husbandless are disqualified. . . As who knew better than she?

Which was why she would qualify, and qualify again and again.

Because, through Nigel, Jean-Pierre was getting everything – status and position, quality and class – that was owed no less to him than it was to Peter.

And now, sitting under a variety of hot red lamps which were supposed to activate the creams that were meant to be conditioning her hair while her feet rested in a bowl of

194

warm water waiting to be pedicured, Ilsa reflected on the ease with which she had taken to her new lifestyle. For though every day was still something of a discovery her former life became an ever-receding experience; it was almost as if that life had never been possessed by her, it was historically remote, something she might have overheard someone else talk about. Which was, in a way, frightening.

The chrome fittings in the salon reminded her of the chrome in the English suite. There was something intensely physical about having a pedicure, Ilsa felt, like licensed decadence.

And then she recognized the high-pitched voice in the cubicle next door. That decisive imperious voice which always sounded as though it were dispensing charity. She reached at once for her blue squash ball.

That voice had instructed Ilsa on how to cut the shelf linings for the refrigerator. Of all the tasks that Ilsa had found humiliating or absurd or incomprehensible – or a combination of all three – the cutting and the shaping of the thick cream wrapping paper that Madame Pachoud got from her butcher was the most distressing. Because each shelf had to be soaped – but not scrubbed – every morning, anyway. Often Ilsa had been in the kitchen at 5 a.m. At first the voice in the next cubicle froze her into a kind of deafness, and she did not even try to hear what it was saying. Gradually, however, the squash ball in her hand relaxed and soothed so she put it aside and lit a cigarette and listened.

Madame Pachoud was going to dine at the Valloire; it was curious that she had never been, probably because it was only thirty kilometres from Geneva, though it was – after all – the only one of the twenty-one three-star restaurants in France that she had not yet sampled. M. Jouniaux, the chef, had been decorated by de Gaulle.

There was only one detail that interested Ilsa which was *when* the Pachouds would be going to the Valloire. She was reasonably confident, though anxious just the same, that she would learn this within the next few minutes: one could count on hairdressers asking the right sort of questions, usually because they wanted to drop the name of one of their more important customers who had already been and pronounced upon this or that restaurant, or theatre, or whatever.

She did not have to wait too long. Soon she heard M. Jean-Claude begin to use one of his more bored tones (which his customers unfailingly took as a challenge). He said. 'Madame d'Onfrio was slightly disappointed with the Valloire.' Madame d'Onfrio was the wife of the French ambassador; one did not therefore dispute any gastronomic verdict of hers.

'Really?' Madame Pachoud said.

'But yes,' Jean-Claude drawled. 'But yes, it was a disappointment.'

'I'm sorry to hear you say that,' Madame Pachoud said, making it clear that she respected Madame d'Onfrio's opinions.

Jean-Claude dropped his voice.

Ilsa held her breath.

Jean-Claude said, 'Madame d'Onfrio is afraid she made a diplomatic gaffe. They only decided to go to the Valloire on the morning of the same evening. The chef was of course offended.' Jean-Claude was amused; Ilsa knew that from his scornful laugh.

'We booked two weeks ago,' Madame Pachoud said anxiously.

'But when is Madame going?'

'On Monday the seventeenth. In eight days' time. That means we booked more than three weeks in advance. Tell me, did Madame d'Onfrio try their *quenelles de brochet*?'

'Alas! Yes. She regretted that.'

'What a pity,' said Madame Pachoud.

And Ilsa knew – just as Jean-Claude and Madame Pachoud knew – that on Monday, the seventeenth, Madame Pachoud would counsel everyone not to have the *quenelles* which had so disappointed Madame d'Onfrio. Which transparent little ploy was of little interest to Ilsa.

She opened her diary. Dinner with the Zellers she read. Good, that meant she could suggest the Valloire – no difficulty about that – though how to get a table only eight days hence was another matter. For a moment she felt weak – almost faint – and put it down to those absurd red lamps being used for that ridiculous treatment. She called for the young apprentice. 'Alexandre. . . Alexandre. . . *Please*. Stop this barbecue at once!' And then, in only a few moments, and by the time Alexandre had rushed over to her, a solution had occurred, and a plan formulated. Zoreh would say they were too late to get a reservation, Ilsa would then offer to telephone herself – indeed, by the time she suggested the Valloire to Zoreh she would have already secured the table, because when she phoned she would tell the patron – whose name she would make sure to discover in advance – that Madame d'Onfrio had told her about the silkiness, the lightness of their *quenelles*.

Alexandre switched off the lamps. 'Oh no,' she said, 'I've still ten minutes' suffering to go through. But turn it down.'

'Sorry. One can't. There is only one temperature, Madame.'

'I suppose I'll just have to suffer. No choice. No choice for me.' She began to giggle.

Alexandre was mollified.

There was something particularly uplifting, Ilsa discovered, about making some casual but extremely costly purchases from the receptionist at the same time as Monsieur Jean-Claude's bill was being paid. It was activities like these that made her know so fully how she was admired, adored, protected; it was the sort of concrete affirmation she understood.

Because one could also buy seemingly thoughtful masculine surprises like a Sulka dressing-gown, or bikini underpants, or silk socks, and while one made one's apparently careless selection one asked for one's change so that the receptionist, or any other customer who happened to be close by, would know the size of one's tip. Today Ilsa collected a new frame for a new photograph of Jean-Pierre, a pair of underpants – navy blue with white spots – and a dressing-gown to match. It was easy to imagine Nigel's delight: Caroline had not been given to this sort of sexy extravagance.

But the projected dinner at the Valloire made her feel the kind of expansive excitement she had not felt for years.

When she reached her car she was pleased to note that the meter was just about to expire: this meant that she had spent two hours at the salon and so would be exactly on time to fetch Jean-Pierre from school. She placed her exquisitely wrapped parcels carefully on the back seat, and then, like most women, carefully inspected Jean-Claude's expertise in the rear-view mirror. Now she was ready to drive away, but the traffic was heavy, and she was blocked by a large black car. One of the men in the car beside her must have been watching her, for he patted his own hair, and smiled. Which was in itself an almost alarmingly unusual act in Geneva, where strangers do not smile at one another and where men never flirt with women unless they have been introduced.

Something other than the oddity of the stranger's smile – the depth of the blackness of the black suits they were wearing? – made her stare more closely at the car. Her eyes registered shock, the stanger in the back seat smiled hugely, smiled devilishly – and then plucked a red rose from one of the garish wreaths on the coffin he was meant to be guarding, and waved it at her. In spite of herself Ilsa felt a smile begin to spread, it turned into a giggle which sent the watching men in the car into paroxysms of laughter; they reversed their car and with much waving, bowing and smiling insisted she precede their hearse. Exhilarated, she drove faster than usual, the hearse kept up with her, and in a few moments her exhilaration turned to annoyance and then panic, but salvation was in a changing traffic light, and very soon she had left the hearse behind.

But the incident left her with oddly conflicting sensations: fear clashed with triumph, dread with optimism. Ilsa disliked disorder and decided not to think about the hearse. She thought, instead, of Jean-Pierre, about the way his face would lift and light when he saw her, about the way he would say, 'Have you brought my chocolate, Mama?' It had drawn into one of those little – though immeasurably important – routines: Jean-Pierre always asked if only because he knew he would never be disappointed.

Zoreh accepted Ilsa's suggestion, and with a bonus, too; she wanted to know whether Ilsa and Nigel would mind if the Chablaises joined them. Would Ilsa mind?

Ilsa giggled just how much she did not mind – the Chablaises were the owners of the Chablaise waters (the universally acknowledged champagne of all mineral waters), the Chablaise casino, the Chablaise spa and thermal waters, the Chablaise golf course. Chablaise water was sent all over the world – it was as well known as Coca Cola. Besides, it was there, at that golf course, there among all those Monet greens, that Ilsa had, come to know Maître André Pachoud, it was there that she had first come to know what the real force of a real golf swing could mean.

Frantically feverish though she was, the week that preceded the dinner at Valloire was more like a single coalesced day that would not move: Ilsa could not shake the sensation of time arrested, frozen in a mix of uncertainty and unreality, as if there could be no possible guarantee that Monday the seventeenth would ever materialize. She inspected, each sleepless day, the tissue that surrounded her eyes as if reality could be wrested from darkening circles, from puffed skin, but there were no circles, and no puffiness, so she examined the white for broken corpuscles but there were none. She would have welcomed any facial blemish or pimple; it would have given her something concrete on which to fasten her anxiety, would have at least diminished the air of unreality that she found so threatening. A dream finally about to be transmogrified into reality is also a sense of imminent loss. Ilsa cursed her own superstitious nature, but did not try to fight it.

And yet it was to turn out that in all her thirty-eight years Ilsa had never been more conscious of her own reality than during the dinner at Valloire. The only pity was that Zoreh was seated where she was able to catch glimpses of herself in a mirror while Ilsa was not. For all that it was as if she could see herself all the time, as if she's moved out of her body in order to observe its every movement, so conscious was she of the shape of her lips whether moving or still, of the language of her eyes – they spoke sadness best – of the contours of her cheeks – strong and helpless at the same time – of the pulse that beat at her throat and temples, of the heart which roared in her tiny diamond-studded ears, and of the cadences and tones of her giggles.

Because after nine years she had at long long last glimpsed Maître André Pachoud.

She willed Pachoud to see her. What if he did not see her? She had not given a moment's thought to the possibility of his not seeing her, though she had thought that some catastrophe might force the Pachouds to cancel their dinner engagement, she had known that the Valloire was a small and intimate restaurant.

But perhaps, if he did not see her, seated as she was with her back to the ancient stone wall, then he would see and recognize M. Chablaise whose face was, after all, more important. . . With her back against the wall or not, she was well within his line of vision; he reminded her of the telephone that refuses to ring, and she waited with the same tension of the lover who has not yet quite believed that the phone will never ring again. Already they were on the second course. She began to feel ill, and gave way for a moment, and covered her face with her hands.

Nigel, who saw this at once, said, said, 'Are you all right, darling?'

'I'm fine,' she said rather too brightly. 'I'm very happy. Too happy, perhaps.'

'Good. You seemed so far away.'

'Young lovers,' Zoreh said, and laughed.

The others at the table laughed too, and it was probably inevitable that six voices raise simultaneously in laughter in that sort of serious restaurant where serious food is being seriously eaten would attract attention.

Maître Pachoud looked up from his *loup de mer* – Ilsa thought he saw her; he stared. He attended to his plate, and seemingly dreamily, stared again. Ilsa looked down, looked up, looked straight ahead, as if she were being examined by an ophthalmologist, and, instead of the small red torch, was confronted by André Pachoud's burning bright blue eye.

Their stares intersected and then set. Now Ilsa willed her lids to lower but by way of default they lifted and widened – frozen – as if in fright – in their sockets. She was trapped, she thought, trapped in her own frozen eyes. Pachoud raised his napkin, and then patted the corners of his mouth with the gesture she knew and loathed too well, and said something to his companions and crossed the room as if searching for something – the men's room? – when his single eye chanced – it seemed accidentally – on Madame Chablaise. And it was only when he raised Madame Chablaise's hand to his well-remembered lips that Ilsa's shy lids lowered.

'Madame Chablaise, what a pleasure to see you! And Monsieur Chablaise!'

Politely Pachoud scanned the rest of the table. The men had risen to their feet, their serviettes held like wilting flags in their left hands, and Madame Chablaise's hand was still clasped in his when he chose to recognize Ilsa. 'Ah, Madame du Four,' he went on smoothly, 'what a pleasure and a surprise to meet you here. You are well, I see.' And as he spoke he gave a bow to M. Chablaise and moved, lightly but slowly, nearer Ilsa, so as to raise her hand. How vaguely he brushed her hand against his lips! Introductions were effected, and neither Nigel nor Pachoud gave any clue to their recent correspondence. 'What a charming coincidence to find the family Chablaise here tonight. Our party is about to make unwise investments at your establishment, M. Chablaise.' Pachoud permitted a loud sophisticated chuckle. 'We intend tonight to insult the chef of the Valloire – your roulette tables, monsieur, will turn our gastric juices into adrenalin!' Ilsa took her turn and allowed a series of giggles to take over. 'Why not join us?' Pachoud continued, 'unless, of course, you don't gamble.'

As always Nigel responded to one of Ilsa's giggles. 'I should be delighted to join you,' he said. 'That is if the others agree, of course. Ilsa, darling?'

'Sounds like fun,' she said. And giggled again.

The Chablaises were most gracious. 'Champagne on the house,' M. Chablaise said.

'Don't let him fool you,' Madame Chablaise laughed. 'Tuesday is the Casino's quietest night. Champagne is always on the house on Tuesdays.'

'So then we are agreed. We shall meet too soon after the delicious meal. By the way, have you tried the *quenelles* tonight?'

'Yes,' Ilsa said.

'And how did you find them? I was advised not to make the error of choosing *quenelles*.'

'Excellent,' Ilsa said softly. 'A symphony, I would say.' Ilsa giggled.

'It seems you were badly advised, Maître Pachoud,' Chablaise said.

Pachoud agreed.

Now Ilsa became animated, became serious, became interested, became modest. She reminded Nigel of the way she was when Jean-Pierre brought home an A+ grade.

Perhaps the original owners of the Chablaise casino, formerly known as the casino Rivarol, and the largest in all France, had decided, way back in the twenties, that gambling was too important to be troubled by beautiful surroundings, for the casino was neither elegant nor sumptuous. Instead that aura of seedy and official state-ownership clung like stale sweat to the large over-lit rooms, the deeply purple carpet, the bored croupiers. The food, though, was excellent; there was a restaurant at the farthest end of the largest hall. A small and ornate concert hall, a golf course and an hotel were all attached to – and financed by – the casino and the thermal waters. Sometimes there were music festivals, and parties given by the Chablaises were held at the casino and omelettes and cakes would be shaped in treble clefs and quavers, but nothing, not even chamber music, could disturb the settled sordidness of all that ultimate, perfected materialism. The French, after all, love gold best. The casino had never lacked customers – buses left Geneva every twenty minutes – amateurs and professionals and even women were all treated with equal severity.

But for Ilsa, that night, the casino became not only beautiful, but even glamorous; it was, she thought, the most perfect evening of her life. Nothing really mattered to her, except that Pachoud joined their table. It didn't matter that her number, eight, chosen because Jean-Pierre was eight, kept winning, and twice, even when she left her chips in place after number eight had already come up as the winner, it came up again. Her luck was stupendous, but it was not luck that kept her there. Pachoud decided to test number eight as well, and he won, and the others followed him, but number eight deserted them, and so they had to stay on – as they said – to recoup their losses, like thieves. Once, during the flurry of congratulations to her number eight, Pachoud pressed his lips to her ear, and whispered, 'Tell me, are you still so beautiful, naked?'

'I don't know,' she said. 'Are you? How long ago is it anyway?'

'Almost nine years.'

So, he knew. He did know. He knew after all.

And of course Monsieur Chablaise's very presence meant that the entire staff all but crossed themselves and knelt before all his party. The service flowed as freely as the champagne.

And all the while Ilsa knew that André Pachoud would phone her again; perhaps she would see him, perhaps not.

She could not say. What really counted was that the choice would be hers.

But in the car, on the way home, when they stopped at the French customs, Nigel said, 'I didn't know you knew Maître André Pachoud. If I had, I would have asked you about him.'

'Oh,' Ilsa said. 'Why? What did you want to know?'

'What sort of chap he is. Caroline's London solicitors, Garratt, Hartley and Williams appointed him as their Swiss correspondent.'

'But you didn't tell me. Why?'

'Didn't seem important. Garratt, Hartley and Williams are about to sign what my chaps want them to sign. I told you about that, didn't I?'

'Of course you did.'

She squeezed his hand.

Because her lids were frozen again, this time, in anger. Now the choice was not hers, now she would have to see Maître André Pachoud. Caroline must know about her, must know *all* about her – it was obvious. And André Pachoud would tell her whatever he knew. He wanted her again, at last. Every time he'd brushed past her she'd had incontrovertible and outstanding proof of that.

'What happened to his eye?' Nigel asked.

'His eye?'

'Yes. He wears a black patch.'

'You know, I wasn't thinking. I'm getting worried about Jean-Pierre, I suppose.' She scowled in the dark. 'That eye? It was an accident. It happened on the first fairway.'

'The first fairway?'

'Yes. On the Montesquieu course.'

'How?'

'He was about to play his second shot to the green. You remember the practice tee nearby? They've raised the fence, it's higher now. Rather too late, but still.'

'Yes, I know that practice range.'

'Well, someone, a powerful golfer of course, sliced his

shot. He cut the ball over the fence and it hit Pachoud's right eye.'

'How terrible! How long ago did this happen?'

'About eight years or so. I remember I was expecting Jean-Pierre, or perhaps it was soon after he was born. I can't remember. Anyway, Pachoud gave up golf after that.'

Ilsa did not say that the accident had happened exactly three weeks before Jean-Pierre was born. Her distress had hastened the birth: Jean-Pierre was born five weeks ahead of time.

She felt restless, and thought Nigel drove too slowly. She said anxiously, 'I didn't phone home and tell the children the number of the Chablaise. I didn't even tell them we were going there. I forgot. I don't understand how I could have forgotten. Why didn't you remind me?'

'I didn't think of it. Sorry, darling. But it was midnight by the time we got there, you know. Jean-Pierre would have been asleep by then. We'll be there soon,' he said.

He patted her knee.

But drove faster.

'We'll be home soon, darling,' he said. 'I'll undress you, and put your things away, and tuck you in, and put you to sleep, like a good little girl.'

'I should have phoned,' she said restlessly. 'I should have phoned, you know.'

Even some distance from Ripaille, at the entrance to the little street, they saw that the house was ablaze with light. He drove faster still, but the driveway was blocked with police cars, and police lamps, and ambulance lamps that flashed like heartbeats. A man whom Nigel did not at first recognize, and then identified as Stephen Bowen, stood at the front door with his arm about Peter's shoulders. Still in the car, Ilsa kicked off her shoes, the faster to run. She was at the door in a flash.

'What are you doing here?' she said calmly. 'Where is Jean-Pierre?'

'I'm sorry, Madame du Four – Dr Genthod is with him.'

'Dr Genthod? He's not our doctor.'

She raced to the staircase, and half way up it, was met by a man who told her he was Dr Genthod.

'Madame,' he said, 'my profound condolences. I am very very sorry. madame – '

'What's happened? For God's sake get out of my way.'

All that took less than a minute and then Nigel, having a word with Stephen Bowen, weeping, took her in his arms.

'It's Jean-Pierre,' she said. 'He's not dead? Not dead? Let me go to him. Let me go to him.'

She pushed Nigel with so much force that he fell back down the stairs.

They heard her screams.

'I must go to her,' the doctor murmured. 'I must give her an injection. Sedation.'

But she was calm even before she submitted to his hypodermic. She was silent. She wanted only to be alone, alone with Jean-Pierre. She said so, and said it all with so much intractable authority that the others were compelled to obey.

In the end, the doctor, who could not bear his feeling of uselessness, sedated Nigel and Peter, and even Stephen Bowen. The doctor was himself shaken.

It seemed Peter was unable to speak. Dr Bowen spoke for him:

'The boys had gone to bed late; they'd been playing with that new electronic war game of theirs and then they'd had a pillow fight, practised some judo, and then they'd got hungry, and had a snack, and then they'd started playing with water pistols. It was about eleven o'clock, and they were still in the kitchen because they'd played there because they hadn't wanted to wet the carpet and Peter had just wiped the water from the floor, and was wringing out one of the those flat sponges, when Jean-Pierre went into an attack. The bronchodilator in the kitchen was empty or dried out, and Peter rushed upstairs, but Ilsa's bedroom was locked, so he couldn't get to the bathroom – he forgot all about the other bathroom – and then he found a spray in

Jean-Pierre's room, among his paints and crayons, and he used it and used it, but Jean-Pierre got more and more frightened because it didn't seem to help; Jean-Pierre was sitting on the kitchen floor and leaning forward with his hands on his knees, taking great heaving gasps and then he lay down on the kitchen floor, and Peter half carried him to the living room and somehow lifted him on to the couch, and placed cushions under his head.

'And Peter telephoned the doctor, but got the answerphone, and then he tried the number the answerphone had given him, but that number was engaged, and then in desperation he phoned me. I phoned the emergency service and the school doctor and they got there within minutes, probably four or five minutes after Peter's call but it was too late. When they arrived they found Peter wiping the sweat and his own tears from Jean-Pierre's face – Jean-Pierre was still breathing, though his breaths seemed very far apart. He was already in a coma, so the doctor was too late. They were all too late.' Too late – the saddest words in every language. . . And as for what this would do to Peter he would not dare guess. . .

They carried Jean-Pierre up to his bedroom: Ilsa was in there now.

Stephen Bowen had no sooner finished than Ilsa called out for the doctor. She wanted an explanation, she said; she wanted Dr Genthod and Dr Bowen; no, she did not want Nigel; and no, most certainly she did not want his son.

Dr Bowen went away, and then, finally, the police and the ambulance men and the doctor went away.

Ilsa would allow no one near her; would not tolerate the sight of Nigel; she made that very clear. She did not want anyone to be informed, not Zoreh Zeller, no one.

Peter and Nigel stayed downstairs. The sedatives the doctor had given Peter took their blessed effect. Once, during those long dawn and pre-dawn hours, Nigel thought he heard the phone tinkle. Perhaps Ilsa was phoning someone; perhaps, after all, there was someone who could comfort her?

At about six a.m., fairly soon after he had thought he had heard Ilsa make a phone call, Madame Blanc arrived. She didn't bother with her usual elaborate courtesies, but went upstairs at once. Peter awoke. Nigel took him to the kitchen to give him some tea – what else, he wondered, was there for him to do? So far, Peter had said nothing – he wept merely, and wept with an ancient and horrible silence.

Ilsa, accompanied by Madame Blanc, came downstairs. She stood at the kitchen doorway, and from there, said, 'I sent for Madame Blanc. She will stay with me. She will pack your things – ' She raised her arm. 'No, Nigel, don't stop me. Don't come near me. I am not hysterical. I have never been more calm. I want you to go away. I want you and that son of yours out of my house. I cannot suffer the sight of your son. I never should have had your son in my house. I should never have been asked to have your son in my house. It should be your son who is dead, but it is not your son, it is *my* son. Now, get out. Take him back to his own house – he's got his own key. You caught me there once didn't you Peter? But because you are so good at keeping secrets you kept that a secret, too, didn't you? I hate both of you – I wish you were dead.'

As if she were a nurse, and Peter and Nigel her patients, Madame Blanc took charge. 'Take the little boy away, Monsieur. You must take him away at once.' She turned Ilsa around and said, 'I will take care of madame. Go now. Please.'

Obediently, Nigel and Peter left. Somehow they got to their former home where Nigel telephoned their own doctor, and, of course, Caroline.

24

It's a very long time since last I wrote in my diary. The packers came in yesterday, to take measurements and give estimates of the costs for shipping all our stuff back to London. For some reason I'm shaking while I'm writing this – it's just that I don't know what I should do with all these diaries, now. Because as soon as we move I'll have lost my hiding place, and I don't know whether I should take these diaries to London or not, I don't think I'll ever want to read them again so I don't know why I want to keep them.

The funny thing is that my Mom hasn't asked about them. I wish I – I don't know what I wish. If only Raffles could talk. He's at my feet now, even though I'm writing on my bed, he's right beside me. It took ages for him to get used to the idea of being with the whole family again. He goes mad when my Dad comes home -- my Dad and he have got a new game. My Dad throws the ball onto every single chair in the living-room, and Raffles jumps in advance from chair to chair to catch it. His hairs are all over the place, and Frederica grumbles, but we all know she doesn't really mean it. Together, Frederica and I burned that ugly voodoo doll in the cellar. She's taken off those horrible black clothes of hers, now, and seems to love yellows and oranges. She told me the sun had come back into our lives because Monsieur Nigel was home again. She's coming with us to London – I'm teaching her English. Now she says, 'I no spick Hinglhish.' She thinks that's a joke because it makes my Mom and my Dad laugh.

No one giggles in this place.

It took a long time though, after we came back, before any of us laughed. Since then I've discovered something about time – it's what happens inside time that matters. It's a bit like this – when you sleep, you don't know anything about time – it goes even before it can be remembered.

And when you are shocked and very very very frightened time moves the way it does when you sleep, and it is as if it's not happening. Of course that's a silly idea of mine – time never stops, it only vanishes.

The time we stayed with Ilsa lasted about 152 days, and $152 \times 24 = 3,648$ hours. The terrible thing is that I'd rather have lost than win the way we did. If only I had realized how ill Jean-Pierre was – but I didn't, and everyone says it would have made no difference at all. Dr Gaud told me that it has even happened to doctors – even doctors have not been able to do anything to help, even doctors do not always realize how dangerous the situation is. But I don't believe him, I don't believe anyone who tells me that, not even Dr Bowen, not even my Dad. I told my Mom I didn't want to talk about it, and we don't talk about it. They lie to me because they want to be kind to me, my Dad especially. I don't blame them for lying like that.

I have to stop writing now. My Mom is calling me.

My Mom called me because Madame Zeller had arrived, and wanted to see me. I stood at the doorway, and listened, I'd never done that here before. I heard Madame Zeller say that she was honoured to meet my mother again, she said she thought my mother was a very clever woman. My Mom murmured something about that being the last thing, the very last thing she would say of herself. She called me again, and so I went in. Madame Zeller looked different from the way she usually looks, but perhaps that was just because things look different to me in this house. I could see, here, that she was the sort of woman boys whistle at, tight blue jeans, long sunny hair in different kinds of yellows, long eyelashes – the kind you see fluttering on a windy sweeping yacht in cigarette advertisements. Fun-loving, I suppose. Now, if my Dad had gone for *that* sort – well, perhaps I could have understood that a bit better!

She seemed pleased to see me, Madame Zeller. She shook my hand, told me she thought I'd grown even better-looking, said she wished me lots and lots of luck at my new school, and then said she'd stopped by, actually,

210

because she had a parcel for me – from Ilsa. I couldn't help it – when she said that name I glanced at my Mom, but she was looking in another direction, at the lake, and so I couldn't help getting all red. I thanked her, and she said not at all, Madame Blanc had forgotten to empty one of my drawers. Madame Zeller had been at Ripaille when my things were found, so she had offered to bring them over at once. I thanked her again. I wanted her to go, I was dying for her to go . . . So my Mom took over – she said that was most kind of Madame Zeller, most kind – it was possible, but probably unlikely, that one or two things were so vital that we couldn't do without them. She sounded rather doubtful, though. It made me stand up very straight. Of course, Madame Zeller said, of course one can never tell with children, what is important, or vital, can one? Perhaps, my Mom answered, perhaps, although one usually knew about the really vitally important things, didn't one? My Mom began moving toward the door, she even walked sarcastically, and I followed her, and Madame Zeller followed both of us.

As soon as we reached the entrance hall my Mom opened the front door, and stood there holding it open. At that moment Madame Zeller remembered that she had something in her large sling bag to give us. She had an envelope for my Dad, and a gift-wrapped package for me. She'd brought me a farewell gift from the Zeller family, she said, and the envelope contained the tremendously exciting plans for that new Chamonix development the men were going in for. My Mom would be excited too, she was sure. My Mom laughed then, and thanked her again, and said she knew all about *that*, of course. She glanced at the folded cartons the movers had left in the hall. I suppose she wanted Madame Zeller to see them. It was a mistake, looking at those cartons, because it made Madame Zeller stay even longer. Then she wanted to know when we were moving, whether we had found a place to live in London, where it was, where I would be going to school. She was trying to be friendly, I could see, but my Mom answered very coldly, very quickly, and then ended everything by asking to be excused, she'd just remembered an important phone call that couldn't wait. She began to close the door, and we got rid of her!

For some reason both of us looked at the larger parcel first. The one that was supposed to contain all those important things I'd left behind. Neither Madame Zeller nor Ilsa could have known that *all* the contents of *all* the suitcases and packages that had been sent on to us had been given away without ever having been opened. Or, if they were opened, no one ever told me about it. That meant all our clothes, even those that had never been worn. I don't honestly think my Dad or I cared one way or the other about stuff like clothes at that time. It was only three days after Jean-Pierre . . .

Getting rid of those things was my Mom's idea – probably it was Frederica who gave her the idea in the first place. I don't think she cared about clothes herself, then. Nothing was normal, we all sort of talked in whispers, my Dad looked terrible – I'd never seen him unshaven like that, his face was a kind of sticky grey, like the streets in the sunlight, and the doctor came, and talked to me, privately, and talked to him, privately, and my Mom talked to both of us, sometimes together, sometimes singly, and Frederica came back, and Aunt Pamela kept phoning and wanting to come, but my Dad didn't want to see anyone. He wouldn't even talk to his people at the bank! My Mom said that it was a terrible time, but that terrible times had a way of becoming less terrible. Meanwhile, she was sleeping in the spare room, the one with the photograph of her as a bride. Frederica has been given that photograph, now, my Dad told my Mom something about it, and she decided – at least this what she said she'd decided – that it had outlived its usefulness, she didn't want it, and Frederica, who was sentimental, like all old maids, was welcome to it.

After about a week my Dad began to get better, and a few days after that I went back to school. We had Graduation Day the other day, and at our school all the prizes are given out on that day, and the students who are about to leave – no matter what grade they are in, or how long they have been at the school – are given an elaborately scrolled certificate to mark the time they spent at the school. My Dad says he thinks it's a bit of a con – he doesn't really like Dr Stephen Bowen, I can tell, even though he hasn't said so. He is grateful to him though – he even says so. He bought him a Piaget watch as a token of appreciation for all that he had done for me on that terrible night. I wasn't on the merit list – it was the very first time I'd been excluded, but I didn't care. Dr Bowen must have thought that would upset me, because he announced to the whole assembly that he had created a special prize that year, and it was a prize that the school would continue, it would eventually become part of the school's tradition. It was a prize for bravery, and it was awarded to me – for having been clear-headed enough to have turned to the school for help during a time of desperate need. The prize was a certificate in a frame, and when we got home, I broke the frame, and tore up the certificate and flushed it down the drain. Neither of my parents asked what had happened to it. It turned out that Dr Bowen had informed them that he intended awarding the prize, because everyone at school knew what had happened, it was best not to try to keep it secret.

There are some secrets that can't be kept, and there are other secrets that must be kept secret forever – especially forever, especially when it is especially difficult. *If you keep a secret properly, so that nobody but you knows about it, then it hasn't happened . . .*

After my Dad got better my Mom moved back into their big bedroom. That was better for everyone. We talked for hours in that room, the three of us all on the same bed, and my Dad would often interrupt and say. 'Your mother's saved me, saved me, saved me.' He said this so often that I stopped being embarrassed long ago. He says it still. One night I told him about the day I had caught Ilsa in that very room – at least that was one secret I could get rid of. My

Dad told me that he was glad I'd mentioned it at last, he's been waiting for that moment, he said, waiting for me to show him when I was ready to talk about things. He knew about that, he hoped I didn't mind, but my Mom had told him about that, about the daily phone calls, about her secret visit, about Dr Gaud, about the missing comfort blanket, and he had told her about our secret lunch. There are no secrets in our family any more, he said, and when he went on to say that the time for secrecy was over, and it was time to start trusting one another again, I looked at my Mom because I couldn't be sure whether she had told him *all* our secrets, every single one, especially . . . But she was looking away, she did not look at me. I don't think she could look at me . . . My Dad saw that she could not look at me, and he moved over and kissed her and kissed her, and said how sorry, sorry, sorry, he was, it was all his fault, he couldn't bear to think of what he had done to all of us, but he'd been self-destructive, he hadn't been able to help himself, he hoped, he prayed we would all find it in our hearts to forgive him, because, so far, he had not been able to help or forgive himself. So my Mom stopped crying, and I couldn't help it, I couldn't stop, I was thinking about Jean-Pierre, and I sobbed and cried, and wept, and howled, and I don't know how long it lasted, and I don't care even now, how long it lasted, or if they knew why I was crying, because I didn't want to stop – not ever. And my Dad got off the bed eventually, and though I'm quite tall for my age – I'm much taller than Ilsa, for example – he picked me up, as if I were much smaller, and half slung me over his shoulder, and walked up and down the room, telling me to cry as long and as often as I needed to, but not a second longer than was absolutely necessary. His voice was not shaking when he said that, but it sounded as if it could easily begin to shake.

All that happened ten days after we had all started living together again, and then everything became normal. We all had a late breakfast the next morning, my Dad had been to the bank the day before, but he decided not to go that day. They told me I had fallen asleep in their bed, and that they had not slept, because they talked and talked, and came to the conclusion that they should include me in the discussion, because they were thinking of leaving Geneva, permanently, and moving back to London, and they wanted to know how I felt about all that, because I was getting on so well at my school, and because I'd lived almost all my life in Geneva.

So I told them I'd love to leave, nothing would make me happier, I preferred London, preferred British television, preferred, in fact, the British. I did not say that I wanted to get as far away from Geneva as I possibly could, and as soon as I possibly could. I'm still keeping secrets, I'm still a secret.

I wanted to know about the bank, I wanted to know what would happen to that, and my Dad told me that his people in London had been trying to get him back for years and years, he was pleased I'd be happy to leave Geneva, as for him, his only regret was that he had not left sooner! But it had got to him, Geneva, the calm tranquil traffic, the remoteness from pressure that made him feel safely outside everything, the repetitiveness of ideas because it was not necessary nor even welcome to think of new ideas, all this had got to him. He said I was a young man now, I would soon be shaving, and I had already been through far too much for my years, and so I was probably older and wiser than my chronology, which was why he could speak to me like this, man to man, so to speak. And then he said he was going to tell me something important that he had learnt – because he had learnt more in these past months than he had learnt in all his years, and what he said was this – if you don't think a new thought, there is no thought. Of course he had applied his mind to the bank, and he had to admit that it had prospered. But he could have done much better with it, if he'd thought instead of conformed. It was complicated, he knew, but though he'd been conscientious, and even efficient, he had not stretched or really exercised his mind, so it had fallen into disuse, and from

215

there it had gone to boredom, and well, he supposed I knew where that boredom had taken him. He wanted me to know that he knew he was one of the lucky ones – he'd a loving, clever wife, and a loving, clever son, and together we'd saved him.

We don't talk about this sort of thing any more, and I'm glad about that.

I have not shaved yet, though my Dad went out and bought me a razor.

We took the stuff Madame Zeller had brought into my Mom's room. I don't know why, but neither of us wanted Frederica to see the things. I could tell Madame Blanc had wrapped it because of the kind of yellow string and thick orange paper she'd used. She uses that paper to wrap her vegetables, and brings quantities of it to Ripaille. There was my microscope, my camera, some lenses and film, two dictionaries, a few photographs – one of them was of my Mom with President Reagan – some pencils, a maths set – I'd forgotten about all these things, even the microscope. My Mom said she didn't think we'd want to give any of *these* away, it just showed you how preoccupied we'd all been, otherwise how could we have forgotten about them, the way we had forgotten?

And then we came to a small thin cardboard box – it made me turn away. She'd even sent back the broken little remote control boat I'd given Jean-Pierre – all the pieces seemed to be there. It hurt me to look at them. My Mom said she could see these were not mine. I told her they were not. She put them back in the little box. Another box held an incomplete jigsaw of a golfer – he had liked that very much . . . Not yours, either? No, not mine. My Mom wanted me to leave the rest to her, but there was only one other smallish parcel to unwrap, and something made me determined to see what was inside it. And there they lay, our water pistol collection, looking so harmless, so colourful, not in the least like guns. My Mom said nothing. I said nothing. My Mom stretched over and quickly unwrapped Madame Zeller's family gift – and there it was,

216

the largest water pistol I had ever seen, only this one really did look like a real rifle, it had darts to go with it. You could shoot water and darts at the same time – you pulled the hammer for the darts, and the trigger for the water. My Mom gasped. Finally, she said, 'What are we going to do with them?' I told her I didn't know, I had no idea. She said she'd thought of something, all we had to do was cross the road, go straight to the little harbour like we've so often done before, hire one of those little motor boats like we've so often done before, and take these parcels with us, and sink them. I agreed, except I suggested that we leave the camera, and the microscope, leave everything but the water pistols. And the little boat, and the jigsaw? We'd leave those, too.

So my Mom took her sun hat, and her cigarettes, and her purse, and we crossed the road, hired a small motor boat, and went out into the middle of the lake. Once we were there, in the middle, far away, although we could still see our balcony, our royal-blue awning, even our curtains, we stopped the engine.

Something in my Mom's face had changed, she looked more like Madame Blanc or even Frederica then like herself. She was breathing very fast and just as loudly – her cheeks were bright red, exactly like mine when I blush, her eyes seemed to have turned yellow, and they reminded me of the wild eyes you see in westerns whenever the hero discovers his best friend is a traitor. Except that the hero never looks scared, and my Mom's eyes had that scared, hunted, haunted look in them.

She said, 'This was the one?

'Yes. It's the kind you use with cartridges. We had lots and lots of spare cartridges, you see. A few of them are in here. See?'

'Yes.'

'See how easily they slot in?'

'Yes.'

'You just fill them and slot them in. We had others. Not all the cartridges we used are here, you see?'

'Yes.'

'When I was waiting for Dr Bowen I put some of them in my pocket, you see? Two of them were still full. I hadn't used them.'

'How many did you use?'

'Three.'

'Three? But they hold so little. Look how small they are! Not as much as a dessert spoon could fit in each.'

'But even half a coffee spoon can be a gallon too much.'

'You can't be sure. The work's still experimental.'

'Some experiments work too well.'

'But how were we to know that? How could we have even dreamed.'

'I know. I know. It was an accident.'

'You – we – can't be sure of that either. It could have happened anyway.'

'I don't think so.'

'But you must think so! You've got to!'

'Yes. I know.'

'I wish I'd never heard that story about Lucky the horse.'

'I know. I wish you hadn't myself.'

'Peter, you can't think I knew? Planned . . .?'

'No. I don't think that. *I'm sure you did not know.*'

'I suppose we'd better bury them?'

'Yes.'

Neither of us did anything.

Then my Mom said, 'He had a very small burial, you know. I wanted to go – at least, I did not want to – I thought I ought to.'

'Who told you about it? Dad didn't go.'

'You remember Madame Fleur? From the tabac?'

'Yes. Of course.'

'She told me. Her daughter is Madame Blanc's neighbour. Madame Blanc went, you see, and Madame Zeller, and her doctor, a man called Spengler. There were five in all.'

'Who was the fifth?'

'A man called Pachoud. André Pachoud.'

'Never heard her talk about him. Who is he?'

'Curiously enough he was my lawyer over here. Maître André Pachoud. She knew him years and years ago. He was the first to teach her golf, and then he had an accident on the golf course – a golf ball hit him in the eye – and so he lost that eye. According to Madame Fleur's daughter she sees a lot of Pachoud now. He's more her type, I suppose.'

'Is there a Madame Pachoud?'

'Of course.'

'I thought so. Will we tell Dad about the water pistols?'

'I've been thinking about that. Yes. I think we should. We don't have to mention those other cartridges, though.'

My Mom and I watched the water pistol until it sank, and it was terrible.

We went back home after that, and my Mom went to supervise cupboards, possessions, books, and sort of thing, and I went back to write all this down.

I had actually gotten to like Jean-Pierre, that's the funny thing. I know I'm not supposed to say 'gotten' but I feel like saying it. Jean-Pierre loved playing with the water pistols, though he and I called them squirt guns. I wish I'd never found the cartridge type – I don't think it could have happened with the other kind. This was so easy – you could put the liquid in the cartridge, and no one could tell that it was a yellow colour. I used one of those flat sponges to soak it up. It was so easy to drop down to my knees on one of the paved footpaths in the school garden, soak the dog urine in a sponge, squeeze the sponge in a wide-necked bottle, pour that into a slim medicine measuring jug, and then pour that into the cartridge. I used three cartridges that night, only one of them had water. When I was waiting for Dr Bowen I put those in my pocket and filled the ones that Madame Zeller just returned with water.

Even when he was so ill I honestly did not realize he was so ill. I honestly did not think he would die. I honestly don't think I even ever wanted him to die. I don't know why I carried out that experiment – I only know that it worked.

My Dad never mentions his name. I wonder what my

Dad would do if he knew about the experiment? I wonder if he will ever guess how I really think about him, about both of them, both my parents.

I wish I could go back to the time when secrets were surprises instead of sins. Ilsa was right about one thing. She was – is – right about my having too many secrets.

I wonder what will happen to me if anyone ever finds out about my secret experiment that worked. And what will happen to my Mom if anyone ever finds out that it was her idea . . .?

If anyone anywhere has a really bad secret that they need to tell someone about they should tell me. I can be trusted with the worst of the worst secrets. I know how to keep even the most murderous secret. I am an experienced secret-keeper.